BOOK ONE

The Summoning

For Lyla Lynne Firuza Osmanov-Fitzgerald,
who brought joy back into my life, and
also for my very patient editor, Jennifer Besser.
Thank you both.

CHAPTER 1

Sleep did not fall away from Sudi at once, but in slow swings between dreams and wakefulness. She fought the dream world, struggling to come back, and when finally she rose up from deep within her mind, the sharp, cold air made her reach for her covers. She flung her hand out, searching for her quilt, and lost her balance. Her eyes flashed open, and she let out a startled cry. She was no longer in her bed, where she had gone to sleep, but outside, and falling down her front-porch steps. She grabbed the iron railing and caught herself. Her elbows and arms scraped over the twisting balusters.

She pulled herself up and stood, too frightened to do more than stare out at the grayish white clouds skittering across the moonlit sky. She couldn't remember climbing from her bed or walking down the stairs, yet she stood in front of her house, barefoot and dressed in a long, loose T-shirt that flapped wildly in the autumn wind.

The front door stood open behind her, and she could feel the heat coming from the house. Her father must have forgotten to turn the thermostat down again. Maybe she had been sleepwalking to escape the high temperature. That would explain why her nightmare had seemed so real. In the dream she had been wandering over scorching desert sand, lost among endless limestone mountains and barren valleys, her lungs barely able to take in the hot air.

But her logic didn't calm the trembling in her knees and hands. What would have happened if she had continued down to the canal or the

Potomac River and fallen into the water?

She started back inside, and as she crossed the threshold, a new worry seized her. Her parents and sisters were asleep upstairs, unaware that Sudi had left them vulnerable to predators. Sudi didn't know how long she'd been standing outside. She touched her cheek. Her skin felt cold. She hoped she hadn't let in something that didn't belong, and at the same time she didn't understand why such a concern should cross her mind. Her family lived in a safe part of the District.

As she started to close the door, a long, doleful howl made her pause. She stared out at the night, suddenly aware of another presence. She searched the shadows, sensing something staring back at her.

The cry repeated, more human than wolf, and for the briefest moment she thought someone was trying to scare her. She tried to convince herself that the wail came from a foreign breed, a diplomat's dog. After all, she lived in Washington, D.C., and unusual animals were brought here from faraway countries. Maybe this one had a peculiar bark, a feral cry.

She shut the door and slipped the deadbolt in place, then turned the thermostat down and went into the kitchen. She switched on the overhead light. If her best friend, Sara, had been there, the two of them would have been falling against each other and laughing at how frightened Sudi had become, but alone Sudi couldn't find the humor in her fear. She opened the refrigerator with tremulous fingers and pulled out a carton of cherry-vanilla ice cream.

Her cat, Patty Pie, rubbed against her leg, begging with purrs and meows for a bite. Sudi found a spoon, scooped a tad into Pie's dish, then stood over the sink and spooned a larger bite into her own mouth. She let the ice cream melt over her tongue.

As she started to dip her spoon into the carton again, Pie hissed. Sudi turned to see what had upset her cat, and as she did, she caught an image in the corner of her eye. She turned back and glanced up. Behind her reflection on the windowpane, a long, snouted face with lurid eyes and tall, pointed ears glared back at her.

The spoon fell from her hand and clanked

against the porcelain sink. Sudi stepped back, dropping the carton of ice cream. She switched off the light and stood in the dark, gazing back at the empty window frame. She wasn't sure what she had expected to see, but the wraithlike image was gone now.

She tried to convince herself that a lost dog had seen the light in the kitchen and had stood on its back paws, nose against the window, begging for her company. But such an animal would have needed to stretch to a height of seven feet at least. She didn't think that was possible.

Without considering it more, she picked up the carton of ice cream, then took a roll of paper towels and cleaned up the mess on the floor. A soft thump on the back steps near the mud porch made her freeze. She was too afraid to go and see what was making the sound.

Reason told her that it was just the stray dog, trying to get inside, but still her heart continued to pound. She didn't believe in ghosts or demons, and she had never been afraid of the night. She tried to talk herself out of her uneasiness—but then she saw Pie.

The yellow cat crouched low and backed away, appearing afraid, the fur on his back standing straight up.

Sudi's instincts took over. She raced up the stairs to her bedroom, Pie scampering beside her. The cat darted into the room ahead of her. She turned on the light, and when she closed the door, the sudden movement stirred the air and the pile of torn-up photographs on her desk fluttered before settling again.

She had spent the afternoon ripping up all of her pictures of Brian. She wanted zero reminders of him. But now she wondered if maybe the breakup with Brian was affecting her more than she wanted to admit. Brian had scared her. Did he still? Could anxiety have caused her sleepwalking?

She grabbed the masking tape from her desk drawer and tore off several pieces, then stuck them over the doorjamb and across the door. The tape wouldn't stop her from leaving her room, but she hoped that untangling it would be enough to awaken her if she did start sleepwalking again. She crawled into bed, wanting nothing more than to huddle under her covers and lose herself in dreams.

Pie jumped on the quilt, curled up beside her, and began purring noisily.

As Sudi drifted off, she thought of Brian again. They had broken up on Saturday, but the real break had come the day Dominique Dupont had transferred into Lincoln High School. Her father was the cultural attaché at the French embassy. Usually the diplomats' kids attended Entre Nous Academy, but Dominique had wanted to experience the "real" American teen life, so she had enrolled in public school.

Sudi shuddered, trying to push memories of Brian away. She should have felt grateful that they were through, so why did she keep crying? It wasn't as if she had really been crazy about Brian, anyway. She had liked Scott, but Brian had asked her out first, and by her third date with Brian, everyone was calling them a couple.

Then Brian had revealed a darker side, and everything about their relationship had changed. What had made her go back for more?

She drifted off, her mind replaying the memory of the night she wanted to forget.

* * *

Morning came before Sudi was ready. She blinked at the sunlight, grateful to find herself in bed. The masking tape still bridged the crack between her wall and the door, and the fear she had experienced the night before felt like a fading dream. She pulled the covers over her head and rolled over.

Her cheek hit something hard. Her eyes opened.

A snake lay beside her.

She jumped out of bed and choked on a scream. The reptile was made of bronze, maybe four feet long, and inlaid with blue and green stones that mimicked a viper's skin. She picked it up, surprise mingling with curiosity. It might have been someone's staff or walking stick. She smoothed her hand over the symbols etched in the sides. The tiny pictures looked like Egyptian hiero-glyphs. Her fingers caressed the beetles, frogs, and baboons.

The images squirmed beneath her touch until they were streaming down the rod.

She cried out and dropped the snake. The rod clanked on the hardwood floor.

She rubbed her hand down her T-shirt, trying

to erase the unpleasant feeling on her skin. Sunshine reflecting off the bronze had probably given the impression that the images were moving, but that didn't explain the strange throbbing beneath her fingers. She looked around wondering how the snake had gotten into her bed.

A sudden gust blew through her open window and caught the pile of torn-up photographs. Bits and pieces of Brian's face whirled around her. The sheer panels between the drapes had been pulled aside, and the window screen rested against the wall. Maybe she had gone sleepwalking again after all.

Panic-stricken, she examined her hands and knees for proof that she had crawled out onto the porch roof while still asleep. She imagined herself digging through a neighbor's trash, finding the horrible walking stick, and bringing it home.

She picked it up again and ran her fingers over the markings. The symbols remained still. She sighed and closed her window, then ripped off the masking tape and threw open her door.

The doorknob continued thumping against the wall as she ran down the hallway and into the bathroom. She locked the door, then stared at her swollen eyelids in the bathroom mirror. Everyone was going to know she had been crying. But that wasn't her biggest concern. She and Brian shared the same friends, so what happened now? Did Dominique just replace Sudi, or did they both fit into the same group?

She thought of the three girls in her drama class, loners who didn't belong. Kids made fun of them, and to avoid the taunts the girls ducked through the crowded hallways, heads down, wearing their bulky coats in spite of the furnace heat, as if they were trying to hide inside their winter clothing. Sudi worried that she would share this same fate.

After taking a shower and drying her hair, Sudi went back to her room. She slipped into a silky purple camisole, then pulled on her tightest low-slung jeans. The new stiletto pumps were going to inflict serious pain by the end of the day. She wrapped Band-Aids around her toes and wore the shoes anyway.

Normally she put on mascara, but she couldn't chance it. The forecast of tears made it too risky. She hurried to the stairs, but as she passed her sisters' room, the silence made her pause. They were never that quiet. And why hadn't they been banging on the bathroom door, telling her to hurry so they could take their showers?

Maybe Sudi had let something into the house last night after all. Slowly, she stepped back to their door and wrapped her fingers around the knob, her heart racing in anticipation of what she would find inside their bedroom.

She opened the door and gasped. "What are you doing?" she asked, even though she knew.

Nicole and Carrie sat on the bed under their lacy pink canopy, a Ouija board between them. Their fingers tapped the planchette, and the small plastic triangle shimmied beneath their touch, then streaked across the alphabet printed in a semicircle on the board and stopped on the YES.

"Mom's going to be pissed," Sudi said. Their mother had thrown away the last Ouija board, along with a tarot deck and the dried herbs that had left a lingering scent of licorice in their room.

Nicole and Carrie turned, each tucking a wisp of waist-length, white-blond hair behind her ear. They were identical twins, but Nicole's love for potato chips and chocolate had added plumpness to her cheeks, while Carrie's picky eating habits had narrowed her oval face. They no longer wore the same size, but they still had a similar unsettling way of looking at Sudi as if they could read her thoughts.

"We're doing this for you," Nicole explained.

"Don't put what you're doing on me," Sudi said. "I have enough problems."

"Precisely," Carrie answered.

"I saw the two of you burning something in the backyard," Sudi said. "I thought you were getting rid of bad test grades, but you were practicing magic again, weren't you?"

Carrie shrugged. "We were burning chicken bones to give Brian skinny legs for hurting you. We hate him for making you cry."

"That's not nice," Sudi scolded, taking on her big-sister role even though she hoped the spell worked. "Besides, I'm the one who broke up with him," she said, practicing the words she planned to say at school. "I told him we were through."

Carrie and Nicole stared at Sudi with something close to pity in their large blue eyes. They obviously didn't believe her. If Sudi couldn't convince her twelve-year-old sisters, then how was she going to convince her entire sophomore class?

"You need something to protect you," Carrie said.

Sudi laughed. "I need a charm to protect me from bad boyfriends," she answered, but as she turned to leave, a soft rasping made her look down. The planchette slid across the Ouija board and pointed to the *S*.

"How'd you do that?" Sudi asked. The board hadn't tilted, and neither of her sisters had moved.

"We didn't," Nicole said excitedly. "It's speaking to us."

Nicole and Carrie put their fingers back on the plastic pointer. The planchette slid to the *U*, then twirled back and pointed to the *D*.

"It's going to be a message for you, Sudi," Nicole whispered, as if speaking too loudly might interrupt the board's concentration.

"You know I don't believe in that kind of stuff," Sudi answered and started downstairs.

In the kitchen she grabbed an apple and bit

into it as she walked through the back porch and out into the yard. She stood under the kitchen window and examined the wet grass. She saw no paw prints in the soggy earth or nose smudges on the windowpane. Maybe she had imagined the dog after all.

When she reentered the house, Carrie and Nicole stood in the kitchen, waiting for her, their faces solemn.

"You need to know something," Carrie said.

Sudi rolled her eyes. "I don't need your Ouija board to know my life is trash."

The twins gasped.

"Don't say that," Nicole scolded. "Words have power . . ."

". . . And what you say will come true," Carrie finished. "It's a scientifically proven fact that you'll eventually become whatever you call yourself."

"Then you two had better be careful," Sudi snapped back, "because if you keep messing around with the occult, you're going to turn into little hags who marry toads and—" Sudi stopped. She was taking her anxiety out on her sisters. "Sorry," she whispered and stepped past them.

"Today could be dangerous for you," Nicole warned. "The Ouija board is always right."

"Someone is after you," Carrie added.

"And I suppose it's someone *eeeeviiiilll*," Sudi said, mockingly stretching *evil* into a sinister Halloween melody. She left the kitchen, grabbed her sweater from the hall closet, tugged it on, and turned to leave.

Her sisters stood behind her, blocking her way.

"Listen to us for once," Nicole pleaded.

Their worried expressions almost made Sudi believe that something bad *was* going to happen.

"You have to stop this," Sudi said gently. "It isn't healthy. That's why Mom threw away all that occult stuff. You need to understand that when your kindergarten teacher told you that twins have a psychic connection to each other, she didn't mean that the two of you are psychics, or that you have supernatural powers."

She kissed Nicole, then Carrie, and headed out the door.

At the corner, Sudi glanced back at the house. Her sisters stood together on the porch, their nightgowns waving in the breeze, staring after her. Sudi didn't believe in their connection to another world, but, looking at them, she wondered what message the Ouija board had given them.

The printer whirred, pushing out paper copies of the Web site on sleepwalking. Sudi leaned back and put drops in her eyes, which were dry and red from staring at the computer screen. Then she pulled the band from her ponytail and ruffled her hair.

School had ended, but she had stayed late, searching for information on somnambulism. Stress had probably caused her sleepwalking, and for that reason she had decided not to tell her mother about the episode unless it happened again—and maybe she wouldn't even tell her then—because if she did, her mother would start questioning Sudi, searching for the cause, and Sudi didn't want anyone to know the truth. She hadn't even told Sara about that night with Brian.

Sudi grabbed the printouts and stuffed them into her backpack on top of her shoes, then left the computer room and started up the stairs, barefoot except for the grimy Band-Aids wrapped around her sore toes. The blisters on her heels burned. She'd only worn the killer shoes for Brian, but he hadn't even come to school. Sudi had learned through friends that his dad was being honored at the Pentagon, and Dominique had attended the ceremony with Brian and his family.

As she passed Brian's locker, an unwanted memory came back to her. The first time they had driven over to Virginia, Brian had steered his car down a dark street where no one could witness what they were going to do. She had thought he wanted to take their relationship further, but his mind had never been on kissing her. Instead he asked her to drive his huge old Cadillac, even though she didn't have a license.

Then Brian had put on his skates, and, knees bent like a skier, he had taken hold of the car bumper while she started the engine. She drove down the paved roads, while Brian kept yelling at her to go faster. She pressed her foot down on the gas pedal until wind snapped through the window and tousled her hair.

The oncoming lights flashed again in her mind, and she flinched. If the SUV hadn't swerved, she would have killed Brian and maybe others. But instead of being upset, Brian had said the near-crash had been his best ride ever. He was into skitching and car surfing—anything extreme.

How many times had he forced her to drive down those same roads? Why hadn't she been able to tell him no?

She should have felt relieved that Brian was going out with Dominique now, but Sudi had an uneasy feeling that her bond with Brian wasn't broken. She didn't know what she would do if he called again and she didn't understand why she had taken such risks. It was as if something dormant inside her had awakened, a part of her she had never known before, and it scared her.

By the time she reached the second-floor landing, the sun had set, leaving the corridor in dusky light. The silence made her pause. The band practiced every day after school. Normally, the off-key tones from clarinets and flutes filled the air. She glanced at her watch. It was almost seven. She couldn't have been on the computer that long without being aware of the hours slipping away.

The sound of footsteps in the stairwell broke the quiet, but knowing that someone else wandered the deserted hallways with her did not comfort her now. She tiptoed to her locker, not understanding the intense need to hide. The feeling nagged at her even though reason told her she was safe.

Maybe she should have listened to her sisters' warning after all. She looked up and down the hallway, not sure what she expected to see, before she worked her combination. She opened her locker and caught her reflection in the heart-shaped mirror on the door. Her hair was parted on the wrong side, exposing a section of the birthmark on her scalp.

As she started to fix her part, a hand clamped down on her shoulder.

Sudi tried to turn and lost her balance.

Carter grabbed her arm and steadied her. "What's wrong?" he asked.

"You startled me," she said and started to laugh, but stopped. She had looked both ways down the hallway and hadn't seen him. "Did you sneak up on me?"

"Why would I do that?" he asked with a slow, easy grin, and rested his hand on the locker above her. He edged closer and looked down at her as if he were seeing her for the first time. He tilted his head until his lips were dangerously close to kissing her.

"Carter," she said, flustered. "We're best friends."

"Just testing," he teased.

She shook her head. Girls at school warned each other to stay away from him, but they never followed their own advice. No one could resist him even with his reputation as a heart-breaker.

"Brian is an idiot," Carter said, interrupting her thoughts. "I told him so when he started going out with Dominique."

His fingers ran down her arm. She pulled away, then hesitated. Maybe he was only offering her the comfort of friendship. He squeezed her hand.

"It's pretty funny the way you ruined Dominique's boots," he went on. "Brian told me she's making him buy her a new pair."

"It was an accident," Sudi protested. "The lemonade slipped out of my hand."

"No one believes you," Carter said and shot her a wry smile.

"You know I'd tell you if I'd done it on purpose." She tried to concentrate on which books she needed to take home, but her mind jumped back to Saturday, the day she and Brian had broken up.

Sudi had bought lunch at the Bread Line, a small restaurant on Pennsylvania Avenue near the White House, and as she bit into the crusty bread and sweet Italian sausage, Brian and Dominique had walked inside, holding hands. When Brian leaned over to kiss Dominique, his gaze fell on Sudi. She immediately marched over to Brian, planning to tell him that they were through, but the drink she was holding dropped from her hand, splashing over Dominique's pricey boots. Sudi fled in embarrassment.

"Can I give Scott your cell number?" Carter asked.

"Scott?" Sudi asked, hoping she didn't sound too breathless.

"I didn't know if you were ready," Carter answered. "You look like you landed pretty hard."

"I'm through with Brian," she mumbled, not sure that she was, and reached into her locker. She pulled a folder from under her rolled-up sweater, and a stack of test papers spilled forward.

"Scott's been waiting for you to figure out that Brian's all wrong for you," Carter said, but his eyes never met hers. He stared at the lopsided pile of tests, then ran his fingers through the pages as if checking her grades. He seemed to be looking for something.

"You can give Scott my number," Sudi answered, but a thought occurred to her as she pulled her shoes from her backpack and slipped them onto her wounded feet. "How do you know Scott?"

"He plays rugby," Carter answered, and then, abruptly, he began jogging backward. "I'll catch you tomorrow," he yelled before turning and sprinting away.

Sudi glanced into her locker and wondered what Carter had expected to find. She pulled out her sweater, and a white envelope glided after it, skating across the floor. She picked it up. URGENT was written across the front. She ripped the seal, pulled out a square piece of paper and read the message.

Our meeting cannot be put off any longer. Come to the Hotel Washington, Sky Terrace restaurant, sunset. I will tell you everything.

A thrill rushed through her. The invitation had to be from Scott. Carter's odd behavior suddenly made sense; he hadn't been looking for anything, he had been sneaking the invitation into her locker.

She stuffed her sweater inside, then twirled the combination lock, grabbed her backpack, and hoped she wasn't too late.

CHAPTER 3

Sudi dropped her backpack on a love seat near the door, straightened her lacy camisole and stepped into the crowded Sky Terrace restaurant. The warm evening air wrapped around her, bringing the lush smells of frying onions and seafood. Even the night views of the White House and the Washington Monument were perfect for a first date. Her stomach fluttered in anticipation.

When Scott didn't come forward to greet her, she headed toward the end of the terrace, where people stood clustered in small groups. Maybe Scott had invited her to a gathering of Entre Nous students.

Halfway there, she noticed a young man, seated at a table near the railing, waving at her. At first, she thought he was trying to get the attention of someone behind her, but then he called her name. "Sudi!"

She swerved around a fast-moving waitress and started toward him, assuming he was a friend of Scott's. He had the Entre Nous look: a three-hundred-dollar haircut and a jacket that cost more than Sudi spent on clothing in an entire year.

"I'm Abdel," he said, rising to greet her, and took her hand. Then, motioning to a girl seated beside him, he added, "This is Meri."

Everyone in D.C. knew Senator Stark's daughter. Meri attended Entre Nous and was usually surrounded by photographers and bodyguards. Her mother had made one bid for her party's presidential nomination, and political analysts said that this year the senator would succeed.

Meri waved and looked toward the exit, as if she were about to use Sudi's arrival as an excuse to leave. Maybe Abdel had been a blind date and Meri was unhappy with the match—although on the surface, Sudi couldn't see any reason for Meri to be displeased.

"I'd also like you to meet Dalila," Abdel added.

Sudi had never seen Dalila before, and she definitely would have remembered meeting her. Dalila was breathtakingly beautiful, despite her shaven head and the strange tattoo above her right temple.

"I'm pleased to meet you," Dalila said quietly.

"Hi," Sudi answered, looking around. "Where's Scott?" She took a seat next to Abdel.

"Scott?" Abdel asked.

"Scott Johnston," Sudi said. "He asked me to meet him here."

"I asked you here," Abdel corrected her. He handed her a menu.

"You sent me the invitation?" Sudi asked, surprised.

"I needed to meet with the three of you."

Abdel set his arms on the table and leaned forward. "I've been sent to the United States by the Hour priests, a secret society—"

"Sheesh," Meri said and fell back in her chair. "Is this some weird way to meet my mother?"

"Why would I want to meet her?" Abdel asked.

"Because everyone in this town wants to speak to her," Meri answered curtly. "And FYI, you won't get a meeting with her through me. I only came here because you gave me such a valuable gift." She held up a rod with the head of a snake that looked like the one Sudi had found on her bed earlier. "My mother told me I had to return this to you."

"It's an apotropaic wand," Abdel explained. "The ancient Egyptians used it for protection. And you can't return it to me, because it belongs to you."

"That excuse is not going to work with my mom," Meri said and placed the snake on the table.

"Maybe after I explain why I've been sent here, you'll want to keep it," Abdel said. "The three of you are descended from the divine pharaohs of ancient Egypt."

Dalila nodded knowingly, suggesting that his revelation wasn't a secret to her. But Meri and Sudi just stared at each other, then burst into spontaneous laughter.

"Do I look regal?" Meri asked between giggles. She was thin and tomboyish, her hair falling into her eyes.

"Abdel is telling the truth," Dalila insisted.

"I was born in Nebraska," Sudi answered pulling on a strand of silky blond hair. Her eyes were blue, her skin pale cream. She didn't look Egyptian. "My family has lived in North America since the Dutch settled Delaware in 1631. So how can I be related to a pharaoh?"

"Because you are," Abdel answered. "And now you must stand against evil and defend the world."

"Right," Meri said and folded her arms over her chest, solemn again.

"Because we're superheroes," Sudi added sarcastically and smiled. She'd played enough pranks on other people to recognize this as someone's practical joke, but who would go to such an extreme? Then she thought of Brian and the new boots he had to buy for Dominique. But he was the one who had dumped *her*. Could he really be that upset with her?

Abdel spoke again, "Since the goddess Isis gave the Hour priests the Book of Thoth, the priests have devoted their lives to stopping the forces of darkness. So, when the Cult of Anubis turned up in Washington, D.C., we were concerned."

Everyone in D.C. had heard about the cult: a new age group from California that had opened a spa, offering relaxation and pleasure for overworked Washingtonians. But Sudi had also heard rumors about therapies that sounded more like magic than cures, and elaborate secret ceremonies performed for members only.

"The cult leaders plan to destroy the bloodline of Horus and return the universe to the chaos from which it came," Abdel said, breaking into Sudi's thoughts. "They'll use demons and—"

"Do you expect me to believe that?" Sudi asked. For a practical joke it was pretty lame, but then another idea came to her, and she suddenly wished she had worn makeup and her push-up bra because this had to be a new reality show. It made sense to her now. Dalila looked drop-dead gorgeous and was probably the hostess, and Meri was a celebrity. Sudi had an image of her sisters writing to the producers and proposing Sudi, the ultimate skeptic, for their show. She lifted her glass of water, trying not to look too obvious, and glanced around, searching for the hidden cameras and microphones.

Abdel reached into a worn leather pouch and pulled out three tattered beige scrolls with dark brown striations.

"These are papyri from the Book of Thoth," he said and handed one to each girl. "You'll need the incantations written here to fight the creatures sent to destroy you."

Sudi touched the frayed edges and unrolled the scroll, then ran her finger over the images of rabbits, snakes, and eyes.

"Only the divine heirs to the throne of Egypt have the power to use the magic in the Book of Thoth to stop the dark forces freed by the cult," Abdel explained.

"Oh, okay, sure. I'll just use my Saturday nights to protect the city from mummies," Sudi scoffed, as she imagined her friends laughing when the program aired on TV.

"You don't really believe this stuff, do you?" Meri asked Abdel. "It's bunk."

Abdel scowled. "You must believe me. The cult leaders could be contacting you already, using a spell to make you walk to them while you're still asleep."

A chill swept through Sudi. How could the show's producers know about her sleepwalking? It had to be just a coincidence. Or maybe Carter was in on it and he had seen what she had been researching in the computer room.

"You're wasting my time," Meri said tiredly and glanced at the other end of the terrace, trying to get someone's attention. "I need to go home and study."

"I'm telling you the truth," Abdel said, his voice rising. "And the proof is in the identical birthmarks you each have beneath your hair."

Sudi reached up and touched her head, then looked across the table. Meri had done the same. They both glimpsed the eye on Dalila's scalp, then looked back at each other again.

"Your birthmarks look like the one that Dalila has above her temple," Abdel explained. "It's the sacred eye of Horus."

"I've heard enough," Meri said.

Abdel turned to Dalila. "Help me convince them that I'm telling the truth."

"Why should I, when no one told me the truth?" Dalila asked, her large eyes becoming glassy with tears.

"Your uncle said that he had reared you to be the perfect heir." Abdel seemed truly shocked.

"The heir to some fortune, I thought. I assumed I was being groomed to marry some rich prince from Saudi Arabia," she replied.

"You were taught the old ways," he argued.

"So I would be a treasure to my people when I married and moved to the Middle East," Dalila shot back.

Sudi watched Dalila. She was definitely overplaying for the cameras.

"No one ever told me I had to fight demons. And, although I don't understand your reasons for doing so, I know you're lying." Dalila grabbed a shawl from the back of her chair, flung it around her like an actress leaving the stage, and stormed off.

"That's it," Meri said, picking up her scroll.

"And, Abdel, take me off your invite list, because I'm definitely not coming to another one of your dinners, no matter how much my mother insists that I should."

Abdel clasped her wrist.

"Let go of me," Meri yelled and tried to yank her hand back, but his hold was powerful.

At the other end of the terrace two men got up from their chairs. One had taken off his jacket, and his husky chest and arms barely fit into his short-sleeved shirt. The other, taller than the first, had a hard, sunburned face. He flung his chair out of the way and marched forward, bumping into the table edges.

"Let go of her!" he shouted with booming authority.

Diners and waiters became silent. The thump-thumping of the two presidential helicopters landing on the White House lawn were the only sounds on the terrace.

"You must listen to me," Abdel pleaded, holding Meri's arm. "Your life is in danger. Do you think the cult leaders will let you live?"

"Look behind you," Meri challenged.

Abdel glanced over his shoulder. The two men had pulled guns, and their attention was focused intently on Abdel.

Diners screamed, and a table toppled over as people stampeded toward the exits.

But instead of releasing Meri, Abdel grabbed her head.

Meri cursed and flung her arms, pounding on his back.

Sudi froze, undecided. This wasn't like any reality show she'd ever seen before; Meri looked truly distressed. Maybe Abdel was just a rich guy living in his own fantasy world.

Sudi clutched Abdel's arm, trying to help Meri. She dug her fingernails into his skin, but Abdel didn't flinch.

"Release her," the taller man yelled again.

Abdel ignored the order and spread his fingers in Meri's hair, then bowed his head until it rested against her forehead. He spoke in a language that Sudi didn't understand and had never heard before.

Meri stopped struggling and tilted her head, looking into Abdel's eyes, transfixed.

The two men with the guns lunged forward. The taller one grabbed Sudi around the waist and pulled her out of the way. Then both men wrestled with Abdel, trying to rescue Meri, but Abdel didn't let go until he had finished speaking.

When he released her, she collapsed into the burly man's arms. The taller one slipped his gun back into its holster and tried to handcuff Abdel, but Abdel shoved him aside and turned to Sudi.

Sudi had no idea what Abdel wanted with her, but she no longer believed this was a practical joke, or a new reality show. She eased backward, afraid, and bumped into a table, knocking over a glass. Water trickled onto the floor near her feet.

Still clutching the scroll, she spun around and tried to run. Her feet slipped on the ice cubes and water. She almost fell, then regained her balance and dashed into the hallway. She grabbed her backpack, kicked out of her shoes, and sprinted down the carpet.

A gun fired as she ran for the elevator.

"Come on. Come on." She furiously hit the call button.

Abdel stepped out of the restaurant and ran toward Sudi as the metal doors opened. She rushed inside and pushed LOBBY, then DOOR CLOSE.

She fell back against the wall, gasping for air.

An arm shot between the closing doors, and Abdel slipped inside. The doors shut behind him, and the elevator started down.

Sudi tried to punch the alarm button, but Abdel grabbed her hand and kissed the tips of her fingers.

"Please," Sudi said. "Don't touch me."

"Don't be afraid," he whispered and clasped her head in his hands, pulling her toward him.

Sudi whimpered.

Abdel rested his lips against her forehead, his breath warm on her face, and spoke the same strange language he had spoken to Meri.

"Heb menekh hekau," he whispered. *"Uab ab-ek. Hu en na ek nifu er fet-ef."*

And then, unexpectedly, Sudi understood the words. Or was it that he was speaking English again? She wasn't sure. Her nerves were raw, and her heartbeat thundered in her ears.

"Sublime of magic," Abdel continued. "Your

heart is pure. To you I send the power of the ages."

In spite of being in a closed elevator, wind blew into Sudi's nostrils and filled her lungs. Her chest heaved, trying to catch a breath not tainted with the smell of tombs.

Abdel forced her head down, and then his lips moved against her hair, over her birthmark.

"Divine one," he whispered. "Come into being. I awaken the soul of ancient Egypt, lying dormant in your soul."

He released her.

Her knees buckled, and he caught her before she fell.

When the elevator doors opened, Sudi grabbed her backpack and scrambled out into the reception area. She collided with Meri's body-guards, who had run down the stairs.

As the elevator closed, the two men forced the doors open and looked inside.

The elevator was empty.

"Where did he go?" the taller one shouted at Sudi.

Sudi shook her head. "I didn't see."

"Wait here," he commanded.

But pure instinct was driving Sudi now. She needed to go someplace safe, and that meant home.

When the men ran off, Sudi hurried outside.

Sirens filled the night. Secret Service agents climbed from black sedans and charged inside.

Still in a daze, Sudi ran across Fifteenth Street and headed north, crossing into Lafayette Park in front of the White House. She slouched on a bench in the darkness, her knees shaking too violently to continue.

Her scalp itched, and her birthmark burned. She opened her backpack, searching for her mirror. The tattered scroll was resting on top even though she couldn't remember putting it there. She started to throw it away, then thought better of it, crushed it under her books, and found her mirror. She studied herself, wondering what Abdel had done to her. Wisps of hair stood in a halo around her head as though she had walked through a cloud of static electricity.

"Sudi?" Someone called her name.

She jumped up, ready to run, her bare feet stinging with blisters and cuts.

Scott walked toward her in a slow, even stride. He still wore his school uniform: gray slacks, blue blazer, and white shirt. He had loosened his red tie. His curly brown hair brushed against his collar, and in the dim light he looked more handsome than her memory of him. He still had his California tan even though he lived in D.C. with his grandmother now. Rumor had it that he had gotten into trouble with drugs back in Los Angeles.

"What's wrong?" he asked with true concern in his voice.

"Just a bad case of the frizzies," she answered, trying to sound lighthearted when all she wanted was to fall into his arms and cry. Her day could not possibly get worse—and then she saw Michelle.

Michelle strutted toward them. The Entre Nous uniform jacket fit most girls like a box, but Michelle had had hers tailored to accentuate every curve. The top two buttons of her white shirt were undone, offering a view of her lace bra and cleavage.

"Hey, Sudi," Michelle said and wrapped her hands possessively around Scott's arm. Sudi and Michelle had been best friends through elementary school, but in junior high Michelle had been accepted into the academy, and the two of them had quickly grown apart.

But instead of responding to Michelle's challenge, Sudi walked away, her brain too flustered and confused to let her engage in flirtatious combat over Scott.

"Sudi," Michelle called after her, sounding disappointed.

"Later," Sudi replied over her shoulder.

"Do you need a ride?" Scott yelled.

She shook her head in response and continued to the street. At the curb, she hailed a cab and eased inside. She waved good-bye and closed her eyes, grateful no one would be home yet. On Monday nights her sisters had dance lessons, and her mom and dad always took them out to eat afterward.

A short ride later, Sudi hurried inside her house and ran upstairs to her parents' bedroom. She opened the chest at the foot of their bed. The smell of cedarwood filled the air. She pulled out her baby-photo album and fanned through the pages.

In every picture, a bonnet or cap or blanket covered her head. And then she found one. She tore it out, certain now that the eye on Dalila's scalp had been a tattoo. In the picture, Sudi's birthmark looked like an ordinary dark mole.

She sat on the edge of her parents' bed and considered what had happened. Maybe Abdel, Dalila, and Meri had only been part of some strange initiation that Sudi had to go through before she could date a guy at Entre Nous. The students were known for being snooty and sticking together, excluding outsiders. She imagined Abdel telling Scott everything that Sudi had done. Maybe they had even videotaped it and were watching her now, laughing at the fear in her eyes.

Sudi tossed the photo back into the chest and slammed the lid back down. No guy was worth that kind of trouble, not even a hottie like Scott.

Sudi crunched into the dill pickle she was sharing with Sara, then took a sip of Coke and handed
both back to her friend. She had thought the class
trip to the Smithsonian Institute would be an easy
way to avoid Brian and Dominique, but when she
stepped onto the school bus that morning, she had
found herself face to face with the two of them,
embraced in a kiss.

She had tossed them a friendly smile, even

though she had wanted to spit. But what she remembered most was the way Dominique had smelled of jasmine and roses. The designer perfume was something Sudi's mother would never have bought for her.

"How can Dominique look so beautiful at the end of the day?" Sudi complained. Dominique was walking by herself toward the line of school buses parked in front of the Washington Monument.

Sara turned, her rhinestone skull earrings jangling against her necklaces.

"Dominique is wondering the same about you," Sara said. "I bet she rubs her skin raw trying to get the glow that comes naturally to you. And her curly bun is definitely an add-on." Sara grabbed a fistful of Sudi's blond tangles. "No one can compete with this. Your hair is gorgeous, and so are you."

"You're the best friend ever," Sudi said and hugged Sara.

"Aw, quit with the mushy stuff." Sara tossed the remains of the pickle and Coke into a trash bin. "Where do you want to go next?"

Sudi glanced at her watch. "It's time to go back to the bus."

"We can't leave without visiting Minister Cox," Sara said and pulled on Sudi's arm. They dodged the oncoming joggers and hurried across the treelined lawn to the National Museum of Natural History.

At the security station, Sudi unzipped her backpack. The guard stuck a wooden stick inside and shone the beam of a flashlight around the grinning monkey faces on her Paul Frank pajamas. She was spending the night with Sara so they could finish their class project on space travel.

After Sara passed through the security check, the two of them ran around the African elephant display in the center of the rotunda, took the escalator down to the ground floor, and rode the elevator near the Constitution Avenue entrance up to the Origins of Western Culture exhibit on the second floor.

"I love all the cubbies and alcoves in this exhibit," Sara said, rushing around the diorama of an early man drawing a bison on a cave wall. "This would be the best place in the world for a game of hide-and-seek."

They stopped in front of the outer coffin of

Tenet-Khonsu, an ancient Egyptian high priestess.

Sudi had told Sara everything that had happened the night before with Abdel. Now Sara looked at the hieroglyphs. "Tell me what they say."

Sudi had seen the same pictographs before, but this time she felt she could decipher their meaning. She read out loud, *"I have not sullied the world of the Nile. . . ."*

She stopped. How could she know what the symbols meant? Yet she was confident that she had interpreted them correctly.

"Show-off," Sara teased and playfully elbowed her. "Did Abdel teach you how to read hieroglyphs, too?"

"Lucky guess," Sudi answered. She couldn't, of course, read in any language except English. Yet somehow she knew the meaning of the symbols inscribed on the coffin.

"But it's a cool idea," Sara said with a scampish grin. "We could bring Abdel and Dalila here, and you could pretend like you can read the hieroglyphs, and you could tell them something dire." Sara started laughing, her imagination taking hold of her.

Sudi gave her a look. "I don't want to continue the game with Abdel and Dalila. I just want to forget it ever happened."

"You will," Sara said and moved on to the mummy called Minister Cox. She tapped the glass. "Can you imagine having your bones on display in a museum? They should make it against the law."

Sara talked as she always did about the unfairness of denying Minister Cox a proper burial, but Sudi walked on to the next coffin and concentrated on the hieroglyphs. She understood the text. How was that possible?

Finally, she read the inscription out loud. *"As for anyone who might pass, pause and make an offering, that I might be well remembered—"*

"Stop," Sara said and nudged her. "You're creeping me out now. You made the words sound too real."

Sudi clenched the strap on her backpack, trying to stop a sudden sense of falling. If she could read the ancient writing, then was it possible that the other things Abdel had told her were also true? She took a quick step back and caught herself.

"What's wrong?" Sara asked.

Sudi shook her head. "Nothing," she answered. "Have you ever heard of someone called Horus?"

"The Egyptian god Hor?" Sara asked and didn't wait for a reply. "The Greeks called him Horus. He battled the god Seth. It was that typical fight between good and evil. Horus stood for order, and Seth wanted to destroy the world. Did Abdel talk about him?"

Sudi couldn't answer, because a sudden feeling of nausea had overcome her. She rushed to the restroom at the back of the exhibit, hurried inside, and turned on the cold water, splashing it onto her face. She took several deep breaths, her head in the sink, then looked up and stared at her reflection in the mirror.

Sara appeared behind her, watching her.

"Hey, are you okay?" Sara asked.

Sudi nodded, even though her legs felt wobbly. "I think I'm coming down with the flu," she lied. She had no intention of leaving the museum until she had had a chance to study the hieroglyphs alone and find a rational explanation for what was happening. "Go on without me. I'll catch a cab."

"You know you aren't allowed to do that," Sara said.

"Do you think Mrs. Grumm wants me puking on the bus?"

"Yeah, I guess you'd start a real vomit fest," Sara laughed. She stepped closer and rubbed Sudi's back. "I'll stay with you."

"Go on," Sudi said. "I'll be okay."

"Are you sure?" Sara asked, looking doubtful.

"Please," Sudi answered and rushed into a stall pretending that she was going to be ill. "I don't want you to watch me." She slammed the door and made gagging noises until she heard Sara's retreating footsteps on the tiled floor.

Sudi waited, the leaking faucet counting out the seconds. Then she went back to the glass-enclosed display and stared at the inscriptions. She was definitely reading the hieroglyphs, or at least, in her mind she had been tricked into believing that she could. Abdel must have hypnotized her, given her a posthypnotic instruction to make her believe she could read the ancient writing even though she couldn't.

She imagined the students at Entre Nous laughing at what Abdel had done to her. Even so, she couldn't understand why she had been singled out.

A muffled noise made Sudi aware that someone was nearby. She spun around, and, when she didn't see anyone, she called out, "Hello."

Silence answered her. Something in the quiet made her tense. She sensed someone moving stealthily about.

The exhibit had alcoves, niches, and spaces under the displays where a person could hide, and hide again. But she didn't go looking for the prowler. Her mother had told her to trust her intuition, especially when she felt unsafe, so, without hesitation, Sudi made her way to the elevator.

When she was halfway there, she noticed splotches of mud on the carpet. She followed the trail to a long mound packed against the bottom of the elevator. More clay had been plastered over the frame and door.

Large oval seals were stamped on the surface, and inside each was her name, written in hieroglyphs. A panicked feeling came over her. She had listened to the short documentaries about Egyptian burial customs that ran continuously on the small screen in the museum theater and knew that seals like these had often been placed on tombs.

Someone was going out of his way to frighten her. Entre Nous students had a reputation for having an eccentric sense of humor, but she didn't think they would go this far. Maybe it was someone who had a darker side.

The lights went out, and then she knew.

"Brian," she said angrily. "This is so not funny."

When no one answered, she headed toward the gem exhibit, where the Hope Diamond was displayed, and stopped, puzzled. A wall stretched in front of the hallway that led back to the rotunda. She hadn't noticed it there before. Maybe she had just been so busy talking to Sara that she hadn't seen it.

She hurried toward the exit at the other side of the exhibit, determined not to break into a run and show fear.

But the night lighting shone unsteadily. Darkness waned and pulsed around her. She tried to focus on what was straight ahead, but the mannequins looked more real when half hidden in shadow, and she felt scared. She had an eerie sense that one of them might step from its display and start chasing her.

Finally, she saw the green exit sign and quickened her pace till she got to the bank of elevators. She pressed her finger on the call button, but the light didn't come on.

Still in near darkness, she tried the emergency exit, across from the men's restroom. She slammed against the handlebar.

The door wouldn't open. She stepped back. Locking an emergency exit was definitely against the law. But she wasn't concerned about the legality; she only wanted out. She hated the gloomy cast of shadows that seemed to move and shift around her. She pulled her cell phone from her backpack, flipped it open, and pressed her thumb on the first key, to speed-dial Sara.

Her battery was dead.

She dropped the phone back into the bag, where it landed on top of her pajamas, and realized then that when she didn't arrive home that night, no one was going to start looking for her, because her parents thought she was spending the night with Sara.

She hurried to the other end of the hallway to a door marked STAFF ONLY. She knocked and waited, hoping someone would answer and help her.

The Smithsonian museums were huge, she reasoned and, with so many visitors, people were probably locked inside all the time. If she just waited, a security guard would come through, searching for stragglers. Besides, the place was probably equipped with hidden cameras, motion detectors, and other surveillance devices. If she was patient, someone would find her.

She rummaged around in the bottom of her bag and found a half-eaten candy bar. She bit into the chocolate and walked back to the emergency exit, sat on the floor, and leaned against the wall, listening for the sound of footsteps.

Slowly, the smell of wet earth crept into her awareness. She crawled over to the door and ran her hand along the bottom, over a wet, sticky mound. Clay had been plastered around the door to seal her inside.

Reason told her that no one could take over such a public place to play a game, no matter how powerful or rich their parents might be. So what did that leave? Abdel had told her that cult leaders wanted to destroy the bloodline of Horus. Dark thoughts came to her. Maybe she was their first sacrifice. She imagined CNN broadcasting the gruesome details about her murder inside the Smithsonian.

Fear and panic overcame her rational thoughts, and terror took hold. She needed to find a place to hide. She ran back into the exhibit and crawled into the cubby under the display of Greek vases.

But as time passed and nothing happened, she began to relax. She tried to convince herself that she had no reason to be afraid. No one had ever died from being locked inside a museum overnight.

Finally, near midnight, exhausted from being vigilant, she curled up into a ball and, using her backpack for a pillow, drifted off.

Hours later, a sound roused her from her sleep. At first she didn't know where she was. Then she remembered and glanced at her watch. It read five o'clock.

Footsteps came from the other end of the hallway. She scrambled from her hiding place.

"Hello," she yelled, certain a security guard or

some member of the morning maintenance crew was close by.

She threw her backpack over her shoulder and staggered forward, trying to find whoever it was.

At the next turn, she stopped and listened again.

When she didn't hear anything, she called out, "I'm locked in. Can you help me?"

She waited. Then a soft *thud-thud-thud* came from behind her. Even as she tried to find a rational explanation for the sound, a deeper and more primitive part of her awakened and took control. Someone was trying to frighten her. She didn't believe in ghosts, but human predators did exist.

Without making a sound, she slid around the corner and hid in a dark recess, waiting, the huntress now. When the person passed in front of her, she would see who had been stalking her, without being seen. That knowledge gave her power.

She took another step to the rear of the alcove and bumped into something. She turned around and gazed into the pale blue eyes staring back at her.

Sudi started to run, then realized she was staring at her own reflection in the glass of a darkened display case. She poked her nose closer, feeling foolish. Her heart was still pounding, and fear had left her mouth dry. She wondered vaguely if the odd taste on her tongue was the residue of too much adrenaline.

Her breath fogged the glass, and as she started to write her initials in the steam, an eerie shadow skimmed over her. The air rustled as a woman formed, her hazy image floating in the glass. She wore a helmet, or maybe the headdress was a crown. A golden vulture's head, entwined with that of a hooded cobra, jutted from the front of the headband. The woman had thick black hair and large wings.

Sudi closed her tired eyes, willing the image to vanish, but when she opened them again, the woman was still there, smiling at Sudi with a kind and loving gaze. Her wings fluttered, and the resulting breeze ruffled Sudi's hair.

"Go away," Sudi ordered. This had to be a dream, and moments from now she would awaken and—

"Why is it so hard for you to believe?" the phantom asked.

Sudi wheeled around and faced her hallucination. She took a tentative step forward, then another, and stretched out her hand until her fingertips pressed into warm, soft flesh.

"Listen well, my sister," the woman said softly. "I looked into my scrying bowl and saw that you will need the story I am going to tell."

Sudi nodded and blinked, then pinched herself, trying to wake up.

"Re-Atum emerged from the primeval ocean," the woman began, "and took the form of a Bennubird. Then he flew from the darkness and perched on a rock. When he opened his beak, his cry broke the silence, and with that scream he created what is and what is not to be."

"And how am I supposed to use this story?" Sudi challenged, not expecting the phantom to answer her.

"As you are dying, you will know," the woman said. "But still, you must take care when you speak the terrible words of power."

Sudi nodded and leaned back against the wall, closing her eyes. She just wanted the dream to go away.

"It's safe for you to leave the museum now," the woman said.

Sudi opened her eyes again.

The woman was gone.

Sudi had never been so relieved to have a dream end. She grabbed her backpack and ran toward the elevator.

The clay that had been packed against the metal door the night before was gone. She hurriedly pressed the call button, anxious to get out and tell Sara everything that had happened. But as she stepped inside the elevator, she looked at her hands. Her fingernails were filled with dirt.

She didn't know what Abdel had done to her, but she was determined to prove to herself that the strange things that had been happening to her had nothing to do with magic or ancient forces. As soon as she was safely back in her bedroom, she knew exactly what she was going to do.

Sudi stepped inside her living room and breathed in the aroma of her parents' morning coffee. She listened as she closed the door behind her. Her parents always watched CNN until they left for work. The silence told her that she had the house to herself until her sisters woke up. She hurried up the stairs to her room, sat on the edge of her bed, and pulled the papyrus from her backpack.

She studied the document looking for the right incantation. She still didn't accept that she was actually reading the symbols; her mind had only been tricked into believing that she could. Even so, she picked a spell—or what she thought was one—for transforming into the Bennu-bird.

"Amun-Re, eldest of the gods in the eastern sky, mysterious power of wind . . ." She paused, surprised by the thin quiver in her voice. She cleared her throat and went on. *"Make a path for me to change my earthly khat into that of beloved Bennu.* Xu kua. *I am glorious.* User kua. *I am mighty.* Neteri kua. *I am strong."*

A long minute passed.

Nothing happened.

She grinned, satisfied that she had proven Abdel was a good hypnotist and nothing more. She wondered how long posthypnotic suggestions lasted. She'd google it and get the information after she took her shower. Grabbing clean undies and the ugly green bra her mother had bought on sale, she hurried to the bathroom and claimed it before her sisters woke up. She stripped and climbed under the hot shower spray.

The warm water took away the soreness from sleeping on the museum floor, and as the aches and pains lessened, so did the memory of the night before. She repeated the incantation, making it her own personal rap, a reminder to herself to never let her mind get carried away with fantasy again. She liked the sound the words made and repeated the spell a third time.

"Amun-Re," she said as she shaved her legs, "eldest of the gods in the eastern sky."

She soaped her arms and used her pouf as she continued, "Mysterious power of wind, make a path for me to change my earthly *khat* into that of beloved Bennu."

"Xu kua," she picked up the beat and stuck her face in the water. "I am glorious."

"User kua. I am mighty."

"Neteri kua. I am strong."

A pounding on the bathroom door made Sudi start. She turned off the water.

"We know you're glorious," Carrie yelled from the hallway.

"Yes, but other people have to use the shower,

O mighty one," Nicole screamed. "How long are you going to take?"

"Out in a sec," Sudi yelled back and stepped from the tub. She wrapped a towel around her and began drying off.

A sudden sharp pain in her shoulder, however, made her wince. "Ouch." She rubbed the muscle, trying to work out the pain. Tiny bumps sprouted on her skin. She didn't need a break-out, not while the weather was still warm and she could wear her halter tops.

She wiped the steam from the mirror and turned to look at her back. Hundreds of red welts spotted her skin. Just her luck. She was probably allergic to something in the museum.

She slipped into her panties and felt a feverish ache in her hip bones. Maybe she was coming down with the flu.

As she hooked her bra, downy feathers floated to the floor. She glanced up at the ceiling, but she saw nothing to explain the feathers encircling her feet.

Then, with a jab of adrenaline, she remembered the incantation she had been reciting.

"Three," she said in a shaky voice and stared back into the mirror. Didn't three times have some kind of magical power? People always said the third time's the charm.

"No," she screamed as plumage sprouted from her shoulders, neck, and ears. Her lips grew into a daggerlike beak. She opened the bathroom door as her fingers vanished. Long, slender feathers brushed over the brass knob.

She tried to call for her sisters, but a strange bird cry came out instead. *"Awk!"*

Her vision started changing. Her eyes moved to either side of her head, and each saw separately. She slammed into the wall, disoriented. She had studied the monocular vision of birds in biology, but this didn't make sense—she couldn't be turning into a bird. Things like that just didn't happen.

She pulled herself up and took one step, then swayed drunkenly as she adjusted to her new body. She tipped off the carpet runner, and her toenails scratched the wood floor. She glanced down. Short, blunt claws had replaced her feet. She stumbled and reached out to balance herself. But instead of arms, wings flapped frantically around her.

"No," she yelled in an angry tweet and hopped down the hallway to the full-length antique mirror. The reflection of a red-and-gold bird with a two-feathered crest stared back at her. She had long legs and an *S*-shaped neck.

Then she glanced outside, and for one exhilarating moment she forgot her panic, as she stared at a fanfare of colors that she had never seen before. With her bird vision she was able to see ultraviolet rays.

But her euphoria quickly faded. How was she going to change back into a girl?

She ran to her sisters' room, clucking wildly. The twins studied the occult and magic. They even tried to cast spells. Maybe they could save her.

"Nicole! Carrie!" she shouted, but their names came out as sharp, repeated tweets.

She stood in their doorway flapping her wings and shrieking, "Help me!" but only a hysterical chirping noise escaped her beak.

"A bird's trapped inside," Carrie said and grabbed a magazine. She swept it toward Sudi. "Help me shoo it out," she pleaded with Nicole.

"No," Sudi chirped, and somersaulted backward, becoming even more disoriented than before.

Carrie swung again. The magazine breezed past Sudi. She squawked and ran, spreading her wings for balance as Carrie and Nicole chased her down the stairs. Sudi tripped and rolled down the bottom three steps.

"Open the door," Carrie shouted.

Nicole sprang past Sudi. Her foot landed on the tip of Sudi's wing, pressing on the feathers.

"Okay," Nicole yelled. She flung open the front door.

Sudi jumped outside and stared back at the twins dazedly.

"Fly away," Carrie said.

Then Nicole slammed the door. The wood tapped the end of Sudi's long beak.

"Some psychics the two of you turned out to be," Sudi trilled in an angry arpeggio of peeps. "You don't even recognize your own sister."

She perched on the step and tried to hold on to the belief that this was impossible; it had to be a dream or a stress-induced hallucination. At the same time a scary idea came to her. Maybe she'd remain this way until she died. And if that happened, how was she going to convince anyone that she was a girl?

She should have learned the incantation for transforming back before she pronounced the spell to become a bird in the first place. Her chest deflated, and she squawked sadly.

She thought of her parents and felt even sadder. Would they think she had run away?

Suddenly her body tensed, and her avian instincts tore her away from her thoughts. She sensed a predator and cocked her head.

Pie was crouching toward her, back taut, ready to spring.

Sudi screeched and fluttered her wings. She rose, then fell, only to rise again before crashing back on the sidewalk and hitting her beak on the cement with a loud click. She got up again, determined not to die as a meal for her cat, and ran awkwardly, flailing her wings up and down, down and up. The motion took tremendous energy.

Pie pounced.

Sudi yelped and slipped from his claws, and then, amazingly, she took to the sky. She was airborne but afraid to stop flapping. She couldn't remember if birds continuously waved their wings. She was positive she had watched sparrows glide, but she was too afraid to stop pumping.

On the ground, Pie skulked after her, stalking his easy prey.

Wind rushed around Sudi and took her higher. She skimmed over the treetops, tearing red and yellow leaves from the branches. Then a raucous cry made her look up. A fleet of black birds dived toward her. Glossy feathers were everywhere, smacking against her. She must have flown into their territory.

She reeled, tumbling down, and hit a tree limb. Balancing herself, she perched gracelessly, leaning against the trunk. Her wings ached, her body throbbed, and she felt incredibly hungry. She snapped her beak around a beetle and swallowed it whole before she even had time to stop herself. She felt the bug squirming inside of her. Disgusted, she started to regurgitate it, but a stealthy movement made her glance down. She twisted her head and saw a swatch of yellow-orange cat climbing toward her.

Pie was unrelenting. Sudi made a mental note to feed him more cat food if she survived. He leaped. She jumped and fell from the tree, plummeting down and frantically flapping her wings.

This time the air sucked her up. She spread her feathers and glided upward on the breeze. She soared around the Washington Monument and fought the urge to dive for fish in the Potomac River.

She wondered if strange things were happening to Meri and Dalila. She swooped down and flew over traffic, following the streets to Entre Nous Academy. She didn't know how she would find Meri once she arrived, but she had to try.

Students were gathered outside the three-story red-brick building, waiting for the school day to begin.

A tall guy pointed up at her. "Look at that bird," he shouted.

"What kind is it?" another boy asked.

Sudi couldn't land with everyone watching her. What would happen if she changed back into a girl? She turned and dived into the narrow alleyway between the school and an office building.

The wind currents changed. Alarm rose inside Sudi. Her concentration flagged, and she dropped straight down, landing hard on the concrete.

She sat up and moaned—a completely human sound. The fall had made her transform back into a girl. In spite of the pain, she stood up and limped toward a line of Dumpsters.

No way she could let anyone see her like this, barefoot and naked except for her undies and the pathetically ugly green bra. She glanced up at the rows of windows in the office building and figured that a dozen or more workers had already seen her. She had no other choice—she opened the lid of a blue Dumpster, stood on a crate, and climbed inside. Settling down in the dark, holding her nose against the putrid smell, she wondered how she was ever going to explain this to her mother.

Pounding footsteps and excited voices caught her attention.

"I know the bird came down here," a voice said, from outside the metal container.

"Maybe it caught itself and kept on flying," someone answered.

Sudi winced. Was that Scott's voice? She cringed, sure that it was.

"It must be here," a girl's voice answered, sounding unquestionably like Michelle's.

Someone started to lift the Dumpster lid. Sudi slid under newspapers and flattened cardboard boxes, but there wasn't enough trash to hide her, and no way was she going to crawl beneath the slippery garbage at the bottom. She stared up at the widening crack between the container and its cover.

CHAPTER 7

"The bird's not going to be hiding in the Dumpster," Scott said. "How could it lift the lid and climb inside?"

The hinged cover fell shut again with a heavy clang of metal.

Sudi sighed and waited in the dark, breathing the stench of spoiled oranges and rotten banana peels. A rustle from something skulking over the trash made her recoil; an animal was in the bin with her. She imagined a rat nibbling on her toes and sat up, wrapping her arms around her legs and hugging her knees against her chest.

When the school bell rang, she stood and timidly lifted the heavy lid, eager to climb out, but first she peeked up at the windows in the office buildings. She had expected to see workers gathered behind the glass, watching intently to see what she would do next, but no one was staring down at her.

She threw back the cover. It banged against the wall with an angry rumble. She pulled herself up onto the lip of the metal box, and then eased out onto the crate.

Tears of frustration burned in her eyes as she carefully stepped to the ground. How was she going to get home? Maybe the best thing to do was to face the problem head on: wrap a newspaper around her waist and walk into the main office, lie and claim she didn't know what had happened to her. She imagined herself on the nightly news—a strange case of amnesia; her mother's panicked face staring into the camera, explaining to the viewing audience that Sudi had always been a nice girl. She pictured herself standing in her undies while being interviewed and all the guys at school laughing at her hideous green bra. She should have trashed it weeks ago.

Without warning a cat bolted from the Dumpster, startling her. It scampered away, then turned around and came back, meowing at her and rubbing against her ankle. Sudi leaned over and scratched behind its ears, glad that her companion had been a cat and not some long-nosed rat.

"I wish you were a dog," she whispered. "Then I could send you to find help for me."

The cat hissed at her and flicked a paw, the hairs on its back standing up in anger as if it had taken offense at her comment about the dog, and then abruptly it scuttled away.

Sudi picked a copy of *The Washington Post* out of the bin, unfolded it, and used it as a towel to cover herself.

As she started around the corner, the cat with the surly attitude returned, racing toward her. Meri followed after it, furtively glancing around as if she weren't supposed to be there. She saw Sudi and gasped.

They stared at each other, the cat circling between them.

The white highlighter didn't hide the blue-gray circles under Meri's bloodshot eyes, but far worse was the edgy fear that gripped her features. She looked like the victim of some horrible catastrophe who had been found wandering aimlessly around a destroyed neighborhood, not believing the devastation.

"Are you all right?" Sudi asked at last.

"What about you?" Meri answered. "You were that bird, weren't you?"

"No," Sudi lied.

"The cat told me you needed help," Meri said and broke eye contact. Still not looking at Sudi, she added, "and that's not the strangest thing that's happened to me since Abdel did whatever he did."

"Do you think he gave us some kind of posthypnotic suggestion?" Sudi asked.

"I thought of that," Meri replied. "Until a few seconds ago."

"What happened then?" Sudi asked.

"I wasn't the only one who saw an exotic bird fly over our school and fall from the sky," Meri challenged. "I don't think Abdel could have infected all the kids in the school yard with some kind of group hysteria."

"He doesn't go to your school?" Sudi asked, struggling to hold on to the thinnest hope that he did, and that he had been able to hypnotize the student body, like a teenage Svengali.

Meri shook her head.

In spite of the warm morning air, Sudi began to shiver. "Can you get me something to wear?"

"Wait here," Meri ordered.

Sudi edged back against the wall and wondered why she didn't have the courage to tell Meri everything. But she couldn't tell her what had happened when she didn't believe it yet herself.

Moments later, Meri returned, carrying a faded pair of jeans and an oversize purple sweater. The sneakers clutched in her hands looked as if they had belonged to a boy who climbed trees and ran through mud.

"I stole these from the clothes we're collecting for our charity drive," Meri said and sat down on the crate, watching Sudi. "I hope the shoes fit. They were the best I could find."

"Thanks," Sudi answered and glanced behind

Meri, expecting her bodyguards to round the corner.

"Where are your guards?" Sudi asked.

"Gone," Meri answered. "When weird things started happening, I knew I couldn't have those two following me everywhere. They were like barnacles."

"How'd you convince your mom?" Sudi said, letting the newspaper fall to the ground. Gray newsprint covered her thighs, and she didn't even want to consider what the black smudges were across her stomach. She tugged on the jeans.

Meri picked at her lavender fingernail polish. "I think they were hired to watch me, more than protect me," she confessed at last. "To make sure I didn't do something stupid that could embarrass my mom and ruin her chances."

Sudi stared at Meri, suddenly understanding how difficult Meri's life must be. Meri shrugged as if Sudi's pity made her uncomfortable. "You get used to it," Meri said, and then she asked, "So when did you realize that what Abdel told us was real?"

"I still don't believe it," Sudi said firmly and leaned over to roll up the cuffs. Then she slipped into the sweater. It smelled heavily of the last wearer's sharp perfume. She lifted her hair from underneath the turtleneck and let it hang loosely over her shoulders.

"I keep denying the truth, too," Meri confessed. "It's common. People convince themselves that unpleasant things aren't true so that they don't have to face their problems. Just watch the evening news. Politicians are always accusing each other of doing something wrong, when they should really be examining their own actions."

"There has to be a logical explanation," Sudi countered as she tied the shoelaces. "I just haven't found it yet." Sudi stood and tested the sneakers. They were a tad too large, and the insides felt grungy against her toes, but she was grateful to have something on her feet.

"I read a spell for transforming into a cat," Meri said at last. "Then I fell asleep, or at least I think I did, and when I woke up I was licking the back of my hand and rubbing it over my face."

Sudi looked up at the rectangle of blue sky between the office building and the school. *This can't be real*, she prayed. *Please don't let it be.*

"I think we should find Dalila," Meri said.

By the time Sudi and Meri had located Dalila, through the Egyptian Cultural Center, the sun had set behind storm clouds. Dalila had agreed to meet them in an hour, but two had passed already. Sudi looked down the street. The traffic lights changed from red to green, the pedestrian signal counting down the seconds left to cross the street.

"She's still not answering." Meri closed her cell phone. "I hope she didn't change her mind."

"I wish she'd hurry," Sudi mumbled and brushed a yellow leaf from her wind-tangled hair.

This section of the District was crowded during the day, but it emptied after the offices closed. Even the eateries had turned out their lights. Still, Sudi didn't understand why she felt so uneasy. She had been there at night before, with Sara, when they had snuck out to go to an underground club called the Breeze.

"Scott likes you, you know?" Meri said abruptly, surprising Sudi.

"Scott?" Sudi stuttered. "I didn't know you knew him."

"We hang out," Meri said. "He was really bummed when you started going out with Brian, because he thought you liked him."

"I do like Scott," Sudi answered and started to explain, but stopped. "I see Dalila."

Dalila ran through tumbling leaves, her long coat flapping behind her. She held the rolled papyrus close to her chest as she joined them.

"I'm sorry I'm late," Dalila said. Her fingers plucked at the red scarf wrapped around her head, pulling it forward, as if she were afraid to reveal her royal birthmark. "I couldn't figure out how to work the machine to buy a ticket for the Metro, so I had to walk."

"Why didn't you just ask someone for help?" Meri said.

"Because, since my uncle told me that everything Abdel said was true, I've been too afraid to trust anyone," Dalila confessed.

"Who is your uncle?" Sudi asked.

"Anwar Serenptah," Dalila answered.

"Jeez, maybe he's the one we need to talk to," Meri said. "He's about the most famous Egyptologist in the world."

"Exactly," Dalila went on. "But he's misled me. He must have known that I didn't understand what it meant to be a Descendant. He swore that he thought my parents had told me. How could he believe that? I'm always looking through bridal magazines and planning my royal wedding. If I had any notion that I was going to be a warrior, I would have been learning how to fire a gun. He let me believe my fantasy. Why did he deceive me?"

Her face crumpled, the lines expressing terrible loss, and for a moment Sudi thought Dalila was going to cry, but she remained stubbornly strong.

"I understood that I was being groomed for something special," Dalila continued, "because I live such a sheltered life. But I thought I was destined to marry a prince. I imagined myself becoming like Queen Noor of Jordan, not a soldier fighting ancient gods. I can't do this."

Sudi put her arm around Dalila and hugged her. She was the only fifteen-year-old girl Sudi knew who really believed she'd marry a prince.

"My uncle taught me the ancient ways in magic and religion," Dalila said. "But I thought he was only sharing his love for Egypt with me, not training me."

"Has anything bizarre happened to you?" Sudi asked.

"No," Dalila answered, obviously lying. She tightened her grip on the papyrus. "Why do you ask?"

"Because," Sudi hesitated, then decided the best way to begin was to tell Dalila everything.

{ 83 }

Recalling the night she had awakened and found herself on the front porch, Sudi began. She told Dalila about the invitation she had found in her locker and ended with her time spent trapped inside the museum.

When Sudi finished, she expected Dalila to give her a rush of possibilities to explain away what had happened, but she didn't.

"Maybe it was the Noble Lady," Dalila offered. "The demon Shepeset is like a fairy god-mother. She was obviously protecting you. Demons can be good or bad; some offer protection, some don't."

"The Noble Lady," Meri repeated, eyeing Dalila quizzically. "You think the woman was a demon called Shepeset and not a creation of Sudi's overactive imagination?"

"Maybe hallucinations are just another reality that we don't see most of the time." Dalila shrugged.

"You believe everything I told you, don't you?" Sudi asked, mystified. This was not the reaction she had anticipated. Dalila's ability to believe her was making Sudi uncomfortable.

"Perhaps good forces sealed the elevator as a

way to protect you," Dalila explained. "What if the woman wanted to stop you from sleepwalking outside again, and trapping you in the museum was the only way she knew to keep you safe?"

"You accept this so easily," Meri put in.

"An unseen world surrounds us," Dalila said, "and it became visible to Sudi last night."

Warm rain splattered their faces, but they didn't run for shelter. They stayed in the downpour, staring at each other. Sudi pressed her lips together, feeling a sudden overwhelming sadness. Her future was going to be far different from the one she had planned. Already she could feel her friendship with Sara drifting into the past, and that loss made her chest ache.

At school, Sudi basically ignored the goodie girls, because she had nothing in common with them, and now she was stuck with two of them. Meri had probably never even tasted beer, and she looked too serious to fall into a goofy giggling spell the way Sudi and Sara did. Dalila was gorgeous, but seemed too bookish, and she had lived isolated from kids her own age, content with imagining the desert kingdom she would rule one day.

Sudi wondered if they ever even thought about boyfriends and dating or sex—things Sudi spent most of her time thinking about. She'd have to watch what she said in front of them. No more squealing over some good-looking guy's butt. She missed Sara already.

Then she realized that Dalila and Meri had become strangely quiet and were looking at her.

"I'm smart," Sudi blurted out defensively. She hated being stereotyped, even when she knew she was guilty of judging them.

"Why did you say that?" Meri asked, wiping the rain from her face.

"Of course you're smart," Dalila answered. "You're a Descendant."

They watched Sudi, and another awkward silence settled over the three girls.

"This is not the way to start off," Sudi said at last. "Let's just forget I said anything."

Dalila smiled pleasantly, but Meri frowned.

"Things like this don't happen," Sudi went on. "There has to be a reasonable explanation. We'll find it, and then we can separate and go back to our normal lives."

"Assume it's real," Meri said.

"I can't," Sudi answered in a low voice and licked at the rain on her lips.

"Just assume," Meri said, "if it's real, then we have to tell Abdel we're not going to take on this job as Descendants. He can't force us to fight against our will."

The idea had never occurred to Sudi. "You're right!" she shouted. Her chest expanded as the anxiety that had been holding her eased. "We'll just tell him we want out."

Dalila brightened. "I know where he lives. Let's go there right now and be done with this."

They linked arms and ran across the street. As they passed an alley, Meri stopped and looked around, cupping her hands around her forehead to shield her eyes from the rain.

"What's wrong?" Sudi asked, and felt the peculiar drop in her stomach that she got before tests.

"I don't know, I just . . ." Meri stared across the street at an empty black sedan. The raindrops on her face sparkled red, reflecting the light from the neon sign buzzing overhead. "Ever since my mother declared herself a candidate for president I've had photographers stalking me."

"Did you hear that?" Dalila asked and hooked her arm around Sudi's elbow.

"What?" Sudi listened to the pattering rain, and then, over the burble of water, came a sharp howl, followed by two longer cries.

"The cry of the jackal," Dalila whispered, pressing closer to Sudi. "We heard the jackals calling to each other when we camped on the west bank of the Nile. Jackals always howl before they begin their hunt."

"This is Washington, D.C.," Meri countered.

"The jackals cried the evening my parents were killed in the cave-in," Dalila went on. "My parents were excavating a tomb, and a tunnel collapsed on them."

"Maybe we should go back the other way," Meri suggested, nervously scanning the alleyway.

"It's just a dog," Sudi said, trying to reassure them. "It's probably lost and hungry." She started forward, intending to rescue the poor animal, but Meri latched on to her arm and pulled her back.

"The howls sound human," Meri said. "Maybe it's some guy—"

Another wail interrupted her. The mournful cry seemed closer, but with the noise from the rain, Sudi couldn't be sure.

"I've got a creepy feeling it's someone from the homeless shelter who's having a breakdown," Meri whispered.

"No," Dalila muttered and stepped back.

"What now?" Sudi asked, and brushed her hair from her eyes. She couldn't see what held Dalila's frightened gaze.

Meri pointed. "There!"

A shadow darted from behind a forklift stacked high with pallets and disappeared again, hidden by darkness and rain.

"That was Anubis, Neb-ta-djeser, lord of the sacred land," Dalila said. Her fingers fumbled with the papyrus as she tried to open it. "He has power over evildoers and the underworld enemies of the dead." She unrolled the scroll. "Help me find a spell."

"Don't be so panicked," Sudi said, not understanding her friends' fear. "It's just a dog, and

I bet it's more afraid of us than we are of it."

Sudi tried to see the animal, but the falling rain reflected the light cast from a security lamp, and the glistening drops acted as a shield, hiding the deeper shadows at the end of the alley.

This time Sudi ignored Dalila and Meri when they tried to stop her. She stepped forward until the brightness was behind her. Then she waited for her eyes to adjust to the dark, but before the moment came, a low growl filled the air and she realized her mistake. She was backlit by the security light, a silhouette easily spotted.

She hadn't thought this through; she had failed to consider that the dog might be rabid, or worse; maybe it was a military animal, one trained to kill, that had escaped its handlers. She imagined sharp teeth biting into her skin and instinctively pulled her sweater collar up around her neck.

Another howl pierced the night, and then, without warning, something splashed through water at a quickening pace, charging toward her.

Sudi darted forward. Her fingers brushed over the rough bricks in the building as she ran through the runoff water. The insides of her shoes became uncomfortably soggy.

She edged against the wall, her heart pounding painfully. Her shoulder slipped into a recess, and she quickly eased into the alcove behind her, then squatted against the door, trying to make herself small and less noticeable.

Through the pelting rain came another sound. She listened intently, trying to make sense of the tap-tapping. Perhaps a cane, or a baseball bat, was hitting the pavement with a repeated beat. A dog couldn't do that. Maybe Meri had been right after all, and the howls had come from a man.

Sudi's eyes had adjusted to the gloom, and she looked frantically around for another hiding place. Beyond the veil of water, a short ladder led to a loading deck. She ran to it and climbed up, her shoes slipping on the rungs. She caught movement in her peripheral vision, and dived behind crates that were stacked high. She prayed that whoever was pursuing her hadn't seen her hide, but she wasn't taking any chances. She crawled to the other side of the platform, then waited, shivering and terrified.

The tapping stopped, as if the person had paused, listening, waiting for her to make another sound.

She held her breath, her heartbeat thudding in her ears.

Moments passed with only the pulse of the rain and her heart, and then a scraping sound followed; someone was moving the crates aside, trying to locate her.

Any remaining illusion that a dog was hunting her vanished as she watched three crates topple. The person had to be high on PCP to have such strength. She rolled to the edge of the platform, dangled her feet over the side, and jumped, then crouched low.

Gushing waters swirled around her ankles before gurgling down a drain. She looked around and then ran across the alley to a truck. She slid under the front bumper, scraping her stomach on grit and dirt. She cowered behind the front wheel and hoped it hid her.

Within moments, the tapping started again, but the constant patter of the rain made it difficult for her to know how close her stalker was. She started to peer out.

The tip of a rod came down in front of her, barely missing her face. It hit the pavement with a loud bang.

She jerked back and waited, unable to breathe.

A bare foot splashed into a puddle, sending grimy water over her face. The person continued around to the side of the truck.

She pulled herself forward until she was under the bumper, then cautiously crawled out and, holding on to the front grille, peered around the truck.

A huge man stood in the rain. His legs were bare up to his knees. A soggy white skirt clung to his thighs, but nothing covered his back. He carried a large walking stick that looked like the snake she had found on her bed.

She brushed the rain from her face, certain her vision had deceived her, and looked again. Sudden intense terror shot through her. Her stomach tightened, and in spite of the water everywhere, her throat became too dry to swallow. She held her breath, transfixed, unmindful of the rain pelting her eyes.

The man was wearing a headdress—a full

head mask of a black dog with slender, alert ears and a long, pointed snout like that of the canine that had gazed back at her through the kitchen window. A thick mane of black hair covered his shoulders.

Slowly, the head turned, as if the man had become aware of her watching him.

Sudi sucked in air and let it out in a mumbled prayer.

A low, rumbling, growl issued forth from the man's throat. He stepped toward her before she could move. His walking stick swung around, the snake head aimed at her face.

She ducked, then scrambled on her hands and knees through the puddles back toward Dalila and Meri, too terrified to scream. She managed to stand, then ran, skidding once on the wet, oil-slick pavement.

The man seized her with unimaginable strength and lifted her, using only one hand. She sensed he was going to fling her to the ground. She tried to hold on to his back. Her palm slid up his shoulder, through the mass of black hair to the back of his head.

She felt no seam, no break, and where there should have been a dividing point between his body and the headdress, unless the man actually had a dog's head. She refused to accept what her mind was thinking, what she knew was fact.

The man yanked her forward. When she felt him start to throw her down, she grabbed the snout of his mask. Her hand slipped into his mouth. Her fingers traced over a warm, slippery tongue and teeth, but worse was the carrion stench of his panting breath and the sticky saliva that clung to her skin.

He hurled her to the ground, and she landed hard on her side.

"Don't let him point the walking stick at you!" Dalila shouted, charging toward her. The red scarf had slipped, revealing her royal birthmark.

Sudi let her head fall back on the pavement. "Right," she moaned, struggling to get away as the man reached for her again and started to pick her up.

"Stop!" Meri screamed and ran at him. Her feet splashed water into Sudi's face as she charged the creature.

Sudi jumped up in spite of the pain and

dizziness. She struggled forward and caught Meri, pulling her back.

"He's real," Sudi said jaggedly. "He's not a man wearing a costume."

Meri whipped around, her head bumping into Sudi's chin, and she stared up at Sudi, her eyes widening and terror-struck.

"He's the jackal-headed god Anubis," Dalila explained.

Anubis turned his attention away from Sudi and regarded Dalila, seeming to stare at the birthmark on her scalp. He snarled threateningly.

The three girls eased back, then stood, huddled together, in front of Anubis. Meri's teeth chattered. Dalila raised the papyrus in front of them. "We'll call forth the magical protection of the goddess Ipy," Dalila explained and pointed to a line of hieroglyphs. "The goddess Ipet."

"Ipy or Ipet?" Meri asked.

"It's the same goddess," Dalila answered. "Different names."

Rain splattered the papyrus, and the colors began to run together.

"Other gods fall down in terror before

Anubis," Dalila said. "But Ipy will stand against Anubis and protect us."

"How are you going to call a god?" Sudi asked, unable to control the trembling in her knees.

"Medu neter," Dalila said.

"What?" Meri asked.

"Divine words," Dalila said and pointed to the hieroglyphs again. "We'll use the words that our ancestors spoke." She cleared her throat and began, "Mistress of magical protection, Ipet-weret, the great Ipet, we call you forward."

Meri spoke the spell with her.

Anubis started toward them again. His yellow eyes focused on Sudi.

Sudi pinched the edge of the scroll and tried to work her tongue around the foreign words. Terror made her speak louder than both Meri and Dalila combined. "Thy hidden name we use," Sudi said. Her throat and mouth burned as she spoke the secret name of Ra, and then at the end of the incantation she added, "To call forth Ihy."

Dalila turned, her eyes stricken with horror. "You spoke the wrong name."

"I said Itchy or Ithy," Sudi said defensively. "Whatever you said, that's what I said."

"No, you didn't," Dalila argued. "You said Ihy, not Ipy or Ipet."

"Are we going to argue about that now?" Meri asked. "Find another spell, and hurry."

A rattling sound made Sudi look behind her. She saw nothing. Maybe it had only been her nerves, but the short, sharp jangle repeated, and something touched the back of her jeans. She looked down.

A naked boy stood behind her, shaking a sistrum. He waved the wooden handle, and the metal rods slid from side to side, making a tinkling noise. His head had been shaved except for one black lock, and he was sucking his free thumb.

"That's the god we summoned to protect us?" Sudi asked, dismayed.

"That's the one you called forth," Dalila answered. "Not us. That's the child-god Ihy. His musical instruments make people fall in love. He can't fight a death god."

The boy looked up at Sudi with a naughty sparkle in his eyes and rattled his sistrum, before he gazed behind her and saw Anubis. He screamed and ran off, his bare feet smacking against the rain-slick pavement.

Sudi turned as Anubis lifted the walking stick and pointed it at her. She sensed something dreadful building in the air. The rain stopped falling around the tip and slid to the sides as if the power circling it were too dense for even water to penetrate.

"What's he doing with his walking stick?" Sudi asked.

"It's not a walking stick," Dalila corrected. "It's a magic wand. Ancient Egyptians used wands to command malevolent spirits and demons."

"Is that what he thinks we are?" Meri asked, clutching Sudi's arm.

"Of course not," Dalila answered, her head bent over the soggy scroll, trying to find another spell. "He's going to use magic to destroy us."

The earth rumbled, and the pavement cracked. Bricks snapped beneath Sudi's feet. She lost her balance, and as she started to fall, a deep, steep-sided hole opened in front of her. She remained suspended on the edge, and then the alley tilted and she plummeted into the abyss, her stomach turning from the rapid fall.

Meri and Dalila spun after her, their screams rising along with Sudi's piercing shriek. Clods of dirt and broken bricks tumbled over them, and then the ground overhead closed, sealing them in the dark chasm.

Soon moist, sticky-cold air gave way to intense heat, and just when Sudi thought she'd pass out, the free fall ended and her feet came down, settling on whitewashed limestone.

She blinked at the sudden brightness, and as her eyes adjusted, she saw shadows scampering about and hiding.

"Where are we?" she asked, her voice echoing around her as if she were in a vast, empty tunnel.

"Surely not under the earth," Meri said.

"We're standing at the entrance to—" Dalila started to answer, but before she could finish, another force washed over them, tightening its hold.

They shot forward.

In front of them, two monumental lions were joined back to back, guarding a gateway. The head of one giant statue faced east, the other, west.

"It's the first hour," Dalila screamed, and the red scarf that had been tied around her head whipped free.

"What?" Sudi yelled back.

"We passed the gate which swallows all," Dalila answered, clutching the papyrus close to her body with one hand and trying to grab on to the wall with the other. Her fingers thumped against the next gateway, but the pain didn't stop her from trying again.

"Where are we?" Sudi repeated her question.

"We passed the entrance to Duat," Dalila warned. "We're in the other world."

"Do you mean hell?" Meri shouted.

"We have to stop whatever is dragging us through the gates," Dalila said. "Once we pass the last pylon we'll enter eternity, and we won't be able to return."

Sudi flung her hands out and tried to hold on, hoping to catch a ledge, or protruding stone. Her fingernails scraped along the wall, and then the nail bed on her pinkie tore.

Unexpectedly, they stopped again, their feet landing softly on the stone floor.

"What now?" Sudi asked, and braced herself against the wall.

Dalila placed her hand against Sudi's mouth and looked around, her eyes alert.

Then Sudi heard the scuffing sound. Something large scraped furtively across the floor, coming toward them.

"What is it?" Meri said in a soft voice.

"Did we pass the seventh gate?" Dalila whispered anxiously. "I should have counted, but I didn't."

Sudi and Meri shrugged, and together they stepped away from the wall, Dalila between them, and stopped.

A huge snake slid toward them, leaving a frothy track of scum on either side of its massive body. It slithered forward, eyes filled with a killer's lust. Sudi couldn't see an end to its long, cylindrical body. It curled around column after column, seeming to fill the room.

"The fiend of darkness," Dalila whispered. "It's the soul-hunting demon, Apep. He'll take our souls."

An aura of evil pulsed from the serpent, and Sudi could feel its hatred for her. Even so, she couldn't pull her eyes away. Its gaze held her spellbound, tugging her forward, entrancing her and inviting her in to its widening mouth.

"Do something," Meri said. "Find a spell."

Dalila held up the dripping papyrus and unrolled the mushy scroll. The colors had run together, and the hieroglyphs now looked like blotches in a finger painting.

The giant serpent squirmed closer, its underbelly slipping over the steps with a wet, plopping sound.

Tears filled Sudi's eyes as all of her dreams fell away; she had never thought she would die so young.

"Don't cry," Meri said and pinched Sudi. "You have to help get us out of here. I'm not ready to die. I haven't even kissed a guy yet, and half my friends back home are seriously discussing birth control."

Sudi's head whipped around. "You haven't been kissed?" she asked, breaking out of her trance. "Never?"

"Would I lie to you, now?" Meri asked.

"A bird can escape," Dalila said and clasped Sudi's arm. "I'm sure that's what my uncle told me. A bird can fly out of Duat, because it can rise above Apep. Turn into the Bennu-bird, and you'll have the strength to carry us out."

"Fly out of here?" Sudi asked. "How? We're sealed underground."

"Just try," Meri pleaded.

Apep roared as if it understood what Sudi was about to do. It pulled its head back, ready to strike.

Sudi spoke the incantation three times and began flapping her arms, as feathers sprouted through her skin. Soon, huge, graceful wings stirred the air, but she didn't fly. She needed the help of the wind.

Dalila seemed to understand and began spinning. She raised one hand above her head, leaving the other down, and continued circling. "The breath of the gods, comforting and warm," Dalila spoke. "Bring your gift to lift Sudi's wings."

Suddenly, a breeze fluttered, following the direction of Dalila's dance. Meri joined her, clumsily at first, and then with grace, and they twirled together.

The wind lifted Sudi's wings. Dalila and Meri ran after her and grabbed on to her tail feathers, but Sudi didn't feel pain the way she had when her sister Nicole had stepped on her wing. She felt strong.

"*Neteri kua.* I am strong," she chirped.

Apep struck, but missed, then pulled back to strike again, and bellowed when Sudi soared away.

Sudi glided through the gateway, the tailwinds pushing her forward. She flew past the lion statues and then ascended with incredible speed, blindly flapping her wings.

Without warning, they burst through into the muggy night, landing back in Washington, D.C., on the steps of the FBI building.

Sudi moaned, a girl again, but racked with pain, unable to move. She lay on the concrete, smelling the rain and staring up at the night, watching the ragged low clouds skating across the sky beneath the larger and darker thunderheads.

"They probably caught all that on closed-circuit TV," Sudi said. "But I'd rather face an FBI agent than that snake."

"At least it wasn't a giant insect. I would have died," Meri exclaimed. "I hate bugs more than anything in the world."

Dalila sighed. "This is worse than I ever could have imagined," she said solemnly. "I probably won't even live long enough to become a bride."

"But we're okay right now," Meri said, sitting up.

"Because Dalila saved us with her dance," Sudi said. "How did you do that?"

"It's simple," Dalila explained. "All natural phenomena are manifestations of the divine, and if you concentrate hard enough, and the gods bless you for your devotion, the wind will come to you."

"Dalila, you're the perfect Descendant," Sudi said, slowly pulling herself up. "But I don't think I have a chance. It's not like the Book of Thoth makes us invincible and calling forth the protection of an ancient god is hard."

"I know," Dalila agreed sadly. "Egyptians worshipped hundreds of deities, and a slip of the tongue can summon the wrong one, as we found out when we called forth the child-god Ihy, instead of the protector goddess Ipy."

"You also called her Ipet-weret," Meri said. "Why did you use the other name?"

"That's just one more problem," Dalila explained "Even the names of the gods are confusing, because they have the Greek name, the Egyptian name, and the Roman name, and probably names I don't even know, because some were worshipped in Mesopotamia."

Dalila became silent, staring down at the scrapes and cuts on her right hand. The bruised knuckles were swelling.

"What is it?" Sudi asked with renewed apprehension.

"I was thinking about the jackal-headed god," she said. "Anubis was once the most important Egyptian funerary god. That is, until his cult was taken over by the priests devoted to Osiris; but some of the priests who served Anubis didn't want to lose their power, so they desecrated the temple and used Anubis and the Book of Gates in unholy ways to call forth demons and resurrect the dead."

"Did your uncle tell you that?" Meri asked.

"Many times," Dalila replied, "but until now I thought it was only part of mythology, not history."

Sudi edged closer to Dalila and put her hand on her shoulder, sensing that fear was making Dalila hold back something important. "What else did your uncle tell you?"

For a long time Dalila stared at the leaves skittering across the street, and then she spoke. "The

Cult of Anubis wants to return the universe to the chaos from which it came, and now they worship the ancient god Seth." She looked from Sudi to Meri and back to Sudi again. "I don't see how we can survive."

"We'll spend the night together at my house," Sudi said firmly. "Then, tomorrow, we'll find Abdel and tell him we want out."

"You've got to see this," Dalila yelled the next morning as Sudi entered the bedroom, carefully balancing three cups of hot cocoa on a tray.

Meri and Dalila were already dressed in clothes they had borrowed from Sudi's closet. They stood at her window, watching Pie. The old yellow tomcat stretched in the sunlight, his back paws on the windowsill, forepaws wrapped around the lock.

"Pie thinks you've been careless," Meri said. "You need to lock your window at night, because evil things have been hanging out in your backyard."

Sudi set the tray down and grabbed Pie, rolling him into a ball and rubbing her nose against his. "Are you part of the feline underground?" she joked.

Pie looked at her with a slight nod of his head, and for the briefest moment Sudi felt that her pet had understood her. She set him down on the floor, and just when she decided that she had only imagined him nodding, Patty Pie meowed.

Meri took her cup of cocoa and poked at the marshmallow with her finger, watching Pie. "He says the cherry-vanilla ice cream you've been feeding him is too sweet and he wants you to buy chocolate next time."

Sudi paused. "You really are communicating with Pie," she said in wonder.

Meri nodded.

Dalila glanced at her watch. "We'd better get going."

The girls finished their cocoa, and then they

headed downstairs, stealing past the kitchen. Sudi glanced into the room. Nicole was crushing potato chips between two slices of white bread covered with globs of mayonnaise. Their mother stood next to Nicole, staring out the kitchen window and drinking her morning coffee.

Sudi hurried outside and didn't turn back when her mother called after her. She was determined to end whatever it was that Abdel had started.

Six blocks later, Dalila, Meri, and Sudi stood on a cobblestone street in Georgetown, staring up through red maple leaves at a yellow row house.

"This is where my uncle brought me," Dalila said. "He told me Abdel belonged to a secret society called the Hour priests. I had never seen my uncle so excited to meet anyone before, and he's met a lot of famous people."

Sudi walked up the iron steps, the metal clanging beneath her boots, and knocked on the door.

Abdel opened it.

"You're here," he whispered, seeming surprised. "I've been trying to find all three of you."

"We want out," Sudi said, barging inside. She

turned to face him. "You need to find someone more mature, someone with military training. Maybe the whole U.S. Marine Corps!"

"No way are we doing this," Meri added, joining Sudi.

Dalila shut the door behind her. "How can I fight demons?" she demanded. "I don't even know how to ride the Metro."

"There's nothing I can do to change your fate," Abdel answered calmly.

"It's never too late," Meri said. "Besides, you had the responsibility to explain everything to us and you failed."

"You failed big-time," Sudi added.

"I'm probably not the best priest to advise you in this battle," Abdel confessed, "but I am the only one you have."

"Battle?" Dalila looked suddenly pale. "I learned the proper way to bow to kings," she went on in a thin voice. "I know how to receive diplomats, but I never learned how to fight."

"Please," Sudi said. Her throat burned as anger rose to cover her feelings of helplessness. Her sisters were probably the ones he wanted anyway, but she definitely wasn't going to mention that and put the twins in danger. They were too careless as it was.

"You don't understand how this could hurt my mom," Meri added. "She wants to run for president."

"It's too late," Abdel answered. "You left me before I was able to explain the spells on your papyri—"

"That's not our fault," Meri interrupted, angrily. "You were scaring us."

"The ceremony was needed to awaken your divine spirits," Abdel countered.

Sudi looked at the overstuffed armchairs in the living room. "You should have brought us here and told us everything."

"You never would have come," Abdel answered. "But I knew you wouldn't refuse an invitation to the Sky Terrace restaurant, and none of you did. My only mistake was in assuming that the three of you would listen to me until I had finished telling you everything you needed to know."

"Any rational person would have left long before we did," Meri charged.

"Even so, I can't do anything to change what

has happened," Abdel said and leaned back against a table near the door. "I can see the difference in your eyes, and I know that each of you has already accepted her fate."

"We did not agree to this," Dalila said.

"But you did," Abdel answered. "You've used the spell to awaken your power of transmutation."

"Our what?" Sudi asked.

"Like Horus, who could transform into a falcon and fly over his kingdom, each Descendant has the ability to change into an animal. That power came alive when you recited the proper spell from your papyrus. Once the spell is spoken, the ability remains for life, and by speaking the incantation you accepted your destiny. Usually it's done in a ceremony—"

"It's not like I knew what I was doing," Meri said. "I ate a mouse! Do you really think I wanted to do that?"

"And my cat almost ate me," Sudi added. "I hate being a bird. It's scary to fly so high."

Dalila hesitated, then pressed her hands against her cheeks. "I turn into Ammut, the monster with the head of a crocodile and the forepaws of a lion. I have the hindquarters of a hip-popotamus. How am I ever going to find a husband looking like that?"

"Dalila," Abdel said gently. "You're supposed to turn into a fire-breathing cobra like the goddess Wadjet. You must yield to your power and not be afraid. You're limiting yourself and not becoming what you were meant to be because of your disbelief and fear."

"I can't do this." Dalila leaned against Sudi. "Don't you see? You're sending us to our deaths."

No one spoke for a long moment. Sudi felt defeated. Dalila's soft crying was the only sound in the gloomy room.

Finally, Abdel spoke. "As long as all three of you are here, we should begin your training."

"We refuse," Sudi answered with a bravery she did not feel. "You'll have to find others."

Abdel started up the steep stairs anyway, the old wood creaking under his weight. When he reached the first landing, he turned back and looked down at them.

"The longer you wait to learn what you need to know, the longer you will live in terrible danger.

The cult doesn't care that you don't want to fulfill your destiny. The leaders will send demons to kill you, and if you're not concerned for your own safety, then at least consider the welfare of your families."

"Our families," all three girls said as one.

Sudi couldn't let anything happen to her sisters or her parents. She clutched the newel post. "I don't know if I can," she said, her stomach churning.

"It's hard," Abdel whispered. "No one would freely choose the life you have been given."

Sudi started up the stairs. Meri and Dalila followed after her with slow, reluctant steps.

"You tricked us," Sudi said when she reached Abdel. "You gave us the scrolls with the right incantations knowing we would speak them."

"That deception has been done before." Abdel nodded, but he didn't seem to take any joy in his trickery. "I knew that once I had awakened the soul of Egypt within you, destiny would find a way to make you read the incantation and bind your fate to that of a Descendant."

On the third floor, Abdel took a large key from his pocket and undid the lock on a door with three clicking turns. He pushed the door open and stepped into a dark, stuffy room.

A flame flared, and Sudi watched as Abdel continued to light the white wicks floating inside oil-filled clay bowls. When he finished, twenty or more flames flickered, and a soft haze hung in the stale air.

"Please, take a seat," he said when he noticed that they were still standing in the doorway.

The girls circled a low, round table in the center of the room and sat down on roughly made stools.

Abdel set a copper chest on the table, opened it, and took out three cylindrical leather cases. "This is only the first of many from the Book of Thoth that you will be required to study." He reached inside the first worn pouch and carefully pulled out a scroll.

"The secrets of the gods, written by Djehuti," Dalila whispered, and reverentially touched the tattered papyrus. "The Book of Thoth is mentioned in many papyri, but no copy has ever been found by archaeologists. Scholars thought all copies were lost in the fire that destroyed the library in Alexandria."

"The Hour priests have kept the scrolls hidden to protect the knowledge written on them," Abdel explained, "because whoever possesses the Book of Thoth has the power to command the gods of ancient Egypt, and even understand the language of animals and fly through the night unseen. Of course, there are risks."

"Great," Meri said and folded her arms.

Abdel sat down, seeming pleased with himself. "Now I will take you back with a story to the beginning of time," he announced, "so you will know your enemy. Many myths are told to explain creation, but all stories originate with the primeval waters and the mound which rose from them. The story I tell you is the true one."

He paused as if he were beginning the recitation of a text he had memorized as a boy. "From the primordial waters of chaos came the mound of creation, and on it sat Amun-Re. The great god brought forth life, and, soon after, the opposing gods of order and chaos, Osiris and Seth, were born."

Sudi had an odd feeling that she wasn't in the row house anymore, but when she glanced around, she saw the same tall bookcases, the flickering flames, and the thin smoke rising to the ceiling.

"Osiris married the goddess Isis," Abdel continued, "and together they ruled Egypt and brought order to the land. Isis was a devoted and faithful wife. Everyone loved her. But the evil god Seth grew jealous of his brother's good fortune. He killed Osiris and seized the throne."

Abdel shuddered as if he had witnessed the crime. "Grief-stricken, Isis stole the Book of Thoth from the gods and used its magic to resurrect Osiris long enough to conceive an heir, a son named Horus.

"When Horus came of age, he challenged his uncle Seth, and, after much struggle, the gods declared that Horus was the true pharaoh. Isis had her revenge, but she feared Seth would retaliate by freeing the demons that lived in the chaos at the edge of the universe."

Abdel looked at each of the girls to make sure he had their full attention before he continued. "For that reason, Isis gave the Book of Thoth to the Hour priests and directed them to watch the night skies. When the stars warned of evil forces threatening the kingdom, the priests were instructed to give the Book of Thoth to the pharaoh so he could use its magic to protect the world."

"That is why I am here," Abdel said. "The stars are warning of terrible days ahead unless the Cult of Anubis is stopped."

He glanced up, and the firelight made his eyes glint. "No one can change your fate, not even the gods. You must stand against evil and protect the world. You are the Descendants of the great kings of Egypt."

Sudi cursed under her breath and slouched against the table. Her throat tightened as daydreams of falling in love and losing her virginity were replaced by hideous kung fu images of running from monsters and losing her life.

Blue smoke spiraled around the closed room, coming from incense burning within reddish gold plates. The scent settled over Sudi, too sweet and strong. She had worn a halter top, and the sticky vapor felt as if it were seeping into the bare skin of her arms and back. She wondered if kids at school could smell the cloying fragrance on her. For three weeks she had come to Abdel's house to read the Book of Thoth and memorize spells, but her thoughts kept jumping ahead to Michelle's party.

More than anything, Sudi wanted to go, but Abdel had told her it was too dangerous for her to be out at night until she learned more magic. She hadn't bothered to tell him that so far she hadn't memorized any spells. She glanced down at the invitation poking out of her backpack. Abdel wasn't her parent, so he couldn't actually keep her from going.

Everyone said Michelle's extravaganza was going to be the social event of the year. No one cared that it was on a school night, because Michelle's parents had hired Grammy-winner Sienna to sing, and Sunday night was the only time available in her frenzied schedule.

Sudi leaned back and opened the shutter, feeling the familiar longing to be outside. Meri's driver waited in the black Lincoln Continental parked at the curb. Red leaves from a maple tree fell on the car hood.

"Abdel is stifling our fun," Sudi blurted out.

"He's only being cautious," Dalila said, without looking up.

"If he really cares about us," Sudi argued, "then why does he always disappear when we come over here? I thought a mentor was supposed to guide us, not leave us in a stinking room with boring translations to do."

"I love doing this," Dalila said, and looked up this time. She smiled, as if studying were bliss.

"Some of us aren't scholars," Sudi explained.

"I hear footsteps upstairs," Meri put in. "I think Abdel stays nearby in case we do need him."

"Let's go somewhere," Sudi said. "We need a break."

"You don't understand the seriousness—" Dalila began.

"I think I know," Sudi snapped. "I'm the one who got jackal saliva all over her face."

Sudi regretted her outburst, but Dalila stood and began rolling up her papyrus. "You're right," Dalila said. "We need a break. Then we'll come back and study."

"Let's go to Dean & DeLuca," Sudi said, grabbing her backpack. "It's not far from here."

Meri started for the door. "My driver will take us."

A few minutes later, Sudi ordered a cappuccino at the outside counter of Dean & DeLuca. She breathed in the rich scent of coffee, then sipped the frothy milk from the top as she sauntered toward a table in the sunlight.

The sunshine warmed her bare arms and back, and she was glad she had worn the loose halter top. She dropped her backpack beside the metal chair, but just as she started to sit down, she saw Michelle push through the doors.

Michelle walked with an exaggerated swing of her hips, her feet coming down like a runway model's as she carried sandwiches to a table in the shade. Then Sudi saw the reason. Scott, Brian, and Carter lolled on the chairs. They wore shorts and long-sleeved rugby shirts with horizontal stripes in alternating blue and red. Brian's knee was bleeding, and he stretched his leg out into the aisle so that everyone passing could see the gash. Scott sat in a corner, his arm slung over the back of the chair. Sunglasses hid Carter's eyes, and even though he didn't wave, Sudi sensed that he was watching her.

"What's up?" Meri asked, setting her latte down and biting into a cookie.

"Carter told me that he played rugby with Scott, but I didn't know Brian played on the same team," Sudi said. "Do you think they talk?"

"About you?" Meri said with a teasing grin. "Sure, and right now Michelle is probably leading the conversation. She's so jealous."

Sudi glanced back. Michelle was standing behind Scott, rubbing his shoulders.

"Let's leave," Sudi said, grabbing the strap of her backpack.

Dalila surprised her by blocking her retreat. "You can't leave now."

"Why not?" Sudi asked.

"Because there are no coincidences," Dalila said, setting an espresso on the table. "Fate brought you here. Now be brave enough to see what destiny is going to offer you."

"My last big encounter with destiny was a jackal-headed god named Anubis," Sudi argued. "I don't think I want to know what providence is handing me today."

"Sit down," Meri said. "They probably won't even notice we're here."

Sudi slumped in her chair. Something tickled

her neck. She brushed back her hair, but instead of going away the feeling crawled across her collarbone. She scratched at her skin.

Meri sat straight up, jarring the table. Her eyes widened. "A bug," she said, pointing to Sudi's chest. "A really big bug. It's as long as my finger."

"It's a cicada," Dalila said, unconcerned. "Just flick it away."

"Get it off me!" Sudi cried.

"I hate bugs more than anything," Meri said. "I'm not going to touch it. What if it bites me?"

"Do cicadas bite?" Sudi asked and jumped up. Her chair scraped the ground with an ear-piercing shriek of metal legs on stone. If Brian, Carter, and Scott hadn't been aware of her presence before, they were definitely watching her now.

She slapped at her neck.

The frightened cicada flitted back and forth, then scrambled under her halter. Tiny, prickly insect feet scurried across her chest. The bug quivered and made a high-pitched, droning sound.

"Get it out. Get it out." Sudi grabbed the hem

of her halter and waved it up and down, trying to shoo the bug away.

Dalila jumped up, looking horrified.

"It's not a cicada after all, is it?" Sudi shouted, as new terror found her. From the shocked expression on Dalila's face, Sudi knew the insect was something poisonous.

"Stop!" Dalila yelled.

"What is it?" Sudi screamed and shook the halter vigorously, flapping it up and down. "Am I going to die?"

"Calm down," Dalila ordered and tried to grab Sudi's hands.

People gathered and looked alarmed. But no one stepped forward to save Sudi from the lethal insect.

"Help me," Sudi pleaded.

Then Scott pushed through the crowd. His hand darted forward, and his fingers brushed over Sudi's breast. He scooped the bug into his hand, then held it in his palm as if it were a pet.

"It's only a cicada," he said. "You don't need to be afraid."

"Put your top down," Dalila said, prying

Sudi's fingers from the hem of the halter.

Sudi gasped and let go. Finally, she understood.

"It's all right," Dalila whispered and went back to her seat.

Sudi smoothed her bodice, making sure the halter top covered her breasts. A blush burned her cheeks.

"A cicada can't hurt you," Scott continued. He tossed the broad-headed insect into the air. "It was probably afraid of you."

Sudi couldn't speak. She stared down at the ground, humiliated.

Scott leaned closer. "It's okay," he whispered into her ear. "I was getting a bug off of you, so it doesn't count."

She ventured a glance up, but Scott was already heading back to his seat. Carter stood in front of her.

"Great show," Carter said, lifting his sunglasses. "I'll definitely be there for your next performance."

He followed Scott back to their table.

People who had gathered to watch her hysterics smiled and dispersed.

Only Brian and Michelle remained.

"Nice try, Sudi," Brian said with a lopsided grin. "But even that show won't get me back."

"As if," Sudi answered, more flustered than before.

Meri pushed in front of Sudi. "Please. Why would she want you back?"

"Why wouldn't she?" Brian said with the conceit that Sudi had come to hate. He smirked and walked away.

"I can't believe you," Michelle said, fuming. "You were flashing Scott on purpose."

"I was attacked by a bug," Sudi said.

"Don't think for a minute that I believe you're afraid of a cicada. We used to catch them in my backyard, remember?"

Sudi started to defend herself, but stopped. "Whatever, Michelle."

"You're so déclassé," Michelle said. "Pathetic, really. I feel like taking back your invitation to my party."

Dalila stood up and slowly walked around the table. Her regal bearing made Michelle pause.

"Go back to pretending you're perfect," Dalila said with calm authority, "and let us drink our coffee without your rude comments."

Michelle stared at Dalila, but she didn't reply. She seemed suddenly unsure of herself and glanced at Sudi, then took two careful steps backward before hurrying back to her table.

"Can you believe she and I were once best friends?" Sudi asked.

"You're better off without her," Meri said. "She's such a poser."

"What do you suppose she's doing with them?" Sudi asked.

"Talking trash about you," Meri said and playfully nudged Sudi.

"At least now I don't have to figure out what to wear to the party tonight," Sudi said. "Because I'm definitely not going."

"We'll go with you," Dalila said, still gazing after Michelle.

"I can't face Scott," Sudi said.

"You're going," Meri said. "Because if you don't show up, then Michelle will think she's won."

"But you have to learn at least one incantation to stop an evil creature from attacking you," Dalila said.

"Just in case," Meri agreed.

"Nothing's going to happen at the party," Sudi said. She didn't want to go back to that dark little room with its smelly incense and lantern light.

"You need to know a spell," Meri persisted.

"Fine. I'll learn one," Sudi promised, even though she didn't sense any danger. Who was going to send a demon after her at a party where 300 people could witness the attack? The cult leaders wouldn't be that stupid. Besides she had watched enough scary movies to know the monsters would descend upon them, as before, when they were alone and vulnerable.

One by one the wicks burned out. The dying flames sputtered and hissed, consuming the oil-soaked strips of cloth. Bitter smoke curled into the bluish incense vapors and rolled lazily about, fogging the air.

Sudi carried another copper trunk to the table. She opened it and pulled out a leather case, then blew away the sand and removed the papyrus. Dalila and Meri had left an hour ago, and Sudi still hadn't found the right spell. She needed to leave soon and get ready for the party.

Footsteps overhead startled her. She glanced at the ceiling. *Clunk. Thump.* The dull sounds repeated. What did Abdel do in the attic all day?

She refocused her attention on the papyrus and found an incantation for turning a demon into a small dog: *Goddess of magic, I entreat you, send a burning ring of fire around the one who beholds me. Set fire to his heart and change him into my dog.*

Sudi imagined the demon transforming into a Chihuahua. In her mind's eye, she saw the devil pup nipping at her heels and following her home. Carrie and Nicole would no doubt beg their mother to let them keep the dog, and the evil mutt would probably love the twins as much as it hated Sudi. She pictured it gnawing on her toes while she slept.

She shuddered and began searching for a spell that didn't turn the demon into a household pet.

A new heading caught her attention: *The Tricks of Love Divination.* Her heart raced. Did she dare?

A love spell appeared easy to cast. No ceremony was involved. She had only to recite the words. She pictured Scott falling for her and imagined his lips on hers, his hands . . . Why not? As long as she had to learn magic, she might as well practice on something fun.

The last flame burned out, leaving her in darkness. She opened a shutter, then grabbed a Sharpie from her backpack and, in the dim light cast by the streetlight, copied the love spell onto the inside of her right forearm.

"Goddess of magic, I entreat you." A pleasant feeling came over her as she began the incantation. "Send a burning ring of love fire around the one who beholds me. Set fire to his heart, that he might love me."

She needed another spell to stop evil, but for tonight the Chihuahua hex would have to do. Nothing was going to happen anyway. She quickly copied that incantation onto her left arm. She had to be careful not to confuse the two spells. They were almost the same, and she didn't want Scott to become her lapdog.

She grabbed her backpack and hurried down the stairs and out the front door. As she started home, she decided to wear her new push-up bra and the low-cut green top with the long sleeves that would hide the words written on her arms.

Two hours later, Sudi waited on the front lawn of Michelle's house, near the valets who had been hired to park the cars. Pink, orange, and gold lanterns swung from the oak trees, casting a fairy-tale glow over the yard. Music pulsed through Sudi. She couldn't wait to dance. It might have been Michelle's party, but Sudi felt as if she owned this night.

She stepped off the curb, loving the click of her heels on the pavement, and looked for head-lights, anxious for Dalila and Meri to join her so she could go inside.

Finally, a black sedan pulled up. A valet opened the back door, and Meri jumped out, tug-ging at the hem of her black T-shirt. Silver sequins across the front spelled out PROBLEM CHILD. The low-slung jeans showed off her flat stomach.

Dalila scooted to the edge of the seat, then lifted her legs, pointed her toes, and alighted from the limo as if she had practiced being a queen a thou-sand times. Kohl darkened the rims of her eyelids, and a red sheath clung to her body. She touched Sudi's arm. Her cold fingers trembled. "I only know how to belly dance. I don't think I'll fit in here."

"We'll show you," Sudi said. "Let's go inside." Sudi ran up the steps. She could feel the guys on the veranda watching her. She squeezed in among the dancers on the porch, and swept her hands up her body in a flirty way, then arched her back and ran her fingers through her thick blond hair. She squealed and turned to bump hips with Meri and Dalila—but instead she slid against air.

She glanced back at the lawn.

Dalila looked ready to run. Meri stood protectively beside her.

Sudi hurried back down the steps and joined them.

"You can't be that shy," Sudi said.

"If a boy touches me, I'll faint," Dalila said. "Everyone dances so close."

"Here's a clue to get over your shyness," Sudi said, hooking arms with Dalila and Meri and pulling them forward. "It feels really, really good."

Sudi led them up the steps through the foyer and into the living room. The music played loudly, and a thrill rushed through her.

The furniture had been removed from the rooms, and the walls and ceiling were covered with sheer, gauzy fabric that swelled and rolled, changing shape continually and reflecting pink and orange lights. Sudi doubted that Michelle even knew all of the kids at the party—but she loved the way so many of them knew her, calling Sudi's name and asking her to join them.

She led Dalila and Meri past the dancers. When they rounded the corner, a fanfare of changing lights made her blink.

"Just how much money did Michelle's parents spend on this party?" Sudi asked, but then she saw Tyler and Jeff sitting at the bar, drinking sodas and eating peanuts. She didn't wait for an answer. "Those two are perfect," she said, and escorted Meri and Dalila forward.

Tyler and Jeff were juniors at Lincoln High, one year ahead of Sudi. She could see in their expressions that they recognized Meri. Then their gazes shifted to Dalila. Tyler slid from his stool and couldn't stop grinning. Jeff set his soft drink down and choked on a peanut. His brown hair fell in his eyes; he flipped it back with a nod of his head.

"Hey," Sudi said. "I want you to meet two of my best friends, Dalila and Meri."

"Hi," Tyler said, but his smile quickly faded into a look of concern.

Jeff stared at Meri, his puzzled expression growing into one of alarm.

Dalila turned first and let out a small scream. Then Sudi looked at Meri and gasped. Long feline whiskers had sprouted from Meri's cheeks.

Sudi stretched her arms to hide Meri from Tyler and Jeff. Then she and Dalila pulled Meri toward the bathroom.

"We'll catch you later," Sudi shouted over her shoulder.

"What are you doing?" Meri asked, a head shorter than she had been and shrinking. "I like Jeff."

"You've got cat ears poking out of your hair," Dalila said.

Meri shrieked and ducked low, pressing through the crush of dancers. A long tail wiggled from out of the top of her jeans.

When the bathroom door opened, Sudi, Dalila, and Meri dodged inside before the girls who had been waiting in line could stop them.

Sudi locked the door.

Meri jumped onto the counter near the sink and stared at her reflection. She patted her cheeks with the back of her hand to avoid scratching herself with her extended feline claws.

"I didn't say the incantation," Meri said when she was able to speak again. "So why is this happening?"

"Maybe nerves caused it," Sudi said, unable to pull her gaze away from Meri's unearthly beauty; the cat ears, whiskers, and changed eyes made Meri look like an enchantress from a fairy tale. "I'm sure we'll get control over the power in time."

Dalila began stoking Meri's hair, calming her. "Magic takes getting used to," Dalila soothed. "One day this will come naturally to you. It's like learning how to play a musical instrument. Mistakes are made at first." Slowly, Meri began changing back; the vertical pupils became black circles in the center of her eyes, whiskers disappeared leaving smooth skin, and the tail vanished.

Finally she slid off the counter, returned to her full girl size. "What if a photographer takes my picture and I end up some weird cat-freak girl on the cover of *Star*?"

"We'll deal with that if it happens," Sudi answered.

"I'm all right now," Meri said and took a deep breath before opening the door. "I'll concentrate on staying calm."

The three girls stepped toward the edge of the dancing crowd. The music pulsed around them and Sudi began to move, her eyes wandering, looking for Scott.

Jeff waved from across the room. He bumped around a line of dancers who were pressed together, moving back and forth in unison, and shoved his way toward Meri.

"Go dance with Jeff," Sudi said.

"Are you sure?" Meri said, waving back at Jeff.

"Go on," Sudi said, and mischievously pushed Meri toward Jeff. "Have fun."

When Sudi turned back, a flash of red among the dancers caught her attention. "I thought you said you couldn't dance," Sudi said and joined Dalila, bumping hips with her. "You're incredible. I want you to teach me."

Dalila swayed her body sensually, her shyness

gone. "I've been belly dancing since I was a little girl. It's in my blood."

All the guys began watching Sudi and Dalila dancing together, and then Carter stepped between them. He rested his hand on Sudi's shoulder, but he never stopped looking at Dalila.

"Introduce me to your friend, Sudi," he said.

"No, Carter," Sudi said harshly.

"What's wrong?" Dalila asked, and stared up at Carter like someone falling in love for the first time.

"Let's get some air," Sudi said but when she started to lead Dalila from the room, Carter put his arm around her friend, pulling her back to him.

"I'm not going to hurt her," he said to Sudi.

"Dalila doesn't know . . . she's lived a really protected life," Sudi argued.

"I'll watch over her," he insisted, gazing into Dalila's eyes. "I won't let anyone hurt her."

Dalila looked up at Carter with the same dreamy expression Sudi had seen on the faces of too many other girls. Sudi didn't understand their infatuations, and she couldn't comprehend how quickly Dalila had lost her shyness.

"I give you my word," Carter said. "Trust me, Sudi."

Carter tenderly kissed the top of Dalila's head before turning her around to face him. Maybe Carter was falling for Dalila. After all, she had been reared to enchant kings. Sudi watched as Carter guided Dalila outside and across the lawn to a stage that had been set up over the swimming pool.

Sudi followed them outside. The yard stretched on and on, sloping gently into a wooded area. She stepped onto the grass, and the aroma of chocolate drifted into the cool autumn night.

A buffet had been set up near the gazebo. The velvety candy dripped down three silver tiers into a huge bowl that was surrounded by fruit and marshmallows.

Sudi pushed into the group of kids gathered around the table and picked out a strawberry. Her mouth watered as she dunked it in the chocolate. But when she tried to ease away, a girl accidentally nudged her and Sudi stumbled into someone, dripping chocolate onto his shirt.

"Sorry," she said and looked up.

Brian glared down at her. "Real mature, Sudi. I know you did that on purpose."

Dominique tugged on Brian's sleeve. "She was only getting chocolate," Dominique said. "It was an accident."

"No, it wasn't," Brian argued. "She's desperate to get back with me."

Sudi rolled her eyes. "If I wanted you back," Sudi said, holding up the strawberry, "I think I could come up with a better scheme than this." She flicked more chocolate on him.

"Yeah," he blustered. "Like what you did earlier today."

Sudi hurried away as Brian started telling everyone the way she had flashed him at Dean & Deluca. Her perfect evening was spinning out of control. She sat down alone on a bench near the woods and stared at the rising moon, her back to the party. She licked at the chocolate on her fingers and wondered what she'd ever seen in Brian.

Someone tapped her shoulder. Before she could turn, Scott straddled the bench and sat beside her. His clothes smelled fresh and new, his aftershave musky.

"I was hoping you would still come tonight," he said.

She glanced down, suddenly self-conscious.

He touched her chin, lifting her head until she was forced to gaze into his eyes. "I barely looked," he teased. "Promise. So don't go shy on me."

Then he stood and took her hand, pulling her up to him. "Dance with me?" She could feel his desire; or was it her own? She started moving with him, enjoying the warmth of his body. His hand slipped down her back, and she caught her breath.

"I'm glad you broke up with Brian," he said, his minty breath mingling with hers.

"Me, too," she answered, and wondered if her eyes had the same dreamy expression that she had seen in Dalila's eyes.

"I'm the one you should have dated," he said, taking her hands and placing them around his neck. Then, his fingers caressed her waist and rested on her hips.

Maybe she wouldn't need to cast a spell on him after all.

She sensed someone watching her and glanced

back at the party, expecting to see Michelle glaring at her.

Instead, Michelle stood on the porch. Five guys crowded around her, all dressed in matching red shirts. Michelle's parents had hired professional dancers to make sure the party didn't lag. Sudi wondered if they had also hired escorts to hover around Michelle and give her a false sense of popularity.

The music changed. Michelle's entourage began clapping, and then all five broke into a hip-hop routine. Michelle danced with them, strutting and flaunting herself, moving toward the stage.

Sudi watched, stunned. "What is Michelle doing?"

"Michelle is Miss Diva," Scott said, his hand on Sudi's shoulder. "She's going to perform."

Sudi looked up at him, astonished. "I thought Sienna was singing."

"She is, but so is Michelle," Scott explained. "It's her special surprise for all her guests."

"I was hoping her special surprise was a goody bag," Sudi answered and stared back at Michelle, feeling sorry for her. "This is going to be a major embarrassment. Didn't anyone bother to tell Michelle that she can't sing?"

"I did," Scott said. "I was over here earlier listening to her rehearse. She's really bad. Carter and I tried to talk her out of it."

Sudi imagined that Brian had encouraged her so he could have a good laugh at Michelle's expense.

Kids began moving toward the stage, clapping and whistling, excited to see Sienna perform.

Two dancers lifted Michelle onto their shoulders. She must have thought all of the commotion was for her, because she smiled and waved, throwing kisses the way celebrities acknowledged cheering fans.

"I warned her," Scott said as he placed his arm around Sudi. "Come on."

Sudi had expected Scott to pull her toward the stage. Instead he steered her onto a path cut between the trees.

"What about Sienna? Don't you at least want to hear her sing?" Sudi asked.

"I can hear her anytime," Scott answered. "I have her CD. And I definitely don't want to listen to Michelle ruining my favorite songs."

"Is Michelle planning to sing *with* Sienna?" Sudi asked, surprised again. "Did Sienna agree to that?"

"I don't know," Scott said. "I have a feeling it's going to be a big surprise for her as well."

Sudi followed him down the path, crushing leaves under her shoes.

"Where are we going?" she asked.

"I want to show you something," he answered.

The thought of walking alone with him through the moonlit woods caused a pleasant chill to rush through her.

The party noise became muffled. Kids screamed and applauded, but the sound seemed far away. Minutes later, Sienna's sultry voice drifted into the night. Scott slowed his pace.

"What did you want to show me?" Sudi said breathlessly.

"This." He slipped both arms around her, and then bent down until she could feel his breath on her face. His lips lingered over hers, and when she didn't pull away, he kissed her.

Her stomach fluttered, and longing filled her body. Why had she wasted time with Brian? She wrapped her arms around Scott's waist and invited him closer, her hips slinking against him.

A twig snapped. She opened her eyes. A shadow slid from behind one tree to the next.

"It's probably only a rabbit," Scott said and nuzzled her neck.

But she had definitely seen something bigger than a rabbit move between the spindly trees. It was probably only a guy and a girl kissing in the shadows, the way they were.

Scott kissed her again, and this time she felt his tongue. She closed her eyes and relaxed in his arms.

A scuffling of leaves made her alert again. She pulled back. In the darkness beneath the trees, she spotted a lone figure, watching them.

"If you want to go slower, that's okay," Scott said, taking her hand. He started toward the path.

Sudi took a deep breath, trying to decide. The shadow was gone now. Maybe it had been nothing. But if the cult had sent a creature to harm her, she couldn't let it follow her back to the party, and she couldn't let Scott stay with her and put him in danger, either. She had to face whatever it was alone.

"Go back to the party without me," she said. "I'll catch up with you later."

"What?" He gave her a confused smile, as if he didn't understand her joke and was waiting for a punch line.

"I won't be long," she said and hurried away from him, ducking under low-hanging branches.

Mud sucked at her spiky heels, and she sank deeper with each step. Then, from behind her, came the sound of other footsteps squishing in the muck. She turned. Her heart raced, pumping adrenaline through her veins. The thin branches waved in front of her, snapping and breaking. She held her breath, waiting to see what had been stalking her.

Scott stepped through the trees. "You'll get lost if you go too far from the path," he said and tugged on her hand, trying to lead her back the way they had come.

"Go back to the party," she insisted.

"Not without you," he said.

She stopped abruptly and turned her head,

sensing something. A creature maybe, or another god that had been sent to harm her. She could feel whatever it was fix its attention on her. Her heart loped crazily in her chest. Evil vibrated in the breeze. But Scott didn't seem to feel the strange shiver in the night.

Her mind spun, trying to figure a way to get Scott to stop playing hero and go away.

"I'm meeting Brian," she lied, her heart sinking. But she had no choice. She had to get Scott to leave the woods, and quickly.

Scott let go of her hand. "He bragged that you would never get over him, but I thought he was just being Brian."

"He told the truth," Sudi said, hating the lie.

"I didn't believe the things Brian said about you," Scott answered.

Sudi wanted to hear what Brian had said and argue in her own defense, but she knew she had to hurry. She whirled around, leaving Scott alone, and ran deeper into the woods, forcing back her tears, wanting more than anything to lure the beast away from Scott and the party.

Her hands trembled, and she fumbled with

her sleeve, trying to roll it up so she could read the incantation she had written on her arm. But fear had muddled her thinking. Which spell was the right one? A pungent smell was wafting around her. She didn't know if evil had a scent, but maybe the creature coming after her did. She held up her arm and blinked back the tears distorting her vision. She had forgotten to consider how dark the night might be. Even with the milky moonlight, she could barely read the incantation.

Whatever was coming had quickened its pace.

She began to speak the spell and stopped. What if it wasn't a creature heading toward her? She couldn't just turn anyone into a dog—

She stopped in her tracks, then crept behind a vine and waited.

A mummy stepped from the foliage and paused, as if it sensed her. Its rib cage protruded where its wrapping had fallen away. Black streaks covered its dried and shrunken orange-brown skin. The eyes had fallen back into their sockets, and the lids appeared closed. Slowly, the mummy's head turned, and through slits, its gaze fell on her.

Sudi held up her arm and read the spell.

"*Goddess of magic, I entreat you, send a burning ring of your love fire around the one who beholds me. Set fire to his heart, that . . .*" She stopped. She was reading the wrong incantation.

If she were going to survive, she had no choice.

"*. . . That he might love me,*" she said, finishing the incantation.

The mummy lunged toward her. Her spell had done nothing.

CHAPTER 13

Sudi jerked back and slammed into the tree behind her. Pain spun up her spine. The mummy's skeletal hands grabbed her, the bony fingers pressing into her waist. Its head bent toward her with an unpleasant crack of bones, and with its closeness came a strong rancid odor.

She groaned with disgust as the mummy's face pressed against her forehead. Then, without warning, its swollen black teeth clicked against hers, and the stale taste of mold and embalming resin settled on her tongue. She pushed the mummy away. Her hands came back covered with bits of dry mummy-wrapping.

"What are you doing?" she asked, not sure the mummy understood. But she felt certain she knew: her spell had worked, after all. The mummy was trying to kiss her.

It tottered toward her again, struggling to keep its body balanced atop its stiff legs.

Sudi felt something in her mouth like a piece of broken tooth. She picked a black nugget off her tongue, then glanced at the mummy. The tip of its nose was missing. She squealed in disgust and spat.

Bile rose to the back of her throat, and she took long, slow breaths to settle her nausea.

The mummy tried to hold her in its brittle arms. Was it trying to comfort her? She ducked out of its embrace, then spat again, wishing the moldy taste would go away.

"I need to get some help," she said, rolling down her sleeves. "Stay here."

She looked into the creature's hollow eyes and

wondered if it understood. She stepped away, and when she thought the mummy was going to remain where it stood, she turned and ran wildly back to Michelle's house.

Leaves slapped her face, momentarily blinding her, but she continued on. Her heels wobbled in the mud, and her ankles twisted painfully back and forth in her unsteady shoes, but that didn't slow her pace.

When she reached the path, she paused, deciding which way to go.

Behind her, footsteps squished in the spongy soil, and then the mummy plodded between two trees, reaching out for her. Its thumbs got tangled in vines as it stumbled toward her. Its chin hit the top of her head with a terrible crack.

She choked back a scream, terrified its jaw had snapped free.

The mummy stared back at her, face intact except for the missing piece of nose. Carefully, she touched its arm. Her fingers encircled the bone. Something dry flaked off in her right palm. She prayed it was only mummy-wrapping.

"You can't come with me," she explained. "I'm

just going to get help. I promise I won't leave you out here alone."

Sudi dropped her hand and took one tentative step away.

The mummy grinned and took a wobbling step forward.

Either it was terrified of the new world in which it found itself and didn't want to be alone, or it was so in love with Sudi that it couldn't bear to be away from her. But she had to find Dalila and Meri, and she couldn't risk having the mummy trail after her.

"Okay," she said. "You can come with me, but if we hear anyone, we have to hide."

She walked with the mummy until they reached the edge of the woods, and then she peered out from behind a tree. Three girls leaned against the buffet table, dipping strawberries in chocolate, but most of the partygoers stood near the stage, snickering and mocking Michelle's performance. Sienna looked ready to run.

Maybe, Sudi thought, she could risk stepping across the lawn with the mummy; but then she saw Scott, sitting alone on the porch steps. Her chest tightened with regret. Her night of magic had deteriorated into a nightmare, and she knew intuitively that her bad dream was just beginning.

"Sudi!" Meri and Dalila called from behind her.

She turned back, surprised to see them hiking through the grass.

"We've been going up and down this path, searching for you," Meri said and displayed the scratches on her hand as proof. "Scott told us you wanted to be alone out here."

"So we knew something bad . . ." Dalila's words trailed off, and her mouth fell open as the mummy moved from the shadows and stood in the moonlight.

Meri gasped and clutched Dalila's arm. Both stood still, staring at the mummy.

"I guess you were right," Sudi admitted. "And so was Abdel. It wasn't safe for us to be out at night yet."

"But you stopped it," Dalila said, stepping closer and touching the mummy's shoulder. She flinched when its head turned.

"Gross," Meri said and took a step back. "He reeks."

"No," Dalila corrected. "Most mummies only have a musty odor. What you smell is the magic the cult used to bring his spirit back to the living world."

"Whatever," Meri said. "He still smells horrible."

"How do you know it's a he?" Sudi asked.

Both Meri and Dalila pointed in reply.

"Oh," Sudi said softly and quickly looked away.

"What spell did you use?" Dalila asked.

"That's the thing," Sudi said, hesitating. "I accidentally put a love spell on him."

She told them about the two spells and how she had used the wrong one. When she finished, Meri couldn't stop laughing, but Dalila looked worried.

"You've made a terrible mistake," Dalila said. "There's a division between the dead and the living, and those who live are not supposed to meddle with those in the underworld. The cult broke that rule, and now you have, too."

"I didn't resurrect it," Sudi argued. "The cult did."

"But what kind of love spell did you use?"

Dalila asked. "Did you bind your soul to his for all eternity? Will your spirit go with him if we find a way to send him back to his world?"

Sudi shrugged; as usual, she hadn't thought it through.

"Let's take him back to my house," Sudi said. "We'll hide him there until we can ask Abdel what to do."

"Are you sure?" Meri said. "Your parents are going to smell him."

"What else can I do?" Sudi asked. "I can't just leave him here. He probably wouldn't stay anyway. He follows me like he can't bear to be away from me."

Dalila shook her head. "The mummy's spirit was brought back, but he can't be one of the blessed dead. He must have done something evil when he was alive, or his soul would have found its way into eternal life. Do you want to take something like that into your house?"

"Especially when he's in love with you," Meri said, and playfully poked Sudi.

"Stop acting like this is a joke," Sudi said and gave Meri an angry look. "We're dealing with a demon."

"Not a demon," a dry voice corrected. "I'm a damned soul."

Sudi, Meri, and Dalila turned and stared at the mummy.

"He understands us," Sudi whispered.

CHAPTER 14

"We can't just stay here," Meri said, studying the shadows. "Other mummies could be coming."

Sudi hadn't considered the possibility that a troop of corpses might be searching for her. "How are we going to get him out of here?"

"Magic," Dalila answered mysteriously. "Wait here while Meri and I get him something to wear."

Sudi watched them leave, but she didn't think their plan to conceal him in clothing was going to work. The mummy leaned against her, his sharp elbow pressing into her, but she didn't push him away. Minutes passed, and when Dalila and Meri didn't return, Sudi began thinking about Scott again. She wiped at the corners of her eyes.

"I guess you're my date for the night," she said cynically, and gazed up at the stars. "I wish it could have been different," she started. "Why did I ever go out with Brian in the first place?"

She turned and looked at the mummy, and before she could stop, she found herself revealing her most inner thoughts and fears. She told him about Brian and Scott, telling him things she hadn't even told Sara.

He nodded sympathetically as if he understood.

Dalila and Meri returned before Sudi had even started on Michelle.

"This is the best we could do," Meri said and unfurled a black trench coat.

"We stole it off the bed where everyone had thrown their coats," Dalila explained. "But we'll return it."

Sudi was certain the coat belonged to Carter,

and she wondered if Dalila was using it as an excuse to see him again.

"People will still see the mummy's head," Meri said.

"Not if my magic works," Dalila replied. She closed her eyes and lifted her arms, with her palms up in supplication. "Queen of magic, Goddess of many names, we bow before your ruling, dear Isis, but if it pleases you, send a burning fire around this one here, and give him the flesh of his youth."

The mummy looked at them with glazed eyes, but nothing happened.

"I guess we'll have to risk walking with him after all," Meri said.

"Let's try again, together," Sudi said, and raised her palms. Meri stood next to her doing the same. They closed their eyes and repeated the incantation with Dalila.

When Sudi opened her eyes, a single red spark floated into the darkness. Other embers joined it, and soon fiery specks swirled around the mummy. Then the cinders fell to the ground, hissing, and the faint scent of charred grass wafted into the air.

Sudi blinked, adjusting her eyes to the sudden gloom. A young man, no more than eighteen, stood in the moonlight completely naked.

"Whoa," Meri said. "What happened to his mummy-wrappings?"

"They're still there," Dalila said. "This is just a disguise that will wear off quickly."

They helped the mummy into the trench coat, then guided him across the lawn.

The girls at the chocolate fountain stopped eating and stared.

"Woo-hoo!" one shouted, wiping at the chocolate on her lips. "Who's the hottie?"

"Introduce us to your friend," Lydia screamed.

"They must be high on chocolate," Sudi said. "Normally Lydia is guy shy."

"Maybe it's the mummy," Meri said, opening her cell phone. "He's really good-looking."

"Evil is always seductive," Dalila added matter-of-factly. "I'm sure that's what they're sensing."

"Great," Sudi said. "Just what all parents want their daughter to bring home."

Meri called her driver, and he was waiting at

the curb by the time they stepped into the front yard. He stared at the mummy's bare feet and ankles but said nothing.

Sudi squeezed into the back between Dalila and the mummy. Meri climbed into the front. They rode in silence, except for the mummy's frightened gasps. He winced at oncoming traffic, and twice shielded his eyes.

Finally, the sedan parked in front of Sudi's house. Dalila and Meri got out with Sudi and the mummy. They huddled near the curb.

"Maybe he should go home with me," Dalila said. "After all, my uncle is an Egyptologist and he'd probably love talking to him."

"The mummy would never stay with you," Meri said. "He'd try to find Sudi, and then he'd be lost and wandering around D.C."

"I'll get him inside," Sudi said, with a confidence she didn't feel.

They said good night, and Sudi started up the walk. She unlocked the front door as the sedan drove away and led the mummy inside.

At the base of the stairs she paused, listening. The refrigerator hummed, but that was the only sound. She gripped the banister and guided the mummy up the steps. Her heart felt ready to explode. What if her mother caught her taking this half-naked guy to her room? She'd never be able to explain this one.

She crept down the hallway past her parents' open bedroom door, feeling totally exposed. When at last she had the mummy in her room, she closed the door and slid to the floor. She didn't stand up again until her legs stopped shaking.

The mummy walked around her room, running his fingers over her dresser, and then he sprawled out on her bed.

Sudi hadn't considered how exhausted he must have felt. She unfolded the comforter and tucked it around him. "I promise I'll find a way to get you through all the gates and into eternal life."

"The beautiful west," he whispered, as if he longed for a peaceful death.

She wondered what his life had been like. In another time she might have loved him. Then a shudder ran through her. What had he done to become a damned soul?

She took a sleeping bag from the shelf in her

closet, unrolled it, crawled inside, and quickly fell asleep.

She awoke with a start. Her mother was pounding on her door. "Sudi, you're going to be late," her mother yelled. "And don't you dare cut school again. I don't want another note from your vice principal."

The mummy leaned over the edge of her bed, gazed down at her, and started to speak. Sudi struggled from her sleeping bag and placed a hand over his mouth. He kissed her palm.

"Don't say a word," she whispered. She felt his tongue on her neck. He rolled over, pulling her on top of him.

She slid off the bed and went to gather some clean underwear from her dresser.

"I have to go to school," she explained, before shutting herself in the closet and taking off her clothes. She rubbed jasmine lotion over her body, hoping it would cover the mummy's stench if it still clung to her. Then she dressed and stepped back out into the room.

The mummy stood by her window, staring out at the backyard.

"You'll have to lock the door when I leave," she said and showed him how to turn the button on the doorknob. "It's really important that no one finds you here."

He nodded and leaned over to embrace her. His lips grazed her cheek as she slipped into the hallway and closed the door behind her. She waited until the lock clicked into place, and then she ran downstairs and burst into the kitchen.

The morning news played on the TV, and the smell of burned toast filled the air. Sudi's mother stood at the sink, scraping black crumbs off her toast with a knife.

"Did you buy birdseed?" she asked when she saw Sudi.

"Yes," Sudi said, and grabbed an apple from the fruit bowl.

"Nicole and Carrie told me that they found a bird trapped in the house," her mother said. "I hope you're not trying to keep a wild bird as a pet."

"Her room smells like the inside of a chicken coop," Carrie said, and Nicole giggled.

"Very funny," Sudi said with a snide grin, but she wondered if Carrie had smelled the mummy.

"I don't want any birds close to the house," her mother continued and bit into the toast. "You've seen the mess pigeons make."

"You wouldn't poison it, would you?" Sudi asked, suddenly panicked, remembering how, as a bird, she had been unable to control the impulse to eat a beetle. "It's not like the bird did anything wrong."

"Are you all right?" her mother asked, her eyes filling with concern.

Sudi wanted to fall into her mom's arms and tell her everything.

"I'm fine," Sudi lied, and started for the door.

Forty-five minutes later, Sudi took her assigned seat in the back of her English class. She pulled out her cell phone, flipped it open, and read a text message from Meri: *Abdel is not home.*

Sudi groaned. She couldn't keep the mummy hidden through a second night. Where had Abdel gone? Surely, he hadn't returned to Egypt. At least, she hoped he hadn't.

An odd awareness made her glance up. Her

classmates were staring at her. A few held their hands over their mouths to hide their snickering.

"Are you all right?" Carter asked, looking at her curiously. He grabbed his backpack, got up from his desk, and slid into the empty one next to her.

"Why is everyone watching me?" Sudi asked in a low voice.

"You didn't comb your hair, for one thing, and you usually wear makeup," Carter said. He scooted the desk closer to her so other students couldn't overhear. "And you smell like you were Dumpster diving. What happened?"

Normally she would have shot back with something clever, but his open and sincere manner made her pause. She reached for a snarled lock of hair and held it to her nose.

"I reek," she moaned.

"Kids are saying the breakup with Brian is affecting you," Carter explained. He placed his hand on her shoulder.

"Who said that? It's not true!" Sudi shouted, outraged. "I am not having a meltdown because of Brian. Why would I miss him? He kisses like a donkey."

Screaming laughter resounded throughout the room.

Sudi glanced at Brian, sorry for her outburst. A flicker of remorse crossed his face as if for a nanosecond he regretted the way he had treated her.

Sebastian, a guy who'd had a crush on Sudi at the beginning of the year, peered out from behind his chin-length bangs. "Sudi, how do you know what a kiss from a donkey feels like?"

Now the entire class was laughing at her.

Brian's voice boomed above the uproar. "Leave her alone," he said. "Can't you see she's losing it?"

"Get real." Sudi rolled her eyes. At least now she knew where the rumor had started. "I am not losing it!"

Carter massaged the back of her neck, trying to calm her. She pushed his hand away.

"You'll get through it," he said soothingly. "Scott's the best medicine. I told him to forget about what you did last night at the party. I mean, we all know you weren't meeting Brian, so why did you tell Scott that you were?"

Sudi shrugged.

"I figured you were still upset about the cicada thing," Carter continued. "So when he tried to kiss you—"

"He told you?" Sudi asked. The heat of a blush rose to her cheeks.

Carter nodded. "He's going to ask you out again."

"He said that?" she asked, eager to hear more.

But Mrs. Grumm walked into the room and tapped a ruler on her desk to silence the class.

"Later," Carter said and turned his attention toward the teacher.

"Good morning," Mrs. Grumm said. She pulled some papers from her carryall and set them on her desk with a sharp slap. Her glasses dangled on a chain around her neck, and her porcupine haircut made her head look too small for her barrel-shaped body.

Sudi leaned back, thinking about Scott, grateful to have almost an hour to mull over everything that was going on in her life.

"Sudi, would you like to start off by reading your essay?" Mrs. Grumm asked and sat down at her desk, biting on the tip of her acrylic fingernail.

Panic seized Sudi. She hadn't done the homework. "I haven't . . ." she stammered, trying to find an excuse, but before she could, Carter tore the title page from his work and handed it to her.

"Are you sure?" she whispered.

"It's not very good anyway," he replied. "You'll probably only get a D."

Sudi headed toward the front of the class, but when she reached the blackboard, she sensed movement near the door.

Black material, the same color as the trench coat which the mummy had worn, fluttered near the entrance. She tilted her head and craned her neck to see. Her heart raced in anticipation. The papers fell from her shaking hands.

The mummy leaned against the open door, still wearing the trench coat. But Dalila's spell had fallen away, and a withered, shrunken corpse grinned back at Sudi.

She gasped and looked at the class, hoping no one had seen him.

The tardy bell rang. The shrill sound panicked the mummy. His nails scratched the door as his hands tried to brace his body. He almost fell, then caught himself and lumbered away.

"Sudi?" Mrs. Grumm looked up and put on her glasses. "What's wrong?"

"I need to go to the nurse," Sudi said and didn't wait for permission. She bolted from the classroom and sprinted down the hallway, her footsteps banging noisily on the hard floor. She didn't see the mummy. Where had he gone? And how had he followed her to school? He couldn't just walk down the streets of D.C.

A scream echoed up the stairwell from the hallway below. Sudi charged down the steps, taking the last three in a leap.

Lydia was hurrying away from the girls' restroom, her face stricken.

"Stay out," she stammered, and tried to say more. Finally, frustrated, she waved Sudi away from the door, but she didn't stay to explain what had frightened her. She darted toward the stairs.

Sudi pushed through the swinging door and almost tripped over a fallen backpack. Lipstick, mascara, and a broken perfume bottle lay scattered on the floor. A cigarette smoldered on the dingy tiles.

The mummy stood transfixed by his reflection

in the full-length mirror. Then he saw Sudi behind him and tried to arrange his bandages.

"Why didn't you stay where I left you?" Sudi asked, approaching him carefully. If Dalila's magic had worn off, then Sudi's spell must have weakened also.

"Love made me follow you," he explained.

Sudi wondered why her magic hadn't diminished, but she didn't have time to consider the reason. She had to figure out a way to hide him.

"No wonder you spurn me," he said sadly, still gazing in the mirror. "I'm hideous."

"We need to get you away from here," she said. "That girl will come back with others, maybe even the police."

"Perhaps if you smoothed oil and perfume over my legs and arms, their beauty would return. I was strong and muscular, my legs thick and brown." He stepped closer to the mirror. "At least let me adorn my eyes. Do you have *mesd'emt* so I can paint my eyes for you?"

"We don't have time," she said.

Anxiety constricted her chest, and she had to concentrate on breathing. She didn't know how long it would be before Lydia found someone and returned. Then again, maybe it was time to let the world know about the cult and the Hour priests. But what would happen to the mummy then?

"Let's leave now," she said.

"If you could have seen me when I wore my headdress," he said. "The long hair fell thickly to my shoulders and framed my face. Queens fell in love with me once." He turned carefully and walked toward her. "Why did you bring me back?"

"I didn't," she explained. "The Cult of Anubis did and sent you to destroy me."

"That's impossible," he said. "I adore you."

"Not really," she confessed. "I cast a love spell on you, and I guess it made you forget why the cult brought you back."

She took his hand. The cold knuckle bones protruded against her palm.

"We can't let people see you," she said, leading him to the door. She peeked out.

The hallway was empty. Teachers' voices came from behind the closed classroom doors and combined in a low, dull drone.

Sudi pulled the mummy forward and guided

him to the janitor's storeroom. She opened the door, switched on the light, pulled him inside, and closed the door. The smells of ammonia and damp mops clogged the air in the small room.

"You have to stay here," she said. "No following me this time. I'm going to get a note from the nurse so I can leave school, but I'll be back."

The mummy nodded.

She opened the door and edged into the hallway, then turned and bumped into Carter. She jumped. "You scared me to death," she said. "Have you been following me?"

"Mrs. Grumm asked me to make sure you were okay," he said, a sly expression on his face.

Had he seen the mummy? Surely, if he had, he wouldn't be smirking; he'd be terrified and screaming. Still, he looked at her as if he knew her secret.

"What were you doing in the janitor's storeroom?" he asked, falling into step beside her.

"Smoking a cigarette," she lied and increased her pace, hoping he would leave her alone.

"You don't smoke," he countered.

"I do now," she said forcefully.

"Mrs. Grumm was worried about you," he

said, trailing behind her on the stairs. "You left the classroom and went the wrong way."

On the second-floor landing, Sudi stopped, and he bumped into her this time. "I told you I needed a smoke," Sudi said. "I can go to the nurse's office by myself. Go back to class, and tell Mrs. Grumm that I'm all right."

"Maybe I should stay with you," Carter said, the smug smile returning to his face.

"Go," Sudi answered and waited until he left before she continued up the next flight of stairs to the third floor.

Minutes later, with the nurse's pass in hand, Sudi returned to the janitor's closet and opened the door.

The mummy was gone.

The sun had set, and the evening damp clung to Sudi's arms and face. She sat with Meri and Dalila behind the Lincoln Memorial and curled her toes in the wet grass, trying to ease the pain of her blisters.

"We're never going to find the mummy by walking around the District," Meri said, massaging her calves. "Maybe we should go back to Georgetown and see if Abdel's home yet."

"The mummy has probably gone back to the cult anyway," Dalila said. "If they can cast a spell strong enough to summon his spirit from death, then they must know one to make him return to them."

"Or maybe he's the lead story on the nightly news," Sudi said, trying to lighten their moods. "We haven't watched TV all day. He could be the breaking story."

She had meant to cheer her friends up. Instead, they stared back at her stone-faced. "What will happen if people discover that the dead can be brought back to life?" Dalila asked.

"I can't even imagine how gross it would be," Meri said.

Dalila shrugged. "I'd like to be able to speak to my parents again."

"But they wouldn't be like they were back then," Meri argued.

Sudi pulled on her shoes and stood. "Come on. We'd better start home."

Meri and Dalila followed her down to the walkway. They had gone only a short distance when three cabs pulled up to the curb. Tourists climbed from the first two, and then Abdel got out of the last one. His normally neat hair hung in his eyes, and his forehead glistened with sweat.

"Abdel!" Sudi shouted and ran to him, feeling an incredible surge of happiness.

Meri shrieked and hugged him.

"Where have you been?" Dalila asked, smiling.

"I've been looking for the three of you," he said, and wrapped his arms around them, squeezing tightly. "You weren't at your schools, and Dalila's uncle didn't know where she had gone off to."

"The cult sent a mummy," Sudi began, but Meri interrupted, her hands flying into the air as she excitedly continued the story. When she ran out of breath, Dalila finished for her, recounting everything else that had taken place.

Abdel nodded patiently, but he didn't seem interested in their troubles.

"If you had come to me first," he said, "I could have warned you that the mummy had only been sent to distract you from something more important."

"If a walking corpse isn't our real problem,"

Sudi said, "then I don't think I want to know what is."

Abdel looked at her. "The cult kidnapped Scott."

Sudi swallowed hard and pressed her fingers against her eyes so she wouldn't cry.

"That's against the law," Meri said. "The authorities will get involved, and I thought the cult wanted to stay low key."

"They won't hold Scott indefinitely," Abdel explained. "They'll release him quickly, but when they do, his soul will have been replaced with a demon's spirit, an evil demon."

"What should we do?" Sudi asked.

"Rescue him," Abdel said simply.

"But how?" Dalila asked. "We're not strong enough to fight the cult. They've had centuries to practice their magic, and we've only studied for three weeks."

"Besides, how are we supposed to know which spells to use?" Meri added. "We've memorized some, but they're for silly things."

Abdel seemed to find humor in their panic. "You're descended from the gods who brought order to Egypt," he said. "I have every confidence that you'll find a way, as your ancestors did when they fought the forces of chaos."

"But wait," Dalila said, clinging to his arm. "You told us that the cult wants to destroy our bloodline because once they do, no one will have the power to use the Book of Thoth to stop them."

Abdel nodded.

"So, what if this is only a trick to make us go to them?" Dalila asked.

"In every encounter, that will be a risk you'll have to take," Abdel answered.

"But what if we can't stop them?" Meri asked.

"The world will be changed," Abdel said.

"And what happens to us if we don't succeed?" Sudi asked.

Abdel looked at each of them before answering. "Legend says that all Descendants who fail are condemned to live with the demons in the chaos at the edge of the universe."

Sudi closed the front door and stepped silently across the dark living room. The smell of chicken frying permeated the air, and when she neared the kitchen she could hear it crackling in the hot oil. She stood in the pantry, spying on her family.

Her mother carried a plate of steaming biscuits to the table, and her father broke into song, serenading her. His deep voice drowned out her sisters' squeals as they tried to sing along. Sudi had been part of that happiness once, but now her mind was whirring with worries that no one ever expected to face. She didn't know how to find Scott, let alone rescue him. And how did Abdel know for certain that the cult had kidnapped him, anyway? After all, he had been a druggie in California, and maybe he had taken a slide back into that lifestyle.

"Come join us." Her father sang the words to the tune of the Toreador Song from *Carmen*.

It took her a moment to realize that he was singing to her. Then she stepped into the overly warm kitchen, and sat down, wondering if this could be her last meal with her family.

"You're late," her mother said. Using a pair of tongs, she picked out a wing and a thigh from the iron skillet on the stove. She placed both on a plate and set it in front of Sudi.

"It's Monday night," Sudi said. "I thought the twins had dance class."

"We finished with this session," Nicole explained.

"We're off for two weeks," Carrie added.

"Tell us about your day," her father said as he passed her the basket of biscuits. "It must have been a good one for you to be so late." He winked.

"Things came up," Sudi said absently and stared down at her food. Normally, she loved her mother's fried chicken, but now she wondered if chickens had dreams and emotions. Did they feel the way she had when she was trapped inside a bird's body?

"If you don't want your thigh, can I have it?" Nicole asked, biting a piece of meat from her drumstick.

"Did you ever think that birds might have feelings?" Sudi asked.

Nicole looked perplexed. "Does that mean you don't want it?"

"Be a cannibal," Sudi said and pushed her plate across the table toward Nicole.

"Sudi, don't you feel well?" her father asked.

"I've become a vegetarian, all right?" Sudi replied brusquely.

Her parents exchanged a quick look, and then her mother spoke. "That's certainly all right." She passed Sudi the bowl of succotash. "Lots of people don't want their bodies to become a graveyard for animals."

"Gross!" Carrie and Nicole hollered in unison.

Sudi stared at the lima beans and kernels of corn. She couldn't eat. Nothing tasted good with tears.

"A guy told me to give this to you," Carrie said, holding up an envelope. Hieroglyphs inside a cartouche formed Sudi's name.

Sudi snapped the envelope away from Carrie. "Don't you know better than to talk to strangers?" Sudi demanded.

"What should I do?" Carrie asked snidely. "Stop answering the door because someone might bring you an invitation you don't want?"

"He came to the door?" Sudi tore at the envelope. In her haste she cut her finger on the paper's edge and cried out, then stopped and sucked the blood.

Carrie and Nicole stared at her.

Her father took the envelope and finished opening it. "It's a gift certificate to a health spa," he said. "What were you afraid it was going to be?"

Sudi shook her head. "I don't know."

Her mother took the certificate. "The Anubis Spa is elegant and pricey. Maybe you can cash in the certificate and use the money for something practical."

"It's a gift," her father said. "Let her indulge herself."

"I don't know," her mother said, absently fanning herself with the card. "The spa is connected with that cult, and I've heard some weird things about them. You know, that California touchy-feely attitude."

"It's harmless," her father said and leaned back, spreading his arms, ready to break into another song.

Sudi grabbed the invitation—she couldn't bear more happiness—and ran from the kitchen, pretending not to hear her father and mother calling her to come back.

Upstairs, she hurried into her room and closed the door, then fell on her bed and flipped open her cell phone. She had started to speed-dial Meri when someone knocked. Her father opened the door and peeked in.

"What's wrong, Sudi?" he asked and walked over to her bed. He sat down beside her. His weight made her side of the mattress lift.

"Growing pains," Sudi answered. "Things have gotten really hard lately."

"Because of Brian?" he asked.

Sudi nodded her lie.

"Sometimes young men can be heartless, because they don't know how to behave yet. They're learning to develop social skills, the same as you." Her father pulled her close to him and kissed the top of her head. "Besides, Brian is a jackass," he added. "I never liked him anyway."

Sudi pulled away from her father and walked over to her open window. "Dad, do you believe in magic?" Sudi asked.

"Of course I do," he answered.

She glanced at him, surprised.

"Today's magic is tomorrow's technology," he explained. "We use things once considered magic every day. When Marconi told his friends that he had invented a way to send messages through the air without wires, they took him to see a psychiatrist, because they didn't believe such a thing was possible. But Marconi invented the radio, and now we send pictures through the air. We all watch TV, and that's a kind of magic, so why couldn't there be more? There has to be."

Sudi leaned on the windowsill and looked out

at the starry sky. "It's scary looking up there and wondering what might be looking back at us."

"That's an odd thing to say," her father said, joining her. "Why would you feel afraid? You have me and your mom to protect you and keep you safe."

Sudi nodded, but she knew she would never feel completely safe again, because somewhere in that night sky lurked enemies: ancient gods who wanted to destroy her.

"Look," her father said excitedly. "A shooting star!"

Sudi gasped and pulled her head back inside. She eased away from the window.

"It's only a meteorite," her father said. "Your hands are trembling. Why are you so afraid?"

"A shooting star is an arrow shot by angels to stop a demon before it can reach the earth," she explained.

"Where did you learn such nonsense?" he asked and hugged her, patting her back.

"The History Channel," Sudi lied. She couldn't tell him she had read it in the Book of Thoth.

"I think we're safe from demons for tonight,"

he said and started from the room, but at the doorway he turned back, a worried expression on his face, as if the terror thrumming through Sudi had somehow telepathically transmitted to him.

"You're safe with me, Sudi," he said. "You don't need to be afraid of shooting stars or anything. If Brian . . ." He left his question unspoken, but Sudi understood.

"I'm fine," Sudi answered. "Brian never hurt me."

Her father nodded and left the room.

For the first time in her life Sudi felt ill at ease with her window open. She shut it and stared back at the black night pressing against the glass. She tugged on the cord and closed her drapes. This had to be a bad dream, some kind of cosmic joke. She couldn't be descended from the god-kings of Egypt's past. She was only a teenager who loved to dance and flirt with guys and had trouble conjugating French verbs.

But the gift certificate in her hand told her that the supernatural world was real, and that she was experiencing the ultimate reality.

Sudi stood in the Penn Quarter near Chinatown and stared across the street at the Anubis Building. Black glass covered the entire facade and reflected the fast-moving clouds. Her thoughts kept jumping forward to Scott. How were they going to find him in there? Moreover, she had thought that she would have been able to sense danger, to know instinctively that her enemy was near, but her shivering came from the cold breeze that snapped the flags and clanged the hoist clips against the towering poles behind her. That's what she told herself, anyway.

A hand touched her shoulder. She winced and spun around.

"Sorry," Meri said. The wind tossed her hair into her face. "I'm a ball of nerves, too. I almost didn't come. I kept thinking, what if it's just a spa and we do something stupid that costs my mom the nomination? She'd never, ever, forgive me."

"Then I guess you'd just have to come live with me," Sudi said, and wrapped her arm around Meri's shoulder. She felt sorry for Meri that her first worry was always about her mother's political career.

Dalila joined them. "I have the spells we'll need." She clutched a leather tube containing a papyrus from the Book of Thoth. "At least, I hope I do."

"Let's go." Sudi started across the street, dodging around traffic. She had hidden the snake wand in her baggy cargo pants, and it thumped painfully against her leg. She'd have bruises, but that was the least of her worries.

"Even if we get inside, how are we going to find Scott?" Meri asked. "The building must have ten floors."

"I guess we'll just look around," Sudi said.

"I've thought about it," Dalila said as she joined them on the curb. "I think the building covers a shaft that leads down to subterranean rooms and tunnels like the tombs in the Valley of the Kings, but instead of a burial chamber, we'll find a temple."

"That's a good start," Sudi said, and pushed through the front door, grateful that Dalila had a plan. She hurried up to the front desk.

A receptionist sat alone. She had a thin nose, large, almond-shaped eyes, and a strong resemblance to the famous bust of Nefertiti. Sudi assumed she'd probably gotten the job for that very reason.

"We don't have an appointment," Sudi said, trying to keep her voice steady. "But we were hoping we could use our gift certificates today." She slapped her card on the marble counter and immediately wished she hadn't made such a dramatic gesture.

Meri pulled a matching gift certificate from her pocket and unfolded it before handing it over. Dalila held hers between two fingers and waited for the woman to take it. They had each received an envelope the night before: a mysterious delivery from an unknown man.

The receptionist smiled, and a look of recognition crossed her face. She leafed through an appointment book too quickly; Sudi sensed that it was a meaningless show. She felt certain the woman knew what she was supposed to do.

"The only treatments available right now are for full body massages," the receptionist said.

"We'll take them," Sudi answered.

"Follow me." The woman stood and ran her hands through her glossy hair, then started down the corridor. A slit in the back of her long black dress exposed perfect legs and bare feet.

She opened a door and escorted them into a dimly lit, perfumed dressing room. Mirrors surrounded them. Sudi caught her reflection and quickly looked away. The stark fear in her eyes unnerved her; she didn't need more to add to the panicky feeling inside her.

"You can undress here," the receptionist said. She opened one of the mirrors and pointed to folded robes stacked on shelves next to bottles of lotion. "Take everything off and put these on. I'll come back in a few minutes." She left, closing the door behind her. The latch clicked into place.

"Why do they want us naked?" Meri whispered.

"That's usually the way it's done for a massage," Sudi said, pulling the wand from her cargo pants.

"It's creepy, like they're getting us ready for virgin sacrifices," Meri said and gave Sudi a meaningful glance.

"I haven't done *it* yet," said Sudi as she answered Meri's look and nervously twirled her wand like a drum major's baton. "But becoming a sacrifice to the god of chaos was never one of my fantasies for losing it."

"They probably won't kill us," Dalila said. "Just replace our souls with the spirits of dead evil-doers."

"Thanks," Meri said sarcastically. "That makes me feel a whole lot better."

"Well, it's true," Dalila answered and squeezed

the leather cylinder against her chest. "Do I have to take off all my clothes?"

"Hell, no," Sudi said. "As soon as we know the receptionist is gone, we're out of here."

Sudi pressed her ear against the door. When she didn't hear anything on the other side, she cautiously opened it and poked her head into the hallway, then slipped out. Meri and Dalila joined her, and together they stole to the end of the hallway and turned down another corridor filled with laundry carts.

"There." Meri pointed to a broad metal door. A sign on the front read: STAIRS.

Sudi hurried toward the door, pushed against the bar and stepped onto the landing. Dank, mildew-scented air engulfed her.

She waited for the door to close behind Meri and Dalila, and then she started downward.

The security lights gave little illumination, and on the next two floors they had burned out. Sudi grabbed the cold metal railing and accidentally hit the wand against the banister. The resounding clang echoed around her and made her feel as if she were descending into an endless abyss. She leaned over and peered into the shadows.

She couldn't see the bottom, and sudden terror seized her. Maybe this was a trap.

"Just continue," Dalila commanded from behind her.

Sudi started again.

A few flights later, a faint rumbling vibrated through the stairs. Sudi stopped, and Meri tumbled against her.

"Is that thunder?" Meri asked, a haunted look creeping into her eyes.

"The lord of chaos," Dalila said and paused.

The sound grew louder until a deafening roar filled the stairwell. The vibration shimmied up Sudi's legs and through her body.

"We're far below street level now," Sudi said, trying to use logic to calm her own fears. "It's probably just a Metro train passing on the other side of the wall."

The sound became muffled. Silence followed, but it was several moments before Sudi had the strength to start down again.

Finally they reached the end of stairs and faced another door. EMERGENCY EXIT was printed across the front.

"It's nothing after all," Meri said and sat on a step.

"The door probably leads out to a Metro platform," Sudi agreed, not sure if she felt disappointed or relieved that their journey had ended in nothing.

"Let's go back," Dalila said and started up the stairs, her footsteps banging noisily. "I suppose they could have hidden Scott in one of the treatment rooms."

"Or maybe he's not here at all," Meri said, gloomily. "Maybe they're holding him on a farm in Virginia. We'd better go see Abdel."

Sudi followed behind Dalila and Meri, but lost her footing on the edge of the next stair and slipped. She caught herself and glanced down. A sprinkling of sand covered the lower steps.

"Wait," she yelled, her voice echoing in the stairwell as she ran back and lunged against the door. It opened, and she stumbled over the threshold.

A blast of hot air shrieked around her, tangling her hair and lashing at her clothes. Her lungs and mouth filled with the sting of desert heat. She stepped forward, letting the door close behind her. Her wand pulsed in warning, the hieroglyphs moving in a never-ending flow.

The wind died and she found herself alone beneath a vaulted ceiling in the forecourt of an ancient temple. She lifted her head, trying to take in all the colors and gold. Paintings covered every wall.

Then, from far away, came the haunting howl of jackals, sweet sounds that awakened an odd longing, and a keen awareness that she was walking toward her death.

CHAPTER 19

Sudi turned, expecting to see the gray metal door, but the building had vanished, and in its place, golden desert stretched across the horizon, dividing an intensely blue river from a turquoise sky.

"Meri! Dalila!" Sudi shouted. The massive walls threw back her voice, and her cries echoed around her.

With a rush of wind, Meri stepped through the air, her hair whipping around her. Dalila followed after her, head bent against another gust. From behind them came the sound of an unseen door slamming shut.

Sand continued to whirl in eddies about Sudi's feet, then settled, covering the floor with swirling patterns of spiral galaxies.

Dalila rubbed her hands over the cut stone in one of the truncated pyramids that supported the pylon. Then she shielded her eyes from the sun's glare and gazed out at the desert. She inhaled sharply. "Is that the Nile?"

"Where are we?" Meri asked, looking up at the monumental gateway towering above them.

"I think we've either stepped into another dimension or we were somehow thrown back in time," Sudi answered.

"Then let's find Scott," Meri said, "and leave, before something happens to keep us here."

They stepped through the gateway and removed their jackets. Sudi took off her sweater, too, glad she had worn a short-sleeved T-shirt underneath. Then they walked between two rows of columns that looked tall enough to support the sky.

Wooden statues of Anubis guarded the next

doorway. Over that entrance, written in detailed hieroglyphs, was a warning: *only the damned enter here.*

"Should we go inside?" Dalila asked, staring at the inscription.

Sudi shrugged, not sure, and glanced at her wand. The hieroglyphs etched in the bronze lay still. She prayed that was a good sign, and started forward, pausing inside the entrance. Oil-burning lamps sat on carved wooden pillars. The flames flapped back and forth, making shadows jump and twitch. The air was stale and smelled strangely of wet copper pennies. Sudi tried to swallow, but her mouth was so dry that she coughed instead. The sudden sound of her cough reverberated down the endless corridor as if she had been leaning over a bottomless well.

The girls huddled together and slowly started down the sloping ramps and steep stairs.

"This is laid out more like a tomb than a temple," Dalila whispered as they continued downward.

The passage ended in a huge room with vivid paintings and hieroglyphs on every wall.

Sudi stared at a drawing of the solar barge passing through the underworld at night and felt a wave of nausea. Beneath the vessel, the condemned stood in fires, flames crawling around them, their mouths open in silent wails, pleading for the sun god's mercy.

"The wall paintings show the ancient Egyptian's concept of hell from the Book of the Hidden Room," Dalila explained. "My parents called the book the Amduat."

"The drawings look so real," Sudi whispered.

Meri traced her finger over the hieroglyphs below a painting of twelve men whose hearts had been ripped out and placed on the ground between their feet. "The bloody ones with torn-out hearts are welcome here," Meri translated the writing. "I bet that's not part of the original test," she added.

"I don't think this temple is a place where the blessed dead would want to find themselves," Dalila agreed.

Sudi looked away. "Let's find Scott and get out of here," she said.

But Dalila lingered, her fascination stronger than her fear.

"I remember how much paintings like these scared me when I was a little girl," Dalila reflected.

"Don't they scare you now?" Sudi didn't wait for an answer but started toward the next passageway.

"The wicked are excluded from the cycle of life," Dalila explained, "and sent to the chaos at the edge of creation."

"Where we go if we fail," Meri said solemnly.

"Maybe," Dalila continued. "Some scholars think chaos is actually in the deepest parts of the underworld. The fierce goddess Sekhmet presides over it. Her minions torture the wicked and drink their blood. But worst of all, the condemned are denied the light of the sun god." She turned slowly. "Maybe these passages lead to chaos."

"Stop!" Sudi blurted out. "Why are you going on as if this is real? These are just myths."

Meri and Dalila stared at her.

"What does it take to make you believe?" Meri argued. "Haven't we experienced enough? Do you have to have a demon dig your heart out before you'll acknowledge that this mythology is real?"

"It can't be," Sudi said; she had a strange

sensation of falling into endless space. "Please, tell me it isn't. I don't want it to be true, because if it is . . ."

"Because if it is, then everything in these paintings is what the cult wants to bring into our world," Meri said, finishing for her.

"Do you think demons will be recruited from the damned to come here and torture . . . ?" Dalila's voice faltered as if that new world were too horrifying to imagine.

Sudi forced herself to look at the paintings again. The misery she saw made her resolute. She was determined to stop the cult, but her determination wavered as a niggling little voice asked her how. She knew no incantations except for one love spell, and turning into a bird wasn't going to scare any of the creatures depicted in these scenes.

"Let's get away from here," Sudi said, marching forward.

"Wait." Meri tapped her finger on the painting of a creature with the head of a crocodile, the forelegs and body of a lion, and the hindquarters of a hippopotamus. "Dalila, is this the creature you become when you transform?"

"For now, anyway, I look like Ammut," Dalila said unhappily. "She lives in the underworld and devours the hearts of the wicked."

"We'd better hurry," Sudi said and hit her wand twice on the floor before starting forward again.

Meri and Dalila followed her this time, and together they continued on until a larger corridor crossed the hallway in which they stood. Sudi headed toward an entrance cut in the rear wall, but paused, as she became aware of faint singing.

Suddenly, Dalila grabbed her arm, and hurried her behind a massive pillar. Meri fell against her, her teeth chattering with fear.

Sudi peered out.

A man marched toward them, carrying a pole; a headless black animal pelt that looked like that of a dog hung from the top like a flag. Behind him, a priest wearing a cloak made from leopard skins walked solemnly, carrying a golden bowl in the crook of his arm. His head was shaved, and thick kohl rimmed his eyes. On his chest he wore a pectoral ornament of a vulture, and several amulets.

Sudi recognized the ankh, the T-shaped cross

with the loop handle. It was a symbol of life and divine immortality. A gold cylindrical tube clicked against the other charms; she wondered what it held inside.

The priest dipped his fingers into the small bowl and sprinkled water over the ground and pillars, ritually cleansing the path to the sanctuary.

A drop hit Sudi's forehead. The water burned, scalding her skin.

Meri slapped her hand over Sudi's mouth and held her tightly to keep her from crying out. Sudi felt defiled and, using the tail of her T-shirt, she frantically wiped at the water. Finally, she was able to peek out again and watch, through tear-blurred vision.

A procession of men and women dressed in white followed the priest into another room. The people looked ordinary; they could have been Sudi's neighbors or classmates. Nothing about them appeared particularly evil. Sudi continued watching, and then at the end of the line, she saw the three girls from her drama club who skulked about the hallways at Lincoln High. Dressed in transparent linen gowns, they danced with sinuous grace, so unlike the shyness they showed at school. Sudi wondered if the cult leaders had deceived them, or did they know they were devoting their lives to bringing chaos to the world? Sudi felt guilty that she hadn't done more to defend the girls when other kids made fun of them. Maybe one word of kindness could have made a difference in their lives.

The three girls spun across the threshold, singing. Then the voices of all the worshippers rose, and the din of rattles, drums, and clappers joined the revelry.

Sudi motioned for Dalila and Meri to follow her. She sprinted across the corridor and snuck inside the sanctuary, easing along the back wall behind a line of pillars. She hid in a dark alcove behind a row of reclining jackals, her heartbeat thudding in her ears. Meri and Dalila squeezed beside her, trying to control their nervous breathing.

The priest in the leopard skin waited in front of a pair of ornate gilded doors.

Two other men, completely shaven of all body hair and wearing low-slung white kilts with pleated front panels, took embers from a stone cauldron and lit incense. As the smoke curled into the room, the two men stepped to either side of the shrine. When the priest nodded, they opened the doors, revealing the statue of a man with an animal's head that resembled an anteater's, with tall, square ears.

The worshippers fell to their knees, but the priest remained standing, gazing up at a statue of his god Seth. A strange aura emanated from the towering image, and soon the air became dense and cold, frosting the pillars and floor with odd patches of ice.

"That's unusual," Dalila whispered. "Only the pharaoh was allowed to stand before a god."

"Maybe the priest is descended from the first pharaohs, like we are," Meri answered in a low voice.

Silence filled the room; the worshippers anticipated something momentous.

Then the priest spoke. *"Du ut des."*

The congregation repeated the words.

"What does that mean?" Sudi whispered.

"'I give in order that you give,'" Dalila replied softly. "They want something from Seth."

"Father of Anubis," the priest said, lifting a vessel in his hands. "We give you this offering."

He poured water from a *heset* jar over a long object covered with a white cloth that lay on top of a wooden funerary couch.

Sudi set her wand down. Then, holding on to the snout of one of the jackal statues for balance, she pulled herself up onto the tips of her toes to see.

Scott lay on the table in front of the priest, apparently unconscious.

Terrified, Sudi ducked back down behind the pillar.

"It's Scott," she whispered. "What will we do if they start to sacrifice him?"

Dalila opened her mouth to speak, but the priest's deep voice interrupted her.

"God of violence, chaos, and storm," the priest said, and the vaulted ceiling amplified his invocation. His words resonated and seemed to come from all directions. "Spirit of anger and rage, bring forth the Descendants of Horus who block our way."

"That's us," Meri whispered, pressing closer to the floor.

Dalila looked as if she were going to faint. "Do they know we're here?"

"I don't think so," Sudi answered, and climbed back on the jackal statue, her feet resting on its forepaws. She strained her neck, trying to see what the priest was doing to Scott.

Thunder shook the walls, and the boom resounded through Sudi. Her hands slipped, and she lost her balance. She fell into one of the patches of slick ice and skidded across the floor.

The congregants turned and gazed down at her, their eyes fierce with hate, and then they broke into jubilant song and prayer.

CHAPTER 20

Thunder shook the room, and the pillars holding the oil lamps rocked uneasily. Flames sparked
and spit red embers into the air. The two lower-
ranked priests who had opened the shrine walked
Dalila, Meri, and Sudi to the front of the sanctuary.

"I'm sorry," Sudi said, even though she doubted
that her friends could hear her over the uproar. She
had been too reckless; it was her fault that they were
all going to be sent to live with the demons in chaos.

They stopped in front of the high priest.

"You two could have done better without me," Sudi said to Meri and Dalila. "You'd probably have already rescued Scott."

"All the votes aren't in yet," Meri answered. "It's not time to give a concession speech."

Sudi nodded, but she didn't know how Meri could remain optimistic.

"We still have the Book of Thoth," Dalila added and faced the congregation, holding her back straight. "I left the leather pouch behind the pillar. The priests didn't know what was inside it, so if we can get back to it, we can still find an incantation to stop them."

Sudi nodded, but she didn't feel confident.

The two lesser priests lifted the funeral couch and carried Scott across the sanctuary. They set him down in front of the line of jackal statues.

"They're not going to sacrifice Scott," Sudi whispered.

"Not when they have the three of us," Meri answered.

Before Sudi could apologize again, the high priest held up his hand and the room became silent.

"Bring Sankhkara forward," the priest ordered,

watching Sudi closely. "Let's see if your love spell is stronger than the power of Seth."

The congregants shuffled, opening a path that led to an upright coffin on the opposite side of the room. The image of a man was sculpted on the gold front. The two lesser priests unfastened the lid. The mummy stood inside, now wearing a headpiece and jewelry made of lapis lazuli.

Sudi wondered how the mummy had traveled from Lincoln High without becoming breaking news on Channel 7. Someone in the congregation must have helped him. For no reason that she understood, she thought of Carter. He couldn't be one of them, but she searched the crowd for him anyway and felt a sense of relief when she didn't see him. But then she caught another familiar face. She looked again, uncertain. Had she seen Brian? Was he part of the cult? Her stomach knotted. Maybe that was her strange connection to him.

The mummy lurched forward, his arms crossed over his chest. Slowly, he brought his hands down to his sides. People stepped back when the mummy passed them as if they were anxious about their safety.

"Sankhkara died on his sixteenth birthday," the priest said to Sudi. "A strong soul, but too trusting. We used his kindness to deceive him. He had a proper burial, but we desecrated his tomb and made it impossible for him to pass through all the gates and join the blessed dead; he no longer had the Book of Gates to guide him because we covered it and replaced it with spells of our own. Now we use his corpse to kill."

Sankhkara stopped in front of the priest.

"Destroy the three," the priest ordered. "Start with the one you love."

The congregants eased back as if they had witnessed Sankhkara's brutality before.

Sankhkara shifted his weight, turning clumsily, and through thin slits, his death-frosted eyes found Sudi.

She cringed and backed up. Her throat tightened around a scream. The mummy had been sent to the party to end Sudi's life, but she had never considered how he had planned to do it. Even now she couldn't imagine what his brittle body could do, but she also knew she didn't want to find out.

He took slow, awkward steps toward her and stopped, his face inches from her own.

Meri and Dalila squeezed closer, wrapping their arms around Sudi's waist.

"He'll have to take all three of us together," Meri said, pressing her cheek against Sudi's shoulder.

Sankhkara raised his arm.

Dalila cried out and buried her face against Sudi.

"I'm so sorry," Sudi said, and tried to remember the spell she had cast on him before. Maybe if she could make him fall in love with her again she could stop him. But her mind spun, and the incantation that came forth was a jumble.

"Send a circle of fire around this one here," she said and stopped. It was useless to try. She closed her eyes and waited for the attack.

The priest laughed, enjoying her failure.

"Beware the priest," Sankhkara whispered. "He's a spirit who feeds upon weak and helpless souls. I'll protect you as best I can."

Sudi's eyes flashed open.

"He's not going to kill you," Meri said.

"Your love spell is stronger than the priest's command," Dalila added.

Sudi glanced at the priest and caught a flicker of rage before his expression turned coldly confident again.

"Why wasn't the priest able to remove my spell?" Sudi asked in a hushed voice.

"Our magic must be far stronger than we think," Dalila answered.

"Great," Sudi said. "Now all we have to do is figure out how to use it."

The priest grabbed Sankhkara's arm and pulled him back. "So, her love spell is stronger than your fear of the second death?"

"What is the second death?" Sudi asked Dalila.

"His soul will be damned," the priest answered before Dalila could speak, "and he'll forever be excluded from the cycle of life."

"You can throw my body to the dogs," Sankhkara responded defiantly. "I'll gladly suffer the fate of the damned. It was worth knowing the love I felt when I looked into her eyes again."

"Again?" Sudi asked. "What do you mean, again?"

But no one answered her.

The priest raised his hands to the statue of Seth.

"Lord of chaos, who brought death into the world," the priest intoned. "We give you the three Descendants and the son of the pharaoh Mentuhotep."

A crash of thunder startled Sudi. The boom reverberated through the sanctuary. The floor shook, and the vibrations quivered up her spine. Cracks shot across the ceiling. Tiny veins ran down the walls. Chunks of plaster fell, and dust clouded the air.

"Seth is going to kill us," Sudi said. "And I don't think he cares how many of his worshippers he takes with us."

"Why should he?" Dalila answered. "He's been trying to end the bloodline of Horus since practically the beginning of time."

Meri pinched Sudi's arm. "Carpe diem."

"Is that a spell?" Sudi asked.

"It's Latin for 'seize the day,'" Meri answered. "Mom uses it whenever she has an opportunity."

Then Sudi saw the reason Meri looked so

happy. Most of the worshippers were staring up at the statue, their faces filled with awe. Others had fallen to the floor, bowing with their eyes closed. A few had hidden their faces in their hands. No one was watching Sudi, Meri, and Dalila.

"Go," Sankhkara ordered and trundled forward, determined to protect them from anyone who tried to stop them.

The girls ran back to the pillar and hid behind it.

Dalila grabbed the leather case and pulled out the scroll.

"Do something while I find the right incantation," Dalila said.

"Like what?" Sudi asked.

"I don't know," Dalila answered. "Try anything." Her fingers fumbled with the scroll, her hands trembling so violently she couldn't open it. She lost her grip, and the papyrus fell. It rolled across the floor away from her.

Dalila started after it as thunder exploded and rumbled through the sanctuary. She lost her balance and pitched backward, slamming into the wall.

Three fire lamps tumbled from their pilasters.

Pottery smashed, and flames raced across the spilled oil toward the scroll.

"No!" Dalila shouted.

Sudi dove after the papyrus. She landed on her belly and skidded toward the flames. The fire reached the scroll first. Flames licked the edges, and smoke curled around the ancient writing.

Sudi tried to grab it, but the blaze shot higher, scorching her. She jerked her hand back and licked the blisters, then reached out again and clutched the scroll. Flames hissed and shot after her. She scooted back.

Meri slid next to her, and together they beat out the fire on the papyrus.

The worshippers watched. Some edged closer.

The papyrus was still smoldering when Sudi handed it back to Dalila.

"We don't have time to look for an incantation," Dalila said, her eyes fixed on the congregants.

The two lesser priests circled around them, crowding nearer.

"Seize them," the high priest ordered, but the lesser priests remained wary. And then Sudi saw the reason for their hesitation. Sankhkara guarded the front of the pillar, bravely ignoring the flames.

Sudi pulled Meri and Dalila behind the pillar again. Smoke stung her eyes, and she coughed as the fires continued to burn toward them.

"Maybe if we used our other powers," Dalila said, holding her hands over her mouth and nose to filter the smoke.

"You mean, change into a bird?" Sudi asked over another roll of thunder. "What good would that do?

"A cat's not going to help," Meri said. "But a cobra could scare them."

Sudi and Meri stared at Dalila.

"I can't," she answered.

"It's our only chance," Sudi said. "Your poison could kill one of them, and maybe that would frighten the rest away."

Dalila turned pale, and Sudi understood. Dalila would never be able to transform into a cobra and strike, because hurting someone was against her gentle nature.

"You don't have to bite anyone," Sudi said. "Just spread your hood and hiss. Maybe that will be enough."

"If we don't do something, they're going to kill us," Meri added.

"I haven't been able to change into a snake," Dalila said. "I become that monster Ammut."

"Just try," Sudi coaxed and held on to the pillar as another thunderclap ruptured the air and made the floor sway.

Dalila closed her eyes and began reciting her incantation. Her face convulsed, and then her lips and chin stretched into a long, tapering jaw with jagged, dangerous teeth. The thick, armorlike skin of a crocodile began to cover her cheeks and snout. Her mouth snapped hungrily.

Sudi and Meri jumped back.

"Maybe we didn't think this through," Sudi said.

Tawny-colored fur spread over Dalila's arms. Her hands turned into paws with sharp, curved claws. Hair grew, circling her reptilian face with a lion's mane.

Finally, her legs bent and shrank into stumps, and within seconds her back end looked like the rear of a hippopotamus. Her short, thick tail twitched. She roared and waddled through the fire out into the congregation.

"It's Ammut!" someone yelled.

"They've conjured the devourer of hearts!" another voice shouted.

Screams became louder than the thunder.

The priest's panicked voice shouted over the cries. "Seth will protect you."

Sudi peeked out and watched the congregants. Their fear of Ammut seemed stronger than their belief in Seth. They pushed and shoved, trying to escape Dalila, but the fires blocked their way. They slammed into each other and stampeded past the statue of Seth in an attempt to reach the exit without running through the flames.

The giant statue swayed.

The priest ran to it and braced his hands against the legs to stop its fall, but the image toppled anyway. Granite splintered. The impact hurled dagger-size chunks of stone around the room.

Sudi ducked as a slab hit the pillar and made it wobble.

The shrieks and wails from worshippers continued to rise, and then the last congregant limped from the room. The panicked voices and running footsteps faded. Quiet returned. The crackling fires were the only sound left in the room.

Dalila transformed back into a girl and couldn't stop grinning. "They think we conjured Ammut," she said. "They were afraid I was going to eat their hearts as punishment for their wicked lives."

"You should have seen yourself," Meri said, and placed a hand over her mouth trying to stop her giggles. "Your butt was humongous."

"We'd better get Scott and leave," Sudi said, "before someone decides to come back."

"I think they'll be too afraid to return," Dalila said, surveying the broken granite. "The statue was Seth's visible body on earth. He'll demand retribution for destroying his image."

A clatter made Sudi turn. Rocks tumbled from a pile of rubble. The high priest pulled himself up and wiped at the blood trickling down his face. His attention focused on Sudi.

"I will appease the lord of chaos," he said as a black aura grew around him.

At first Sudi thought it was only the smoke from the fires, but the nimbus around the priest continued to grow, churning wildly. Demonic shapes formed and darted from the cloud as if eager to attack, only to roll back as other, crueler faces swelled and retreated. The stench of tombs and death saturated the air.

"What is it?" Meri asked, her fingers cold in Sudi's hand.

"I don't know," Dalila answered, pulling Sudi and Meri backward behind a line of flames.

The priest curled his fingers and gathered the spectral streams into a ball. He flung the sphere at Sudi. The orb screeched toward her, and the sanctuary filled with the cries from a horde of demons.

CHAPTER 21

The thick blackness spun toward Sudi. The demons imprisoned within it squirmed and thrashed, writhing over and around each other, trying to be the first to attack. She stood defenseless, watching death hurtling toward her, and forgot to breathe. She had failed her parents, her sisters, and her friends, but mostly she had failed herself.

Sankhkara lurched forward and threw himself between Sudi and the sphere. He held her against his hollow chest. The globe hit his back and disappeared inside him. His mouth opened in a grimace, and he collapsed.

Sudi fell to her knees beside Sankhkara. How many people had to suffer because she had screwed up?

"I think he's dying," Sudi cried out.

"He's already dead," Meri answered, kneeling next to Sudi.

"The demons will take his soul to chaos unless we can cast our spell quickly," Dalila explained, joining them.

"Where's the incantation to send him back to be with the blessed dead?" Sudi asked, turning to Dalila.

"I'll get it," Meri said and raced back to the pillar where they had left the papyrus.

"You can't save him," the priest said as the black vapors began pulsing around him again.

Sankhkara lifted his skeletal hand and touched Sudi's cheek. "It was worth it to save you," he said, and then he began to pray. "Creator, maker, giver of breath, Amon, the one supreme deity."

"That won't help," the priest taunted.

"We'll save him," Sudi countered, and when she looked up, she noticed the priest's amulets.

"The ankh," Sudi whispered to Dalila. "It's a symbol of life. Would it help?"

"It might keep Sankhkara's spirit here long enough for us to recite the spell," Dalila answered in a soft voice.

Without thinking, Sudi leaped up and lunged past Sankhkara. She threw herself forward and tackled the priest. His aura curled around her as she fell on top of him. They skidded together over the jagged pieces of broken granite.

Sharp fragments cut Sudi's fingers, and warm blood trickled down her thumb as she clutched the priest's ankh and yanked hard. The shadows surrounding him gathered hungrily around her face, slipping into her mouth and leaving a vile taste. She choked, feeling her breath being sucked away, but that didn't stop her. She pulled again, and this time the chains broke.

Gold charms bounced and clanked across the floor, but the ankh remained in her palm. The priest tried to wrestle the talisman from her. A black line shot from his aura and encircled her arm, squeezing it until her fingers felt numb.

Then, unexpectedly, the shadow dropped its hold, and a groan gurgled from the priest's lips. The black nimbus retreated inside him.

Sudi rubbed her wrist. "The ankh must have been keeping him alive," she said. With renewed hope, she placed the ankh on Sankhkara's chest as Meri joined them and unfurled the scroll.

"You have to remove the love spell you put on him," Dalila said, "in case it interferes with the one to send his soul to rest."

Meri handed Sudi the blackened papyrus, opened to the proper spell.

In the smoky light, Sudi read the hieroglyphs: *"Goddess of magic, I entreat you, remove your love fire from around the one who beholds me. Extinguish the love in his heart, that he and I might be free from desire."*

She handed the papyrus back, and, as Meri and Dalila began reciting the other spell, she leaned over Sankhkara again and held his bony hand.

"You didn't need magic to make me love you," Sankhkara confessed. "Our souls have been one since the beginning of time, but fate has cruelly separated us."

Then a thin vapor escaped his lips and spread into a golden mist above them before vanishing.

"Let's get Scott," Meri said. She hurried over to where Scott lay.

Sudi wiped her tears and stood slowly. The depth of her sadness surprised her. She walked behind the pillar and found her wand. On her way back, she picked up the golden tube that the priest had worn around his neck and stuck it in her pocket.

"Wake up," Meri said, nudging Scott. "It's time to go home."

Scott sat up and looked around. The white linen that had covered him dropped to the floor.

"He's naked," Meri squealed, and stared brazenly.

Dalila turned her back. "Cover up," she ordered.

Sudi wanted to look, but kept her gaze focused on Meri instead.

"The spa lost your clothes," Meri said with a mischievous grin. "Can you believe that? So you'll have to wear the sheet home."

"Spa?" Scott looked befuddled. He pressed his

fingers against his eyes. "What am I doing in a spa?"

"You got hurt playing rugby," Sudi said as Meri wrapped the linen around his waist. "Your coach thought a massage and a soak in a whirlpool might help."

"I don't remember," Scott said and looked around the room.

"Maybe you have a concussion, then," Dalila said with convincing authority.

"Then why didn't they take me to the hospital?" he asked as he hobbled forward. His bare foot kicked a piece of granite. "What is all this mess?"

"They're remodeling," Sudi answered.

Sudi and Meri pulled Scott into the next corridor. He walked sluggishly, his breathing labored. He kept wiping his eyes, as if his vision were blurred.

"Do you think he's all right?" Sudi asked.

"He's in a daze," Meri whispered. "He's probably wondering if he's been doing drugs again."

Finally they reached the massive gateway that led out to the desert sand. Scott leaned against the wall, shaking his head, still trying to awaken from a bad dream.

Meri stopped. "How do we get back?" she asked. "The door is gone."

The sun rested on the horizon, its heat warming Sudi's face. Even so, she stepped forward, certain the scenery was a sham. She closed her eyes so her vision couldn't deceive her. Then, leading with her hands, she continued until her fingers touched something solid. She smoothed her palms across the cold metal and found a protruding doorknob. She turned it. A latch clicked, and she started to open the door.

Without warning, the still air became filled with violently rotating winds. Gusts shrieked around her and fought to close the door. Her hair whipped into her eyes. Her fingers loosened their hold, and the metal began slipping from her grasp.

She refused to fail her friends this time. Strength rose inside her.

"Hurry!" she yelled, and used her foot to brace the bottom edge of the door.

Meri and Dalila rushed through, pulling Scott with them. The windstorm caught the cloth wrapped around him. The tail end flapped out and snapped against Sudi's cheek.

Sudi grappled with the door, trying to pull herself inside, but the gusts were stronger, and she was losing the struggle. Sand whirled about her, scraping her cheeks and clogging her nose. She couldn't breathe or open her eyes. She hadn't escaped her fate after all. She sensed intuitively that when the door blew shut, she would never be able to open it again.

A sudden, violent gust hit the door, and it started to close. Sudi tightened her grip. Her chest heaved, her lungs struggling to get air, but she only sucked more sand into her mouth and nose. She coughed and spit, then stopped. Something moved within the swirling sand. A dark shape was coming toward her. She squinted, protecting her eyes, and tried to see what was in the storm with her, but before she could make out the profile, warm fingers wrapped around her wrist. Other hands pushed against the door, opening it.

Meri and Dalila pulled her inside the stairwell.

Sudi tripped forward, gasping, and collided with her friends. The door slammed behind them, and then all four lost their balance and tumbled to the floor. Sudi rested her cheek on the cold concrete, and took in deep gulps of the dank air, the odor of mildew replacing the smell of dry desert sand.

"To us!" Meri shouted, jumping up. "We did it."

Dalila clapped and pulled Sudi to her feet. "All of us got out."

Sudi laughed and gave her friends a bear hug. "We survived."

"All right," a deep voice came from the steps overhead. Scott stared down at them. "Enough with the lovefest. Let's get out of here."

"We're coming," Dalila shouted excitedly, and ran up the stairs.

Sudi brushed sand from her clothes and hair and used the tail of her T-shirt to wipe her eyes. When she finished, she studied the door. "Do you think that other place is still there?" she asked Meri.

"You don't really want to see, do you?" Meri asked.

"Maybe," Sudi answered. Her curiosity was becoming greater than her fear. She placed her hand on the doorknob.

"Don't!" Dalila yelled, hanging over the railing.

Sudi opened the door anyway. She and Meri stared out at the Metro platform. The dim lights gave the vast room a gloomy feeling. A train sped by, and from its passage a current of warm air rushed over them.

"The desert vanished," Meri whispered. "How did it just disappear?"

"I don't know," Sudi replied and let the door close. "Scott's right. Let's get out of here."

Meri and Sudi ran up the stairs and hurried after Dalila and Scott. Together, they walked through the spa. No one tried to stop them. An attendant glanced up but didn't even ask if they were lost.

At the front door, Sudi caught a glimpse of herself in a mirror and paused as the others rushed outside. She was encrusted with sand, her hair a tangle. She had lost one shoe and had no recollection of when that had happened.

As she started to leave, an odd sensation made her turn. The high priest stood behind her. The kohl liner no longer circled his eyes, but he was definitely the same man, and somehow alive again. He wore an Armani suit, with a gold ankh hanging over his black sweater. He leaned against a sign posted in the entrance that announced the opening of a new teen club called The Jackal.

"I hope you'll return soon," he said. "I'll leave VIP passes for you and your friends at the front door of my club. I think you'll like the atmosphere."

Sudi pointed the tip of her wand at him and smiled back. "You bet," she said, and twirled the rod dangerously close to his face. "I've got a feeling we'll be seeing a lot of each other."

She turned and ran outside without listening to his reply.

Meri and Dalila were waiting for her in a black sedan that was parked near the entrance. Scott sat between them in the backseat.

"Get in," Meri said. "We'll take you home."

"No," Sudi said. "I want to walk."

"Like that?" Meri asked.

Sudi nodded.

"Be careful," Dalila whispered.

"I have to go to one of those functions with Mom," Meri said, "but I'll call you as soon as I get home." Then she spoke to her driver and the sedan pulled away.

The sun had set by the time Sudi reached her house, and she was shivering from the cold. She had left her jacket and sweater in that other dimension, somewhere in ancient Egypt. She stepped inside and called out a hello, grateful to be home. When no one answered, she assumed that her parents had already left for the Kennedy Center. Her sisters were spending the night with their best friend, Elena.

In the kitchen, she drank two glasses of water and then opened the cylindrical charm that the priest had worn. She pulled out the tiny piece of papyrus rolled inside and read an oath from Seth that cursed anyone who harmed the priest.

Sudi stuck both back in her pocket, then

picked up her wand and started up the stairs. She was too exhausted to worry about curses tonight. She was going to shower, do her nails, and then find a party; she was never too tired for fun.

As she stepped into her room, a cold draft blew over her. Her window was open, the drapes askew, one panel torn from the rod. Her muscles tensed and, as she started to turn, someone grabbed her around the waist.

Sudi dropped her wand and wrestled against the arms restraining her. She bit her attacker's hand.

"Ouch!" her assailant screamed as he let go.

She turned, ready to kick.

Scott stood behind her, head bent, studying the tooth marks on the fleshy mound of his thumb.

"You're lethal," he said, looking down at her.

"Scott?" Sudi asked. "Were you trying to scare me to death?" Before he could answer, a more important question came to her. "Why did you break into my room?"

"Something crazy happened today," he said, stepping closer. He ran his finger over her cheek and then held up the tip of his finger to show her the sand. "I don't know what it was exactly, but I called my coach and he never sent me for a massage, and if that place was a spa it was a really weird one. I have this odd feeling you rescued me."

She glanced back at her torn drapes. "Next time you have a question, do you think you could just call me?"

"Did you save me from something, Sudi?" he asked, his fingers brushing through her hair. Sand spilled onto her shoulders.

She tried to find the words to explain what had happened but only nodded instead. Maybe memories were coming back to him, and if so, what was she going to say?

"You still owe me a kiss," he said and leaned down, his lips hovering inches from hers. "I've waited a long time," he murmured and waited for her permission.

"Me, too," she agreed. He touched her. She

had never felt a kiss as good as his, and when he pulled back, a sigh escaped her lips. Her hands slipped under his T-shirt, her fingers spreading up over his chest. Touching him stirred a longing in her; she wanted more than his kiss. She became suddenly aware that her parents and sisters weren't home, and that her bed was only a few inches away.

He smiled down at her, obviously understanding her thoughts, and gently pulled her toward her bed.

"I like you, Scott," she whispered. "But I'm not ready."

"Ready for what?" he teased and sat on the edge of her bed. He pulled her down until she was sitting on his knee.

"I need a shower and—"

He pressed a finger over her mouth to silence her. "You look beautiful to me."

Doubt shimmered through her as he held her tightly, his lips trailing up the side of her neck. His kisses were muddling her thinking, and his behavior didn't seem like Scott's. Why had he broken into her house? And she didn't like the way he was pressuring her now.

A sudden, frightening thought came to her. She and her friends had rescued Scott, but they hadn't bothered to find out whether a demon had already taken possession of Scott's body. Adrenaline raced through her. Scott should have been stunned to find himself inside an Egyptian temple, but he hadn't been. He had barely asked any questions. With rising panic, she realized that a demon from chaos wouldn't have been surprised.

She pushed herself off his knee and picked up her wand. The hieroglyphs moved from top to bottom, warning her that a demon was approaching. She pointed the snake head at Scott, but he only chuckled, low in his throat. She didn't know how to use the magic, but she had another sport in mind. Her hands trembled as she gripped the wand like a baseball bat, ready to strike a home run. But if she killed the demon with her swing, wouldn't she kill Scott as well? And what if Scott wasn't possessed at all, and breaking through her window was his idea of romance?

"What are you doing?" Scott asked, a puzzled look on his face.

Sudi hesitated too long.

Scott seized the wand and tossed it across the room. It hit the wall with a loud clank.

"How did you figure it out?" he asked, clenching her in a tight hold. The gentleness was gone from his touch; the pressure from his fingers caused her shoulder to throb.

An eerie sound at the open window made Scott turn. Patty Pie arched his back and hissed, his front paw clawing at the air.

Scott chuckled and eased his grip as Pie leaped onto an overhanging branch and ran away.

The interruption was all Sudi needed. She pulled free and ran across the room, with Scott close behind her. She opened the door and spun to the other side, then pushed hard, hitting Scott with the door's edge. He yelled and held his face, staggering. Blood trickled from his nose.

She raced down the stairs, two at a time, and ran out into the night. The porches of the row houses extended out onto the sidewalk like an obstacle course. She dodged one iron railing, only to find herself rushing into the next barrier of stairs. Even so, she tried to stay close to the buildings and under the trees, hoping their shadows would conceal her.

Lights came on in the surrounding houses, and behind her, a door opened. But she did not turn back. The safety within the homes was an illusion, and she knew that if she went inside, instead of finding sanctuary, she would only bring death to the families who lived there. And then, what would happen to Scott if the demon decided to leave him after it had massacred a dozen people? He'd end up in jail for life at best.

Sudi quickened her pace, knowing she had to fight the demon on her own.

By the time she reached the canal, her side ached and her legs burned. She couldn't run any farther, even though she could hear Scott's feet pounding on the hard dirt. She crouched under a bush where no one could see her transform.

Then she raised her hand to the night. "Amun-Re, eldest of the gods in the eastern sky, mysterious power of wind, make a path for me to change my earthly *khat* into that of beloved Bennu."

Immediately, her skin prickled. Feathers grew from her fingers as her arms contracted and her bones popped. Then, with her monocular vision, she saw Scott. He had found her after all. She scurried from beneath the branches and took long strides, flapping her wings before her transformation was even complete. Wind rushed around her, holding her wings, and she lifted off the ground.

Scott screamed and jumped. He grabbed her bird-claw. Pain shot through her, and she spiraled down. She hit the ground, transforming back into a girl, and skidded across moldy leaves. Her back ached, and she thought for sure her leg was broken.

"Now," Scott snickered. Fire burned in his eyes.

Sudi fought against the dizziness and tried to remember a spell that could help her. Her mind jumped from one hieroglyphic script to the next, but each time, she came up with useless incantations. Casting a spell for glossy hair was not going to stop the demon who stood over her.

At first, Sudi thought the murmuring came from the quiet flow of water, lapping against the canal banks, but slowly she realized the soft sounds were whispers, coming from the shadows. She struggled against the pain to rise up on her elbow and listened intently, trying to understand what the hushed voices were saying.

Scott looked up, wary, and stepped into the darkness beneath the trees. He growled, low in his throat, a feral sound, as if warning others away.

Maybe a pack of demons had come to steal her from him. She imagined the creatures pouncing and snarling as they tore her apart.

Then, without warning, a cat sprang from the branches above Scott and landed on his back, its claws ripping into his shirt.

He cried out and flung his hands, trying to knock the cat away.

The feline yowled, an unnatural, half-human shriek. Its sleek black fur sparkled with glitter, an earring dangled from its ear, and a velvet scrunchie slipped from its head. Already its hind legs were turning back into those of a girl wearing spiky red heels.

In the same moment, Dalila crouched beside Sudi. "We have to draw hieroglyphs on Scott's chest," she said breathlessly, "to make the demon's spirit leave him."

Sudi looked at her, surprised. "How did you know I was in trouble?"

"Your cat, Pie, told Meri's cat, Miwsher," Dalila explained.

"The feline underground," Sudi said, and pulled herself up onto her knees, ignoring the jabbing pain.

Scott bellowed and spun around. Meri fell to the ground, transforming back into a girl. Her black dress, cut low in the back, was torn and rumpled, her party makeup smeared. But her skin still glistened with golden glitter.

Dalila and Sudi scrambled to her, each grabbing an arm, and drew her back, away from Scott.

He stood in the dim light, grumbling and baring his teeth in an ugly grimace.

Sudi stared back at her enemy, feeling a queasy dizziness. "What if we can't get the demon to leave Scott? Do we have to—" she stopped. She couldn't say the words.

"Kill him?" Dalila finished for her.

"Don't even think about that," Meri ordered.

Scott retreated into the shadows.

"What now?" Sudi asked. Darkness surrounded them; Scott was probably sneaking about, planning a surprise attack from another angle.

"I'll find him," Meri answered. Her eyes

changed back into those of a cat. "There," she whispered. "He's next to the maple tree."

"Do you think we can really restrain him long enough to write something on his chest?" Sudi asked, feeling doubtful.

"You bet." Meri kicked off her shoes, reached up under her dress, and rolled off her panty hose.

"What are you doing?" Dalila asked, her frightened eyes searching the shadows for Scott.

"We need ropes," Meri replied as she stretched out the legs of the panty hose. "We'll tie his wrists behind his back."

"How can you be so sure?" Sudi asked. She couldn't even see Scott in the gloomy depths.

"Jeez, haven't you ever heard of positive thinking?" Meri said. She didn't wait for an answer. "We charge him on the count of three. One. Two. Three!"

Sudi ran blindly, following Meri's lead. Suddenly, Scott stood in front of her. She screamed and lunged into him. He stumbled backward, tripping over his own feet. His back hit the tree.

Meri grabbed one wrist, Dalila the other, and

before Scott could react, they were tying the ends of the panty hose around his arms.

Sudi pressed hard, pushing her full weight against his stomach.

In the murky light, his stare looked alien and filled with hatred. And then he surprised her. His face came down, mouth wide, and he tried to bite her nose. She pulled back, feeling his teeth scrape over her skin. She cried out, filled with rage, and elbowed him hard, driving the breath from him in a loud whoosh.

"I'll never be able to be a Descendant," Sudi whimpered, afraid that she might have wounded the real Scott. "I hate this."

"All right, we have him," Meri yelled.

Scott kicked and thrashed as Sudi rolled up his shirt, and then Meri handed Dalila the lipstick from her pocket, and Dalila drew the eye of light on Scott's stomach. He heaved and hissed. Apparently, the symbol caused him pain.

Then Dalila stepped back and began to read. *"Hail to thee, Ra, king of the eastern sky in thy rising, even to thee who is called Atum at thy dawning. Yea, great Ra who comes as Khephera, the everlasting."*

Dalila droned on, but Sudi stopped listening. Scott had pulled one hand free and was angrily shredding the panty hose.

Sudi nudged Dalila. "Can we get on with it?"

"We don't need a filibuster," Meri agreed. "Just recite the spell."

Dalila looked up and gasped. Scott had almost broken free.

"Force of the stars, we offer these words," Dalila continued shakily, pointing to the hieroglyphs, and then Meri and Dalila joined in. *"Pierce Scott's heart, and dispel the darkness. Tear the demon from his soul."*

They stepped back quickly and watched.

Nothing happened.

"Should we try again?" Sudi asked.

Then, slowly, a shadow leaked from the eye drawn on Scott's chest. The black mist rose, spiraling up; it curled around the branches overhead. Then it dropped to the ground and thickened into a bent-over creature, taller than a man, eight feet or more in height, with large, thick arms. Eyes formed, and the creature screamed. Its fury filled the air with an electrical charge.

"I don't think we did it right," Sudi said, taking another step back, pulling Dalila and Meri with her.

"Maybe we forgot something," Dalila said. She unrolled the papyrus again. When she looked up, her face was pale. "We should have drawn a protective ring around us before starting the incantation."

The demon fixed its attention on Sudi, its eyes strangely alluring. She stared back, fascinated.

"I think it just wants me," Sudi said, easing away from her friends; she wanted to make sure they wouldn't be harmed.

The silhouette streaked toward her, losing form, and swirled around her. She tried to control her fear and to think, but before she could consider a plan, the shadow engulfed her. The demon's hatred pulsed through her. Its poisonous vapor seeped into her mouth. The taste made her gag.

The pressure became unbearable. She collapsed to her knees and fell forward onto the cold mud, her nose pressed against moldering leaves. She tried to draw a breath, but the effort seemed too great. The pace of her heartbeat slowed. She was vaguely aware of Dalila and Meri calling to her, and then their voices grew too faint to hear.

She was dying, but even as her body wanted to let go and be released from the pain, her soul fought to hang on to life. Then she remembered the words that the woman had spoken to her inside the museum. She mumbled them now: "Re-Atum emerged from the primeval ocean and took the form of a Bennu-bird. Then he flew from the darkness and perched on a rock. When he opened his beak, his cry broke the silence, and he created what is and what is not to be."

Maybe she would have more strength as the Bennu-bird. She tried to transform, but she felt too weak.

She concentrated, and this time feathers fluttered around her, and she changed into the bird. She opened her beak. "I speak these terrible words of power; send the demon hovering over me back to the chaos where he belongs."

The words came out as a primal scream that shattered the night and echoed around her.

Immediately, the pressure lifted and Sudi was transformed back into a girl.

The shadow wavered about her.

Sudi watched the black fog pull itself into a silhouette again. The demon opened his mouth, weeping loudly, and looked at her as if repenting for the crimes he had been forced to commit for the lord of chaos.

"He doesn't want to go back," Dalila said, joining Sudi.

"I know," Sudi answered. She pitied the demon, an emotion she had not expected to feel, and suddenly she wished she had spoken other words. Maybe she could have released him from his enslavement to Seth. She understood the reason the woman had used the word "terrible" to describe the words of power.

Then the demon vanished, leaving only its stench and a withering vapor.

"What did you do?" Meri asked.

As Sudi told her friends, she felt both elated and frightened, but mostly sad that she hadn't been able to save the creature.

"The Bennu's cry is the primal scream of creation," Dalila said. "You have the power to change what is."

Sudi shook her head. "I don't think it was

me," she whispered, "but another force. A greater power came through me."

They stared at each other, and then Sudi gazed up at the stars and prayed to the universe to guide her and help her speak the words of power more wisely.

"I think we've been successful," Dalila said.

"Except for the fact that we still have a love god running lose on Capitol Hill," Meri said with a huge grin.

"Hey!" a voice yelled.

"We forgot about Scott," Meri squealed.

Sudi was already running back to him. He looked bad: bewildered and covered with bruises.

He held up the shredded panty hose, then dropped them. "What did you do to me?" he asked, touching his swelling nose.

"I never did anything to you," Sudi said. She hadn't meant to hurt Scott, only the demon. "It's not what you think."

"I don't even know what I think," Scott said, and started to pull down his shirt. He traced his finger over the lipstick markings on his chest. "What's this eye for?"

Sudi couldn't even think of a lie to explain what they had done to him. She looked to Meri, hoping she could come up with an explanation. Meri shook her head and turned to Dalila, who shrugged.

"Something important," Sudi mumbled.

Scott glanced down at the dried blood embedded in his fingernails, then at the scratches on Sudi's arm. "Do I need to apologize for something?"

"It wasn't you," Sudi said.

"Then what was it?" Scott asked. "You look like someone dragged you through sand and mud."

Sudi shrugged. She knew how she must appear to him. She had seen herself in the mirror at the spa.

"I really like you, Sudi," Scott said. "But I don't know, you do some weird stuff." He shook his head, and, without explaining more, he hobbled away.

Sudi started after him, then stopped as an unnatural breeze curled around her. "Oh, no," she whispered and looked at Dalila and Meri. "Is the demon back?"

Dalila and Meri stared back at her, unsure. The air thickened, then began to spin, glimmering with flashes of gold. Huge wings formed and encircled Sudi. She turned as the downy wreath of feathers was transformed into a woman's arms.

Meri breathed out in a whistle and Dalila's eyes widened with awe.

"I am Isis," the woman said, "she of many names and daughter of Nut. I hold the greatest secrets of the universe, and I give my magic to the three of you."

Three rings appeared, hovering in the air. The sacred eye of Horus was fashioned in the gold with lapis lazuli and green faience.

"Seth caused the loss of the eye," Isis spoke softly. "But I restored it. The symbol is most powerful."

She slipped the first ring on Dalila's finger. "The ring of Isis bestows my favor and protection."

Then she guided the second onto Meri's hand. "All who see it will know you are my sisters."

At last Isis faced Sudi. "You especially have proven yourself strong," Isis said as she placed the last ring on Sudi's finger. "You were called to a life you didn't want, and you have accepted what fate has given to you."

Then Isis started to disappear, her body wavering in the breeze.

"Wait," Sudi said. "I have a thousand questions."

"Many blessings, my sisters," the goddess said, and then she vanished.

The girls stood in stunned silence, staring at their rings.

"Well," Meri whispered, smiling with happiness and triumph.

Dalila seemed pleased; she kept turning her hand to make the stones reflect the street light.

"And now we're sisters," Sudi said with a burst of emotion.

"Sisters!" Dalila and Meri shouted. They caught Sudi and and hugged her, kissing her cheeks until Sudi was laughing and pushing them away.

"I'll see you tomorrow," Sudi said, grateful that she would.

After leaving her friends, Sudi spoke the incantation for transforming into a bird. This time she focused her attention on her arms.

Feathers grew from her fingers, hands, and skin, fanning into wings. She ran down the street, until the wind caught her and lifted her above the trees. She soared, half girl, half bird, pure goddess, toward the rising moon, enjoying the enchantment of this night. They had been victorious, but she knew that this was only the first of many battles.

BOOK TWO

Divine One

For Patty Copeland, my best friend forever,
and her wonderful husband,
my big brother Tom.

The storm was worse than any Meri had seen since she and her mother had moved into the old Victorian house in Washington, D.C. Lightning blazed across the night, and within three seconds, thunder exploded. A short burst of hail hammered the windows, then stopped, leaving only the patter of rain on the glass. Meri couldn't rid herself of the strange and frightening feeling that the storm was somehow directed at her, a prophetic sign of bad days ahead.

A sharp hiss made her look down as lightning flashed again, illuminating her bedroom with shuddering light. A dark form crept across the carpet, tail flexing back and forth.

"Don't be afraid, Miwsher," she said as thunder rattled the walls. She assumed that the storm had frightened her normally bold cat.

She tossed back her covers and jumped out of bed, but as she started to run after Miwsher, her foot landed in something wet. She paused and swept her toes across a soggy groove in the carpet, then looked up, expecting to see rain trickling from the ceiling; after all, the house had been built in 1840. She didn't see a leak, but she did see her cat, perched on top of the tall chest of drawers.

Meri spun around. If Miwsher was there, then what was the other creature?

The backyard bordered on Rock Creek Park, and although bears no longer roamed in the wilderness behind their house, raccoons and foxes did. Maybe a small animal had used Miwsher's cat door to come inside and escape the downpour.

Meri tiptoed after the fleeing shadow, imagining the poor stray shivering with fear—but she didn't follow too closely, in case the trespasser was a skunk.

As she neared the stairs, an unfamiliar musty odor filled the gloom. The scent reminded her of cucumbers and wet soil. Although it wasn't a bad smell, some deep instinctual pulse within her took over—she stepped more cautiously now, not understanding her fear.

The middle landing formed a balcony from which she could see down into the living room below. As she leaned over the banister, wind hit the tall windows behind her, and the sudden noise made her jump. Thin branches slapped the panes. The leafless twigs made odd ticking sounds, louder than the rain.

She eased down the remaining steps, clutching the handrail so tightly her fingers ached. When she reached the last stair, a metallic crash came from her mother's home office, startling her.

It wasn't unusual for her mother to work late. She was the senior senator from California and had made one run for her party's presidential nomination. Everyone said she'd succeed in the next election. That worried the opposition party, but it also worried Meri.

The last time her mother had been a candidate, Secret Service agents had gone everywhere with Meri, including the high school dances. Their constant chaperoning had inhibited her. She was fifteen and still hadn't kissed a guy; not even a tight-lipped peck like most girls got on a dare in sixth grade. How pathetic was that? Some of her friends back home were seriously discussing birth control. She could only imagine how unexciting her love life would be if her mother actually won the election.

Then a bigger worry took over. Eventually, the agents would discover Meri's secret, and as sworn law-enforcement officers, what would they do? Was magic against the law?

She already feared that photographers would take her picture when she was doing something freakish. At one time she'd had two bodyguards assigned to protect her from the paparazzi. But after she'd learned about her true identity, Meri knew she couldn't expose the two men to the dangers she had to face. It had been hard enough convincing her mother that she didn't need the two-man escort. She couldn't picture herself trying to convince the

Treasury Department that the protection of the Secret Service wasn't necessary.

Meri paused in the doorway to her mother's office expecting to see the four-footed intruder padding across the desk. The night-light cast a pallid glow over the bookshelves, but nothing looked disturbed. Meri entered the room, brushing her hand across the polished wood, then gazed out the window and surveyed the backyard. Wind had toppled the iron lawn furniture and pushed it against the stones in the rock garden. Maybe that explained the sound she had heard.

From the corner of her eye, she caught a shadow moving toward her. She whipped around and bumped into someone. Before she could scream, a hand covered her mouth, and she breathed in the almond fragrance of her mother's lotion.

"It's me." Her mother spoke into Meri's ear.

"Mom," Meri said, her heart still pounding from the impact. She started to flip on the overhead lights, but her mother stopped her.

"Someone's in the house," her mother whispered.

"It's only a stray, or maybe a skunk," Meri said. "I forgot to lock Miwsher's cat door."

"No animal could make the noise I'm talking about," her mother said. "I heard the side gate opening."

Twice when they were living in California, someone had bypassed the alarm system and broken into their home. Now Meri wondered why her mother was prowling around the house like a detective, instead of calling the police.

Before she could ask, lightning struck the oak tree in the backyard, splitting the trunk. The night glowed orange, pulsing with spectral brightness, before fading back to gloom. Thunder shook the house. The vibration rumbled up Meri's legs and through her body.

Outside, sparks sputtered and swarmed around the branches, igniting twigs. Small fires spit more embers into the wind as rain quenched the flames. After that, the security lights went out. Immediately, the alarm system began bleeping, signaling that it had switched to battery power. Then the sound died.

For the second time that night, Meri had

an eerie sense that the storm's fury was directed at her. Warmth left her as fear took over, and the strange internal cold made her shiver. She eased in front of her mother, trying to shield her from the swelling shadows.

"Why didn't the backup system work?" her mother asked. She grabbed Meri's hand and pulled her down the hallway and into the kitchen.

Moments later, a match flared. Her mother lit a candle and handed it to Meri, but as she started to light a second one, something banged against the back door.

Meri jumped, almost dropping the candle. Wax dripped onto the hardwood floor.

"Was that the wind?" her mother asked, whipping around.

The knocking came again, in a steady, loud beat.

"It's probably a neighbor," her mother said, heading for the door.

But Meri had something more deadly in mind. "Don't answer it." She grabbed her mother's sleeve, pulling her back. Meri feared the storm had brought more than thunder, lightning, and hail.

The pounding continued, more urgent than before.

"A power line could be down," her mother said. "Maybe they've come to warn us."

"Mom, please don't," Meri said. She couldn't tell her mother about the real dangers facing the nation. She imagined the look of surprise and disbelief in her mother's eyes if she did. She doubted her mother would believe her. No one would.

She tried to think of a way to begin, but before she could, her mother had turned the dead bolt and opened the door. She peered outside. The chain lock, still engaged, jangled loudly as wind shrieked into the room, whistling around Meri and making the copper pans hanging from an overhead rack clang against each other.

A shadowy form slipped between her mother's feet and wiggled outside. Her mother squealed and slammed the door.

In the stillness that followed, her mother turned and faced Meri.

"What kind of animal was that?" she asked breathlessly. "Did you see it?"

Meri shook her head. "I only saw a tail."

The knocking came again, and before Meri could stop her, her mother opened the door. This time she said something to the person on the other side. When she shut the door and turned back, her eyes looked different, widened with shock.

"Please go to your room," her mother said. Her smile might have convinced the American public that she was calm and in control, but Meri didn't buy it.

"Who's there?" Meri asked, disobeying her mother.

"We are not going to discuss this," her mother said. "You don't have a need to know."

Her mother was on the Senate Intelligence Committee and had been called away before in the middle of the night because of urgent matters involving national security, but Meri didn't think an envoy from the president or the secretary of state stood on the other side of the door. Neither office could have inspired the dread she saw in her mother's eyes.

"I think I better stay," Meri said, feeling a rising need to protect her mother.

"Please," her mother added with a strange desperation in her voice. "I must speak to this visitor alone."

Reluctantly, Meri left the kitchen, but in the hallway she paused and listened, hoping to find out more.

"I said, your room," her mother's voice came from the kitchen.

"All right," Meri answered, already forming another plan. If she sat by her window, she'd be able to see the visitor when the person left.

The candle fire spit fitfully as she raced up the stairs.

In her room, she blew out the flame. Then she sat on the tufted seat in the bay window and stared out at the dark, caressing the birthmark on her scalp, near her temple and beneath her hair. She had always thought the mark was no more than an oddly shaped mole, until she had met Abdel. After that, she knew it was the sacred eye of Horus. It stood for protection, healing, and perfection, but also identified her as a Descendant of the royal throne of Egypt.

She thought of Abdel again. Her stomach fluttered pleasantly whenever she pictured his face. A dreamy smile stretched her lips as she traced his name on the window with her finger, then encircled it in a looping heart. Too often she daydreamed of kissing him, hugging him, and more.

She sighed. He was probably annoyed with the way she stared at him and giggled when he spoke. Her crush was pointless, because they could never be together. After all, he was her mentor and guide; at least, he was supposed to train her in the old ways. So far, he hadn't taught her how to handle her powers, or speak an incantation correctly. She didn't understand his reluctance.

Sometimes she had a feeling that he couldn't stand to be around her, and that made her long for him even more. Maybe something was wrong with her, she thought. Love wasn't supposed to hurt, but she couldn't help the way she felt.

The night she'd met Abdel, he had told her that he belonged to a secret society called the Hour priests. Back in ancient times, the goddess Isis had given them the Book of Thoth and instructed them to watch the night skies. When the stars warned of danger, the priests were supposed to give the book to the pharaoh. Nowadays, the priests found the next Descendants and gave them the ancient papyri.

Meri had thought the story was interesting, but she hadn't understood why Abdel was telling it to her until he added that he had been sent to the United States to find her. She was descended from Horus, a divine pharaoh of ancient Egypt, Abdel told her, and like all Descendants before her, she was being called to stand against evil and protect the world. Only the divine heirs to the throne of Egypt had the power to use the magic in the Book of Thoth to stop the dark forces.

Meri hadn't believed him, of course; nor had Dalila and Sudi, the two girls who had been summoned with her.

Even after he had given her a papyrus from the Book of Thoth, she had laughed at the idea that she could be divine. But when she started to leave, Abdel had stopped her, his expression determined and grim. He had clasped his hands around her head and recited an incantation to awaken the soul of ancient Egypt that survived deep within her.

Now she repeated the words, loving the feel of them on her tongue, the sound they made as they met the air. "Sublime of magic, your heart is pure.

To you I send the power of the ages. Divine one, come into being."

That night, a powerful feeling, both frightening and euphoric, had vibrated through her, growing in intensity, until she had thrummed with strange energy, her nerves and muscles tingling. What would have happened if her two bodyguards had stopped Abdel, or even hurt him?

The sound of the back door opening and banging shut startled her and tore her from her thoughts. She leaned forward and pressed her forehead against the cold glass, trying to see the visitor.

Rain and gloomy shadows hid whoever walked beneath the trees, but like the pharaoh Horus, who could transform himself into a falcon, each Descendant had the ability to change into an animal. Meri could become a cat. She didn't have control over the power yet, but she recited the incantation anyway.

As the words formed in her mouth, an ache rushed through her. Her legs trembled, and she clasped the edge of the windowsill, focusing her thoughts on remaining a girl; she needed only the night vision of a cat.

Whiskers prickled and popped from her cheeks, but then her pupils enlarged, and what had been lost in the swirling darkness below her now became visible and distinct.

She gasped.

Abdel stood beneath the trees without an umbrella or a coat to protect him from the storm. He looked as if he had rushed out into the weather wearing only a T-shirt and jeans; she didn't understand what he was doing in her backyard.

He looked up, and she wondered if he had sensed her watching him.

She jumped away from the window and glanced across the room. Luminous yellow eyes stared back at her from the dark. Her heart stuttered until she realized she was gazing at her own cat eyes, reflected in her mirror.

Slowly, she calmed herself and crept back to the window. Rain spattered the glass, and cold seeped over the sill, curling around her, but the draft alone didn't make her shiver. There was no reason for Abdel to visit her mother, unless . . .

A dull ache throbbed inside her chest. Maybe her lovesickness annoyed Abdel so much that he had come to talk to her mother about her behavior.

She sat on the window seat, tears warm in her eyes. She couldn't help it if she was infatuated with Abdel. Besides, she didn't want to stop liking him. She loved the way he made her feel, all pleasant ache and butterflies. She didn't care that her obsession was wrong.

Abdel turned and walked away, rain pelting his back, and in that moment she remembered the desperation in her mother's voice, the fear on her face. Her mother had acted as if she knew the visitor, but where would she have met Abdel, and why would she be afraid of him?

A loud, grating noise blasted the quiet and jolted Meri awake. The high-pitched buzzing made her cover her ears. She jumped out of bed and looked out her window. Workmen with chain saws were already cutting the fallen tree into logs. From the cast of sunlight, she knew it was late and wondered why her mother had let her sleep so long.

She hurried to her closet, kicked aside the stack of new shoes, then stopped and stared at the line of muted gray and navy blue clothes in her closet. Her mother had hired a stylist to change Meri's surf-rat look into preppy, college-bound freshness. Meri didn't feel like herself in the clothes that Roxanne had bought, and no way was Meri going to dress boring and safe.

Then with a shock, she realized that Roxanne had taken down the photos of Meri with her friends on the beach in Malibu and replaced them with lists of fashion dos and don'ts. Meri tore down the papers with the curlicue writing and crumpled them without reading what Roxanne expected from her.

Frustrated, she took off her pj's and began dressing for school.

On Saturday, Roxanne had made Meri take out her nose ring, and in rebellion Meri had hemmed the skirt of her school uniform. Without even looking in her mirror, she knew she had made it too short. The hemline barely reached midthigh. In the public school she had attended back in California, that length would have been fine, but at Entre Nous Academy, the shortness was going to cause a scandal. She'd probably be sent home again.

She grabbed the black-and-white oxfords and a pair of socks, then rushed back to her bed, wishing she could wear flip-flops and toe rings instead.

As she bent over to tie the shoestrings, a curious, meandering path on the carpet made her stop. She looked closer and traced her hand over a thin, opaque membrane that matted the fibers together.

A fine film came off on her fingers. The animal that had broken into the house must have left the trail, but other than a giant slug, she couldn't imagine what kind of creature could have done it. But she didn't have time to puzzle over it. She needed to question her mother about Abdel's visit.

She raced down the stairs and burst into the kitchen. Warm air rushed around her, bringing the smell of fresh coffee and baked cinnamon rolls.

Ten or more candle stubs lined the sink. She didn't understand why her mother had lit so many candles and burned them down to puddles of wax, unless she had stayed up all night.

A clatter made her turn. Georgie, their housekeeper, rolled a bucket and mop across the floor and stopped near the scattered leaves and tracked-in mud.

"I didn't do it," Meri said, answering Georgie's scowl. She hugged the thin old woman, who grumpily remained silent. Then Meri dashed into the morning room off the kitchen.

Her mother sat at the table, dressed in a black suit, watching news programs with the sound turned off on the six televisions in the built-in cabinet that covered the east wall. The remote controls lay on the white linen cloth in front of her.

Meri sensed her mother's tension and wondered what the commentators had said.

"Where is everyone?" Meri asked and sat down.

Normally, staffers crowded the breakfast table, taking notes and talking on phones. Most were interns eager to break into political life, but a few had been with her mother through her entire career.

"Good morning," her mother said, but her gaze never left the screens.

"I saw all those burned-down candles in the kitchen . . ." Meri began as she poured Froot Loops into a bowl. "Didn't you go back to bed?"

Something on one of the middle televisions

caught her mother's attention. She grabbed a remote and pointed it at the TV; a reporter's voice filled the room: "Was it stress or lack of self-control?"

Meri looked up, not even sure her mother had heard her question. The news clip showed her mother walking away, surrounded by aides. The voice-over reported on her sudden weight gain.

Her mother jabbed the remote, and silence filled the room again.

"I could be the first woman president of the United States," her mother said angrily, "and they're focusing on my weight. Didn't they even listen to my speech? I know the opposition party paid someone to point out the pounds I've put on."

"Of course they did," a male voice said. "What's wrong with being full bodied?"

Stanley Keene, a reporter from the *Washington Post*, sat in the rattan chair in the corner, away from the sunlight. His huge belly hung over his lap. He pushed a cinnamon roll into his mouth, then wiped his fingers on a napkin and left it crumpled on the wickerwork arm of the chair.

"You know Stanley," her mother said.

"Morning." He smiled cheerily and brushed crumbs from his mustache.

"Good morning," Meri answered, trying to sound polite, but she had never liked Stanley. Even so, she felt bad that she had interrupted his interview with her mother. The opposing political party had been attacking her mother in order to divert attention away from her criticism of the president's foreign policy. Stanley had probably been giving her mother the chance to explain her views.

"Maybe we should go to my office." Her mother picked up her cell phone without waiting for Stanley's reply and called her driver. She grabbed her briefcase and started for the door.

"Mom," Meri said, pushing back her chair. She couldn't let her mother leave without finding out what Abdel had said.

Meri ran in to the living room.

"Mom," she called again.

Her mother turned, a haggard look in her eyes, and placed a hand on Meri's shoulder.

"Why did Abdel visit you last night?" Meri asked. Now that she had asked the question, her chest tightened in anticipation of the answer.

"Abdel?" her mother said.

"The person who knocked on the door last night," Meri explained, with rising frustration. Why was her mother pretending she didn't know him?

"That was my assistant, delivering a copy of a new bill for my review," her mother said.

"You can tell me," Meri said, her heart pounding. She was shorter than her mother and stood on her toes so she could see into her mother's pale eyes. The color always surprised her, so different from her own. No one would have thought they were mother and daughter. Meri's hair was black and curled in tight ringlets, her skin dark. Her mother's translucent skin revealed the blue veins in her temples.

"You seemed afraid of him," Meri whispered.

"What?" Her mother gave her a questioning look. "You mean last night? The storm scared me. What other reason would I have to be afraid?"

"Have I been a nuisance?" Meri asked, certain her mother was hiding something. "Was Abdel complaining about me?"

"Sweetie, I don't know anyone named Abdel." Her mother opened the front door. "And if I did, I wouldn't keep the conversation from you."

Meri stepped back. Her mother was lying, but Meri didn't know why.

"We really have to go," her mother said and kissed Meri's cheek. She started down the walk as the black Lincoln Continental pulled up the front drive.

"What would Abdel have said?" Stanley asked.

Meri spun around. Stanley was staring at her. A thin smile stretched his lips, making his cheeks rounder. He didn't look away when she caught his gaze. Was he just studying her the way journalists sometimes did, hoping to find a new angle?

After all, her mom wasn't just a candidate for office. She was also a single parent. Magazines loved to run that story. Meri had been an orphan living on the streets of Cairo before her mother had adopted her and named her Meritaten, after the daughter of the pharaoh Akhenaton and his wife, the famous beauty Nefertiti.

"What is it?" Meri asked rudely. "Why are you staring at me?"

Stanley shook his head and pushed past her, following her mother to the car.

Meri was desperate to find out more. She hadn't given up. She sensed that her mother was keeping something from her, and she didn't think it had anything to do with national security.

She eased back inside, already feeling the tingling in her skin as her body anticipated the change. She grabbed her book bag, clutched it close to her chest, and stepped outside, then stole around the corner to the side of the house, where no one could see her. She placed her house key safely in her skirt pocket and faced the morning sun.

"Amun-Re, eldest of the gods in the eastern sky, mysterious power of wind," she whispered. "Make a path for me to change my earthly *khat* into that of your beloved daughter Bastet."

A gentle energy whirled around her, caressing her cheeks and throat and making the leaves tremble. The metamorphosis began.

In response, she said, "*Xu kua*. I am glorious. *User Kua*. I am mighty. *Neteri kua*. I am strong."

A smile crept across her face as her clothing and backpack disappeared. She raised her arms in a lazy stretch, her soul already the essence of cat, and let the sun's rays warm her.

A sleek black pelt covered her skin. The silken fur shimmered in the light. Then her eyesight changed, and the sunshine became blinding. She stepped into the shadows. Her vision grew more panoramic but remained hazy around the edges.

A sudden feeling of pain made her press her fingers against her chest as she shrank down to cat size. She meowed in triumph, enjoying her feline instincts, and sniffed the urine the tomcats had sprayed; it was like reading a gossip column. A toad jumped in front of her, and she had to concentrate to pull herself away from the temptation to spend the day chasing after it.

She rushed to the front yard, her ears erect and facing forward, trying to hear her mother and Stanley over the shrill noise of chain saws.

Stanley leaned on a walking stick that she hadn't noticed him using before.

"Look at the cute cat," her mother said as Meri approached, mewling.

Stanley's head snapped around.

"I hate cats," he said and stamped his foot on the brick walk.

The sound crashed through Meri. Of all

her senses as a cat, hearing was the sharpest. She jumped back, arched her back, and hissed.

"Why did you scare the little cat?" her mother asked Stanley in a scolding tone. "I can't believe you were so mean."

Stanley bared his teeth. For a moment, Meri thought he was going to snarl. Instead, he poked the tip of his walking stick under her belly and nudged her away.

"Stanley," her mother said. "You're going to hurt the little thing."

"Cats make me edgy," Stanley explained.

But immediately Meri realized she had another problem. She recognized the snake-scale pattern on his walking stick. That was her wand. The one Abdel had given to her. What was Stanley doing with it?

The wand had the power to ward off evil, and even though Abdel had not shown Meri how to use its magic, she couldn't let Stanley take it. She leaped and tried to dig her claws into the metal-covered stick. Her nails screeched over the stones embedded in the bronze.

Stanley swung the stick and flung her into the air.

Her mother screamed in disbelief.

Meri twisted and squirmed and landed on her paws. She crouched low to the ground, lashing her tail back and forth in anger, and watched her mother and Stanley continue down the walk.

At the car, Stanley placed his hand on her mother's shoulder. His presumptuous touch made her mother scowl, and he took his hand away.

"Once we're in the car, we won't be able to talk freely," he said. "I need your answer now."

"Then my answer is no," her mother said.

"You have to help me," Stanley continued. "You know what I can do if you refuse."

"When I feel doubt," her mother said, "my answer is always no." She had an intimidating frown, and she was focusing it on him. "And no matter what you may believe, you can't blackmail me into changing my mind."

"Don't give me your final say yet," he said, softening.

The driver came around the car and opened the door for Meri's mother. He wore dark glasses, and even though Meri couldn't see his eyes, she knew by the turn of his head that he was scanning the neighborhood for snipers. His dark suit jacket was buttoned, and he probably had a Secret Service badge hooked on his belt.

"The Cult of Anubis is just a silly fad," her mother said as she climbed into the sedan, "something from California that has become popular here. I could ruin my career by doing what you want."

Stanley crawled into the car, taking Meri's wand with him.

Meri was too stunned to chase after him and reclaim her wand. Instead, she wondered what Stanley had tried to force her mother to do.

Like her mother, most Washingtonians believed the cult was only a fad that had become popular with young people who wanted to enjoy the spa and get in touch with their inner selves. Most members were unaware that the cult was ancient and evil.

Only a few people knew its true history. Anubis had once been the most important Egyptian funerary god. Then his cult had been taken over by those devoted to Osiris. But some of the priests who had served Anubis hadn't wanted to lose their power, so they had used Anubis and the Book of Gates in unholy ways to call forth demons and resurrect the dead.

Now the priests who had once served Anubis worshipped the wicked god Seth and planned to return the universe to the chaos from which it came. The leaders had brought the cult to Washington, D.C., hoping to find the Descendants and destroy the bloodline of Horus before the Hour priests were even aware of their scheme.

Meri shuddered, imagining what would have happened to her if Abdel hadn't found her first.

But her thoughts quickly turned back to Stanley. He knew something about the cult, and it had to be important for him to risk blackmailing her mother. She wondered what he intended to do if her mother refused to help him.

$\mathcal{E}$

$\mathbf{M}$eri needed to hurry on to school, but the inborn pattern of a cat was growing stronger than her desire to transform. She stretched and rolled, soothing herself with a throaty purr, then licked her paw and rubbed it behind her ear. Just as she decided to waste the day lolling in the sunshine, black clouds spread across the sky and hid the sun.

She scrambled across the street and raced toward school, hoping to get inside before the first raindrops fell. When she passed the National Geographic Building, her whiskers twitched. Other eyes were staring at her. She tilted her head. Pedestrians marched around her, feet clomping on the walk. A man almost stepped on her, but no one was watching her with ill intent.

Still, the feeling didn't go away. She jumped onto the stone wall.

Across the street, Michelle Conklin stood sentinel at the entrance to Entre Nous Academy, holding an oversize umbrella, oblivious of the students who had to duck around the huge black canopy.

She was staring at Meri.

Instinctively, Meri's lips curled back, and she hissed. When Meri had started school at the academy, she had wanted to be popular the way she had been back in California, but Michelle had seemed determined to make that impossible. She had spread lies and warned other students away from Meri.

A raindrop landed on Meri's nose. More hit her back. Her feline self curled inward, and Meri could feel the change begin. She dashed around the corner, to an open courtyard directly across the street from Entre Nous. Then she scuttled under the branches of a hedge and crept back until she was certain no one could see her, not even Michelle.

She relaxed, and sweet pain rippled down her spine and tail. Muscle spasms made her yowl. Her bones stretched, and paws turned back into fingers. She lay naked beneath the thick growth of shrubs.

"Darn," she whispered. Where were her clothes? Panic made her hold her breath and concentrate.

Seconds later, her clothes appeared, but not everything did. Her feet remained bare, and her backpack was missing.

Her belongings didn't always make the transformation with her. Dalila and Sudi didn't have this problem. They always changed back fully clothed, in whatever they had been wearing before the switch.

She got up on her knees, spread the branches, and peered out. No one was watching. She jumped from behind the thicket and cursed silently, then brushed the dirt and leaves from her skirt. Abdel had to teach her how to use her power before she ended up naked in a public place and got arrested.

Meri crossed the street, dodging around traffic and hating the grimy, wet sludge beneath her toes. She needed to get to her locker before the first bell and put on her gym shoes. She eased through the crowd near the door. Kids talked in different languages and laughed at jokes that Meri didn't understand.

It was not the first time she had wished she could attend Lincoln High with Sudi instead. Meri's life had been casual in California; she hadn't had to worry about how low to curtsy when she met P. Diddy in a celebrity club. But in D.C., knowing who stood where seemed important. Most of the students at Entre Nous had protocol officers to guide them, and those who didn't took classes on etiquette at George Washington University.

"*Pardonnez-moi,*" Meri stammered as she tried to push around two guys speaking a mix of French and Arabic. "*Assalamu alaikum,*" she said in Arabic. "Hello" was the only word she knew.

When they didn't budge, she became frustrated. "Can you just move it?" she said in her plain California English. That worked. They turned and looked down at her, then stepped aside.

She could feel her blush growing. If her mother expected her to make friends with students whose parents could contribute to her campaign, she was going to be miserably disappointed. Meri's bad manners were probably going to cost her mother votes.

She started up the front steps, anxious to get inside and warm her feet. A black umbrella swung in front of her and barred her way.

"Where are your shoes?" Michelle asked, and lifted the umbrella back over her head.

Meri stiffened. She didn't need this encounter. She already had too much on her mind.

"Is that the California style?" Michelle went on loudly, and glanced around to see if other students were watching.

"Why would you think this is a style?" Meri asked. "And why do you even care?"

"Sorry, I forgot," Michelle said too sweetly. "Barefooted probably comes naturally to you. Weren't you a beggar on the streets of Cairo? I'm sure that's what I read."

Before Meri could answer, Scott pushed

through the students who were shaking out their umbrellas and crowding inside.

"Why are you standing in the rain?" he asked, his wet curly brown hair hanging in his eyes. He didn't wait for Meri to reply, but grabbed her hand and pulled her onto the porch under the overhang.

He still had a California tan, even though he had moved to D.C. to get away from drugs and a bad scene back in Los Angeles. He lived with his grandmother, a physics professor at Georgetown University. His parents had hoped the change in environment would keep him clean, but he ran into other problems in the nation's capital. Meri wondered what his parents would have done if they had known what had happened to him.

"I was just inviting Meri to my party," Michelle said pleasantly, as she squeezed onto the porch between them and pushed Meri into the crowd. "And I hope you'll come, too, Scott."

"Sheesh." Meri rolled her eyes. When Scott was around, Michelle acted as if Meri were her best friend.

Michelle handed her umbrella to Meri, then pulled two turquoise envelopes from her messenger bag. She gave one to Scott and the second to Meri.

Meri folded the oversize invitation and stuck it into her jacket pocket.

"You're having another party?" Scott flicked his finger against the card. "You just had an extravaganza that cost more than most people earn in a year."

"It's practice for what I'm going to do," Michelle said and brushed back her two-thousand-dollar blond extensions before continuing, "I'm going to run the coolest club in the world and let only celebrities in. I'll be more famous than my father."

Her dad had a celebrity-courting lifestyle, but he did it to make money; he was the best fund-raiser in D.C.

"I thought you wanted to be a singer," Scott said and winked at Meri.

"I've outgrown that," Michelle said seriously. "I want to do something more."

"And I'm sure your club will make the world a better place for all of us to live in," Meri said sarcastically.

"Thanks," Michelle answered. "I never quite thought of it that way. Maybe I can make a difference."

Scott laughed. "Are you for real?"

"It's hard to believe one person can do so much," Michelle said, beaming as if he had complimented her. "My father always tells me I'm amazing." She took her umbrella from Meri and ran inside after Cecil, the son of the ambassador from Romania.

Scott rested his hand on Meri's shoulder. "With all the money she's spending on entertaining us, she could practically support a third-world nation."

"I know," Meri answered. "Thanks for rescuing me again."

"Why is Michelle always on you, anyway?" Scott asked.

"I'm friends with Sudi," Meri said, wiggling her toes to get rid of the numbness.

"I don't think that's the reason," Scott said thoughtfully. "I think Michelle is jealous of you."

"Me? Why would perfect Michelle be jealous of me?" Meri asked. "She has everything."

"She doesn't have photographers running after her," Scott said. "You do, and she'd do anything to get that kind of attention. But the biggest reason for her jealousy is me." He smiled broadly. "She thinks I like you." He slid his eyes sideways, and Meri followed his look.

Michelle stood on the other side of the window next to the door. She was talking to Cecil but her eyes were focused on Meri and Scott.

"I think she thinks we're more than friends," Scott said.

"I've told her a dozen times that we're not," Meri answered. "I can't believe she's jealous. She has a life that anyone would want."

"Except for you and me," Scott said. "All we want is to go home."

Meri nodded. They both missed California and felt out of place in D.C. "You're doing a better job of fitting in," Meri said.

"That's because all the girls are crushing on me," Scott teased. He stopped and nudged her. "Come on. Cheer up. My conceitedness alone should make you laugh."

"I'm trying," she said and smiled up at him.

Scott held the door for her, and she stepped inside. A blast of dry, furnace heat hit her.

"So, why haven't you called Sudi?" Meri asked. She had promised Sudi she'd find out how Scott felt about her. "I know you like her, so what's the problem?"

"Strange things happen when she's around," he said. "She's bad mojo."

He tore open the invitation that Michelle had given him and brushed a hand across his forehead.

"What?" Meri asked and grabbed his wrist. He looked wobbly enough to pass out.

"Michelle's parents rented The Jackal, that new teen club. I can't believe she's having a party there," he said.

"Does that place mean something to you?" Meri asked. She had reason to be nervous, but she didn't understand why Scott was.

"The jackal is a symbol of death, isn't it? They used to haunt graveyards and feed on corpses." He looked at Meri and added in a whisper, "Their howling scares me. It's called the death howl."

"Have you ever heard a jackal?" Meri asked, surprised.

"Yes," he answered. Then he blinked, as if an odd flash of memory had left him. "No," he corrected and laughed loudly, making fun of his lapse. "How could I know what a jackal sounds like? It must be the old burnout in me speaking. I wouldn't know a jackal if one came up and bit me."

Her stomach felt queasy. She was suddenly worried about her only friend at the academy. "You're not—?"

"I'm clean," he said solemnly. "I don't know why I said what I did."

But Meri suspected that she knew.

The bell rang, and Scott walked away from her, pushing through the throng of students.

Meri stood in the center of the hallway, letting kids jostle around her, and didn't even move when someone stepped on her toes.

The Cult of Anubis had kidnapped Scott and r eplaced his soul with a demon's spirit. Meri, along with Sudi and Dalila, had rescued him and exorcised the demon, but she wondered if they had been completely successful. Maybe some kind of demonic residue had been left behind—something that Scott wasn't aware of on a conscious level— that made him afraid to go to The Jackal, even if it was for a party.

CHAPTER 4

After school, Meri wandered through the Eastern Market as another storm ripped through D.C. She hadn't eaten since the night before, and her stomach grumbled noisily. She craved a bite of apple or a dried fig—anything!—but her money was in the book bag she'd lost when she'd changed into a cat.

When a vendor turned to pick up a crate of oranges, she stole four green grapes, popped them into her mouth and chomped down. The sour taste made her wince. She squinched up her face, and when she opened her eyes, the man was staring at her.

Sudden guilt replaced her hunger pains. The unripe fruit hadn't even been worth the theft, but she couldn't tell him that.

"I lost my money," she tried to explain.

Before he could scold her, thunder crashed, and its violent shock waves rolled through the block-long market hall.

The vendor made the sign of the cross and stared up at the ceiling, watching the light fixtures swing back and forth.

The butcher across the aisle stopped hanging sausages over a wire and stepped down from his ladder.

Even the two photographers who had been stalking Meri suddenly forgot their prey.

She heard the photographer she knew only as Thimble shout, "This weather's not natural. No storm systems are coming down from the Arctic, and nothing's coming up from the Gulf."

"It's the Pentagon," the butcher announced.

He waited until he had the attention of all the shoppers near his counter. "They've learned how to control the weather."

"Then I wish they'd do a better job of it," the fruit vendor challenged and started rearranging the grapes.

"Just ask her," Thimble pointed at Meri.

Everyone turned and looked in the direction of his accusing thumb.

"She's probably heard her mom talk about these storms," he continued.

Meri shook her head.

Tourists and shoppers wearing plastic head scarves stared at her. Their eyes widened, and smiles broke out across their faces as one by one they recognized Meri. Cell phones and cameras came out.

Meri wasn't sure if it was hunger or nerves that was making her feel so faint.

The crowd inched toward her. The people within it seemed suddenly forged together at the shoulders, their camera lenses like third eyes all focused on her.

Meri spun around and darted past the

shoppers behind her. Her soaked tennis shoes made a wet, sucking sound each time one of her feet came down. She was starting to panic, not sure where to go, when Sudi stepped through the door near the bakery and shook out her umbrella.

Meri slammed into her. "Let's get out of here," she said in a breathless voice that didn't even sound like her own.

Sudi looked up. "Why's everyone staring at you?"

"I stole a grape." Meri pressed her fingers over her eyes, trying to get rid of the weird, spinning sensation. "Can I borrow some money? I need to eat."

"Sure," Sudi said and held the door open for Meri. Then she looked back over her shoulder. "You must have done something more than steal a grape."

Meri dashed out into the rain and waited for Sudi to open the umbrella. They linked arms and hurried toward the corner. The rhythmic squish-squash of Meri's shoes made Sudi laugh.

"What happened to your oxfords?" Sudi

asked. "I thought that was the only kind of shoe you were allowed to wear at that snooty school of yours."

"I lost them, along with my books and homework," Meri said. "The day has been a wipeout."

A vendor in a kiosk held out a spoon with a sample of candied pecan. Meri gratefully took it and bit down, enjoying the sugar seeping over her tongue.

"Did you talk to Scott?" Sudi asked.

"Not yet," Meri lied. She wasn't going to tell Sudi what Scott had said, not until she was able to coax a better answer out of him, anyway.

"Why not?" Sudi sounded disappointed. "Didn't you see him at school today?"

But before Meri could think up another lie, lightning forked across the clouds, curling and scattering into a hundred jagged veins.

Sudi squealed, and within seconds, thunder crackled, shattering the air. Meri clutched Sudi's arm.

"Am I the only one who thinks this weather is creepy?" Sudi asked. "My dad said that meteorologists have called a special meeting to try to figure out what's going on. I hate it. It feels so—" She stopped.

"So directed at us?" Meri asked.

Sudi nodded. "You don't think that's weird?"

"I think that's why Abdel wants to see us," Meri said, and at the same time she prayed that she was wrong.

"Life was easier when all I had to worry about was finding a party," Sudi said with a sulky frown. "I remember when not being able to buy a new push-up bra was a major problem."

Sudi had a key pass to all the trendy teen clubs, and she knew how to sneak into any D.C. party, even the swanky embassy affairs. Her parents were both lawyers at a prestigious law firm and worked twelve-hour days, seven days a week, so Sudi had the freedom she needed to live the party life she loved.

Meri looked across the street.

Dalila waved and ran across the intersection without looking both ways or even checking the traffic signal. The wind lifted her umbrella high over her head, and she didn't notice the car that swerved around her, or the one that stopped just in time. She had lived a sheltered life. Her parents had been killed in a cave-in while excavating a tomb in the Valley of the Kings. Since that time, Dalila had been homeschooled by an overprotective uncle. She didn't know how to do simple things that Meri took for granted, and apparently crossing the street was one of them.

"Let's hurry inside," Dalila said, already opening the door.

The smells of coffee, chocolate, and freshly baked cakes drifted out into the cold air.

"I feel as if the weather is a bad omen for us," Dalila said and whipped a red scarf from her head.

When Meri had first met Dalila, she shaved her head to flaunt her royal birthmark, the *wedjat* eye, which was identical to the ones that Meri and Sudi had. But since learning that the cult wanted to destroy the bloodline of Horus, Dalila had let her hair grow back, and now glossy black strands covered her scalp in a tight pixie. She had known about her royal heritage, but she had been stunned to discover the real meaning of the birthmark. She had thought she was being groomed to marry a Middle Eastern prince.

They followed the hostess to a table near the plate-glass window. Meri sat with her back to the room and ordered German pancakes and cappuccino without looking at the menu.

"Abdel was standing in my backyard last night," Meri said, and then she leaned forward and told Sudi and Dalila everything that had happened the night before, leaving out any mention of her crush on Abdel.

"Why would Abdel need to see your mother?" Dalila wondered. "You have to ask him."

"I will," Meri said, and then she described her morning encounter with Stanley and how she had discovered that he had stolen her wand. "He gives me the creeps, the way he stares at me."

"Do you think he knew what the wand was?" Sudi asked.

"Maybe he just needed it for support," Dalila suggested. "You said he was a huge man. My uncle uses a cane sometimes, because his weight makes his knees hurt."

Meri shrugged. "I suppose, but I'm certain the wand was hidden in my closet. Why would he go snooping around in there?"

"I'll bet he's a pervert looking for underwear," Sudi put in.

"Yuck!" Meri squealed.

"But even if he did take the wand because he needed a crutch," Dalila added thoughtfully, "we'll still have to figure out a way to get it back."

Meri started to tell them that The Jackal had opened but before she could, Abdel joined them.

"Good morning," he said and sat down in the chair to Meri's left.

Meri's heart fluttered, and her cheeks grew warm. Seeing him in person was so different, and so much better, than daydreaming about him. He was always more handsome than she remembered. She loved his dark eyes and hair.

"What's wrong?" Sudi asked and shook Meri's shoulder.

"Nothing." Meri shrugged Sudi's hand away.

"You're blushing," Dalila said, reaching across the table. She placed her hand on Meri's forehead. "Are you feverish?"

Meri pulled back. "I told you I'm fine." She tried to sound lighthearted, and laughed to show them that her blush meant nothing, but the giggle came out as a honking snort. Before she could calm herself, Sudi spoke.

"Ask Abdel why he was standing in your backyard," Sudi urged.

Meri couldn't believe Sudi had just blurted that out.

The waitress set a plate filled with thin folded pancakes in front of Meri. She gazed down at her food, ashamed and bashful. Her hair swung forward, and a strand fell into the syrupy fruit. She grabbed it and licked off the syrup without thinking, then rolled her eyes in embarrassment. Why did she always act so ridiculous when Abdel was around?

"Go ahead and eat," Abdel said in a gentlemanly manner, as if he thought she was waiting until he had his meal before she started chowing down.

Even though Meri felt faint with hunger, she was suddenly too nervous to eat. Her stomach had curled into a tight ball, and she knew if she took a bite she'd vomit.

"Abdel, why did you go over to Meri's house last night?" Sudi asked when Meri didn't.

"I sensed that Meri was in terrible danger." He touched Meri's hand.

Meri's fingers twitched, and she wondered if he could sense how much she liked him.

"But why did you talk to my mom?" Meri asked. She looked into his brown eyes and wished she hadn't. Her strength left her, and she had to place her elbows on the table to keep from keeling over.

Too late, she realized that she had jerked her hand away from Abdel. Had he noticed? Would he think she had done that on purpose because she didn't want him to touch her? When really, she wished she could push her pancakes aside and kiss him.

"I didn't talk to your mother," he said after a long pause.

His lie snapped her out of her swoon. Her mother had lied to her about their meeting, and now Abdel had, too. What were they keeping from her?

"Someone knocked on the back door," she said, more frustrated than angry. "My mother invited the person inside. If it wasn't you, then who was it?"

"I saw your mother look out at the storm, but I never saw anyone standing on your back porch." He held up his palms, as if that would convince her that he was telling the truth. She had never noticed the scar on the pad of his thumb before. "Maybe a friend of your mother's came over before I arrived."

Meri thought of Stanley. Her mother would never have let an ugly old troll like Stanley spend the night. So who had she let in?

"An animal was loose in her house," Dalila added.

Abdel studied Meri with such an intense look that her swoon came back.

"Did you see what it was?" Abdel asked.

"I only saw its tail," Meri answered.

"Is it possible that what you saw was a snake?" Abdel leaned closer to her.

Meri had convinced herself that the dark form had only been the tail of a squirrel, or a stray cat, but she supposed the shadow wiggling up and down and side to side could have been a snake.

"Maybe," she answered, not liking the concerned look in his eyes.

"I think the creature was Apep," Abdel said, sitting up straight again in his chair.

Dalila dropped her fork. "The soul-hunter is here?" She pushed her plate away. "How could Apep escape from the Netherworld?"

"I believe the cult summoned him," Abdel answered.

"But when we saw Apep last, the snake was so large," Sudi argued, "he would have stretched from here to Capitol Hill, so how could he fit inside Meri's room?"

Meri shuddered, remembering the fine film she had found on her carpet that morning. In the Netherworld, the giant serpent had slithered toward them, leaving a frothy trail of green scum on either side of his body. An angry god had sent them to Apep, and Meri had hoped never to encounter the snake again.

Tears filled Meri's eyes as she realized the danger she had unknowingly brought into her home.

"Apep brings violent storms." Dalila crossed her arms over her chest, as if feeling a sudden chill. "And the weather forecasters have no explanation for the thunderstorms."

Dalila's uncle and guardian was the famous Egyptologist Anwar Serenptah. He had immersed Dalila in ancient Egyptian culture, magic, and religion, so she knew things that Meri and Sudi hadn't learned yet.

"But I don't understand how Apep was small enough to fit into Meri's room," Sudi said, voicing her concern again. "You could be mistaken, couldn't you? Maybe it was just a raccoon or a possum."

"It's not easy for something from the Netherworld to come here," Abdel explained. "The creature is weak and small at first, until it adjusts to our world."

"Then what?" Sudi asked.

"The three of you need to stop Apep before the demon becomes too strong," Abdel said and broke eye contact.

"But there's something you're not telling us," Dalila said.

"In the past, only the god Seth has been able to resist the serpent's stare," Abdel said.

"But we escaped Apep once already," Meri put in.

"Yes, you *escaped* the soul-hunter," Abdel

answered. "You weren't fighting Apep, or trying to defeat and vanquish the demon."

"He's right," Dalila agreed. "We only had to run from him."

"I'll study the Book of Thoth," Abdel said, standing abruptly. He looked down at Meri. "And until I find a protective spell, you must be cautious."

"You always have us search for the information ourselves," Dalila said. "Why is this time different?"

"We can't make a mistake this time, because . . ." Abdel seemed to be debating within himself whether or not he should tell them the truth.

"Tell us," Sudi pleaded. "It's always better to know."

"I'm certain Apep has been summoned to destroy the three of you," he said. "I think the creature stole into Meri's house, hoping to kill her in her sleep."

"Why didn't he?" Meri asked as a shiver crept up her spine. "Apep was under my bed."

"Perhaps the spells I cast stopped him," Abdel said, "or maybe Miwsher scared him away."

"That's why you were in my backyard?" Meri asked, feeling a burst of warm emotion. "To protect me?"

"Yes, divine one," he answered. "That is my duty."

Meri smiled, and he looked away from her.

"All three of you must give me your solemn promise that you won't do anything until we meet again," he said. "What I need to do may take some time, and I don't want you venturing out on your own, the way you did with the mummy."

"I promise," Meri said. So did Sudi and Dalila.

The girls had tried to deal with a mummy that had been summoned to destroy Sudi, but instead of getting rid of the creature with a simple spell, Sudi had placed a love spell on it and turned an uncomplicated problem into an impossible one.

Apparently satisfied, Abdel turned and left.

Meri watched him. She couldn't just let him leave. She jumped up.

"Where are you going?" Sudi asked.

"I forgot to tell Abdel that The Jackal had opened," she lied.

"I'm sure he knows," Dalila said. "You haven't eaten your pancakes."

"I'm not hungry," Meri answered over her shoulder.

She ran outside. Rain hit her in a solid sheet, soaking through her clothes. She splashed through the puddles, chasing after Abdel. She wanted to invite him to Michelle's party.

"Abdel!" She yelled and waved.

He turned and held out his umbrella, inviting her under its protection. She stepped next to him and he placed an arm around her.

"You're shivering," he said, pulling her close to him. "Your teeth are chattering. Didn't you bring a coat?"

"It's a long story," she said, cuddling against him.

Now that she stood close to him, pressed against his warm chest and looking up into his eyes, she felt too shy to ask him to go to the party with her. She hadn't thought this through.

"What did you want?" he asked when she didn't speak. "Is something wrong? Did something more happen last night?"

She shook her head. He leaned down, studying her eyes, his breath mingling with hers. She wondered if he could hear her galloping heartbeat over the rain.

"Meri," he said gently, "if nothing is wrong, I need to go home and study."

"I was wondering if you—" Her stomach growled noisily, and she pressed her hands against her waist, trying to stop the sound.

"Why didn't you eat?" He took her elbow and led her back to the café. "You need to finish your pancakes."

"No!" she said loudly.

"What is it?" he asked.

He looked like any sixteen-year-old guy, but if he was an Hour priest, then he had probably lived for a few thousand years. She wondered how many girlfriends he had had in that time. Probably none that looked like a wet surf rat, like Meri. She wished she could be glamorous like Dalila, or have Sudi's confidence. He'd probably never go out with a foolish, simple tomboy.

"Never mind," she said and started to walk away.

He kept pace with her, holding the umbrella over her head. "If something happened, you have to tell me," he said.

"Just go back to all your Cleopatras," Meri said glumly. "I imagine you'll be happier with them."

He chuckled. "How did we get from Apep to Cleopatra?" He stepped in front of Meri and made her stop. Then, with his free hand, he lifted her chin until she was forced to look into his eyes. "Tell me."

"I just wanted—" she stammered and stopped. She should never have followed him outside. She wasn't good at flirting.

Abdel frowned.

"Why do you always act like I'm a nuisance?" she asked. "I can't control the way I feel."

Understanding softened his eyes. "You don't need to feel afraid," he said. "I promise, I'll protect you. I'll find a way for you to stop Apep."

"That's not it." She looked down at a puddle, suddenly realizing that he wasn't going to leave until he knew what was bothering her. She took a deep breath and lifted her head.

"Michelle is——" she started again and stopped abruptly when he glanced at his watch. "Can't you see I'm trying to ask you out?" she asked, completely flustered.

He didn't say a word, and she couldn't read his expression. Then he smiled. Was he laughing at her?

"You're the most irritating person I've ever met in my life!" she yelled.

A sudden burst of light blinded her, and at first she thought it was lightning. But then another flash and another quickly followed the first. Thimble and his companion had jumped from an SUV parked at the curb and were taking photos of what they probably thought was a lovers' spat.

Meri turned and stomped away, her shoes making that terrible sucking sound. She couldn't even ask a guy for a date, let alone have a first kiss. Between the paparazzi, the Secret Service, and her own inability to deal with guys, she probably wasn't going to lose her virginity until she was forty-one, if then.

It felt like the worst day of her life.

The photographers kept walking with her,

jumping in front of her and taunting her, trying to trigger a reaction, but she was too sad to react. After the initial burst of anger, she had been left with a funny, hollow feeling inside. She was glad the rain was pelting her face so they couldn't see the tears welling up in her eyes.

When she didn't make faces at the camera, or try to run, the photographers became bored with her and left.

As their SUV drove away, she let the tears fall. Why had she moved here? She imagined her friends back in L.A., down at the beach. At least there, she had been able to lose herself in the waves.

She had been so deep in thought that she hadn't heard the voice calling her name.

When at last the shouting came into her awareness, she brushed back her dripping wet hair, wiped her nose, and turned with a huge smile on her face, expecting to see Abdel running after her.

"Michelle's having another party," Sudi yelled, holding her umbrella over Meri's head.

Meri looked down the street. Abdel had vanished. She folded her arms over her chest against the cold. Her jacket was soaked and stank of wet wool, but worse, rain was dripping down her back, and her hunger was turning into sharp stomach pains.

"How did you find out?" Meri asked over the

sound of her teeth chattering. "I thought Michelle was only inviting kids from Entre Nous."

Sudi put her arm around Meri and squeezed her tightly, trying to make her warm.

"Carter got an invitation," Dalila explained. "But I don't have a cell phone—"

"So he called me because he knew Dalila was with us and he wanted to invite her," Sudi raced on excitedly, her happiness escalating to a level that Meri couldn't bear. "We have to go," she continued. "Scott will be there. Let me see the invitation."

When Meri didn't move fast enough, Sudi snatched the envelope from her jacket pocket and tore it open.

"Read the fine print," Meri warned. "It's going to be a karaoke party, and Michelle expects everyone to sing." Meri felt miserable, and it wasn't just from shivering and not eating. Without Abdel, the party sounded like a night in hell.

"Singing will just add to the fun." Sudi pulled out the invitation. "Besides, it can't be bad if Michelle is giving it. She spends like a zillion dollars on her gala fetes."

Sudi's excitement ended. A high whistle

escaped her lips. She handed the invitation to Dalila and shook her head.

Dalila began reading; her regal bearing seemed to slump. A sudden gust tore her umbrella from her hand, and she didn't even try to catch it. It cartwheeled down the street, a streak of red in the gray storm.

Dalila stared at Meri. Rainwater ran in tiny rivulets over her perfect features and twisted down her thin neck.

"We have to go." Dalila pointed to the location written on the invitation.

"Just because it's at The Jackal?" Meri didn't finish her sentence but turned and started tramping through the puddles. They couldn't make her go just because she was a Descendant.

Sudi ran after her. "Why are you so upset?"

"We don't have time for parties. We have to fight Apep. All right?" Meri answered, but that wasn't the reason for her anxiety. "I think that's enough to make me tense." She continued with her lie. "My life cannot get any—" She stopped. Every time she had said that lately, another problem had been dumped on top of the ones she already had.

"I'm going to talk to Abdel and see if he wants to go," Dalila said behind her.

Meri spun around. She hadn't sensed any teasing in Dalila's voice, whose expression remained tense.

"I think he should be with us the first time we go to The Jackal." Dalila handed the soggy invitation back to Meri. The blue ink had run until the letters were long blotches.

Meri let it fall to the ground, and the rainwater washed it into the gutter.

Then Dalila and Meri linked arms with Sudi and squeezed under her umbrella. They began walking toward the Capitol.

"Abdel won't go to a party," Sudi said. "He's way too stuffy. He probably doesn't even know how to dance."

Meri started to defend Abdel, but Dalila spoke first.

"Do you think this means that Michelle has joined the cult?" she asked.

"Michelle's too self-centered to join any group that doesn't center around her," Sudi answered bitterly.

But Meri wondered. Perhaps Michelle hated Meri for a reason other than simple jealousy. Maybe they were enemies fighting on different sides of the ancient battle between order and chaos.

Meri stared into her dressing-table mirror and smoothed on lip plumper. She loved the sting, but when she puckered up, she didn't see any change. Then, she worried that the thick layer of balm might make her lips taste like Vicks. She grabbed a Kleenex and rubbed until her lips burned. When she had finished, tiny flecks of tissue covered her chin.

Dalila and Sudi stared at her.

"Why are you so nervous?" Dalila asked.

"I don't know why I care what I look like," Meri complained. "The cult is probably using Michelle's party to trap us, anyway." Meri threw down the tube and sprawled across her bed. "Forget it. I can't go."

"Of course you're going," Sudi said as she added lilac eye shadow above her own spiky lashes.

"I can feel magic gathering around us," Dalila said. She took a kohl liner from her velvet draw-string bag, kneeled beside the bed, and gently began outlining Meri's eyes.

"How do you always stay so calm?" Meri asked, loving the attention.

"I'll share one of my secrets with you some-time, when you really need it," Dalila said. "But if I showed you right now, you'd laugh at me."

"Try us." Sudi pulled a sheer top over her silky camisole. "Do you royals really have secrets that you keep from all the plebeians like me?"

"I have something better than a secret," Dalila said mysteriously. She stood and picked up her velvet bag, then carried it over to the bay window. She pulled out three red votive candles and set them on the sill. After that, she took out a book of matches. "Ancient Egyptians didn't have matches or use candles, but I needed one flame for each of us, and this was the best I could do."

"For what?" Meri asked, bouncing off the bed and joining her.

Dalila seemed breathless and excited. Her enthusiasm spread through the room, infecting Meri.

Sudi sat down on the window seat, still using a fluffy makeup brush to sweep bronze shimmer over her cheeks. "What are you doing?"

Dalila smiled. "Thoughts are like magnets, and we draw into our lives what we think about most."

Sudi and Meri nodded.

"This past week we've been focused on the cult and Apep," Dalila continued.

"What else should we be thinking about?" Sudi countered and tapped the makeup brush against her palm.

"This could be our last—" Meri stopped. She couldn't bring herself to say the word.

"But if it is our last night," Dalila went on, "then let's concentrate on something that will give us joy." The match flared, and she lit the candles one at a time. "Great Isis, goddess of love, hear us," Dalila began. "We entreat you to turn our thoughts to love and romance."

Meri smiled. Unexpected warmth flowed up her arm and into her heart. She touched her chest and suddenly imagined Abdel's lips touching hers. She caught her breath and placed her fingers over her mouth. The sensation felt too real.

"Woo-hoo!" Sudi shouted. "Did you put a spell on us?"

"No," Dalila said. "Isis made you stop worrying about all the bad things that could happen, and she turned your mind to concentrate instead on all the good fun you're going to have tonight."

"But you must have done something." Meri strode over to her full-length mirror. Dalila had made her eyes smoky and sexy. She suddenly felt all glamorous and seductive in her chiffon skirt and lace tunic. Her bare legs looked luxurious and long in her spiky sandals. She wiggled her toes to show off the three toe rings she wore for good luck.

"Wow," she whispered, then spun around. "Dalila, what did you do, really?"

"Nothing." Dalila smiled. "Isis banished your doubts so you could feel the confidence with which you were born. That's all."

"Come on, gorgeous," Sudi teased and grabbed Meri's arm. "Let's go, before all the cute guys are taken."

"You mean, before Michelle gets Scott," Meri teased back.

Sudi stared at herself in the mirror. "With the way Dalila made me look tonight, that's impossible."

"I told you. I didn't do anything," Dalila said lightheartedly. "You're just feeling what's inside you."

Meri set her cell phone on the dressing table and tucked her house key into her skirt pocket. She wanted her hands free—she smiled to herself, imagining Abdel—just in case the mental image she had had of the kiss came true.

Less than an hour later, Meri, Dalila, and Sudi strode down Seventh Street in the Penn Quarter, their high-heeled sandals tapping out their pace. The spicy smells from the restaurants in Chinatown wafted around them as they neared The Jackal, and the pulse of music came through the walls, flowing out into the night.

"We're here to party," Sudi reminded the other two and gave them each a mint from her tin.

"Party," Meri agreed without any enthusiasm and bit into the candy.

"*An arit sen tet er a,*" Dalila recited as they stepped past the gilded wooden figures of pharaohs that lined the façade.

"May they not do evil to me," Meri whispered, repeating Dalila's invocation in English. Sudi mouthed the words with her.

Meri pushed through the revolving door. The rubber edges of the black glass panels made soft, swooshing sounds as the door turned.

Once inside, they stood in an entrance hall paved with glittering gold tiles and flanked with statues of reclining black jackals. From hidden speakers, the wild dogs' howls filled the passageway.

"Do you think it's a trap?" Meri asked.

"There's only one way to find out." Dalila started forward with the confidence of a queen.

At the other end of the entry, two bare-chested men wearing low-slung white kilts opened a second set of doors and waited for the girls to step through the threshold into utter darkness.

"Jeez," Sudi muttered. "Where's the party?"

The doors slammed behind them, leaving them in complete blackness. They waited, clutching each other, as their eyes adjusted to the gloom.

A warm air current encircled them, caressing their arms and bringing the scent of sun-scorched sand.

"Are we sure we're inside the club?" Dalila moved away from them toward a glimmering light.

Meri joined her, spellbound. A starry night covered the huge, vaulted ceiling above them.

"It looks like we're standing near the pyramids on the Giza Plateau," Dalila said, staring at the scene of a desert night painted on the wall.

The angry thump of music broke their trance.

"Come on," Sudi yelled excitedly.

Meri ran down a curving ramp that led out on to a vast dance floor.

Light shuddered across the dancers, and the beat rushed through Meri with a hypnotic feel, enticing her to move.

The fragrances from designer perfumes filled the room, mixing into one blissful scent. She flung her hands over her head and slid between two guys. Sudi and Dalila moved with her, hips undulating, bodies close, pressed next to strangers on the crowded dance floor.

A guttural yell made them stop. They glanced at each other.

"Is someone hurt?" Dalila asked.

"That's someone's pathetic attempt at singing," Sudi explained.

Two voices squawked and bawled, destroying the guitar-driven music.

Meri and Dalila started laughing.

Sudi grabbed their arms. "Let's find out who's ruining the song."

Scott and his friend Carter stood onstage, singing off key and laughing at their inability to read the lyrics scrolling on the prompter.

"You guys need help!" Sudi's ex-boyfriend Brian yelled as he jumped up on the stage, joining them. He swung his head and began playing air guitar. Then he pushed between Carter and Scott, his lips on the mike. His deep, hoarse voice made everyone laugh.

Brian's new girlfriend, Dominique, placed her hand over her mouth and turned her back to the stage so he couldn't see her giggling.

"I love karaoke," Sudi said, beaming. "It's making Brian look like a fool."

Her breakup with Brian had been bad, but she had never told Meri everything that had happened between them.

"Get off it, Brian," someone yelled. "We want to dance, and you're killing the music."

Brian answered with an obscene gesture.

More kids booed him.

Sudi stopped laughing; her nervous stare made Meri take her hand.

"Are you all right?" Meri asked.

"Brian's getting upset," Sudi explained, no longer enjoying the taunts flung at him from the audience. She began easing back, pulling Dalila and Meri with her.

Without warning, Brian broke into a run, his footsteps pounding loudly. When he reached the edge of the stage, he dove onto the audience, his arms spread wide. Kids squealed and ducked. He landed on enough people to cushion his fall and cause pain for others.

Guys cursed and complained and dumped Brian in front of Sudi.

Brian and Sudi glared at each other; Brian's lip curled as if he were going to say something, but before he did, Dominique placed her arms around his waist and leaned against his back.

"You were marvelous," she said in her French accent.

Brian smiled broadly. "Yeah, marvelous."

Sudi rolled her eyes, but Brian didn't catch her look of disdain. Meri wondered what he would have done if he had.

Suddenly, Carter shoved through the crowd.

"I was afraid you weren't going to come to the party after all." He kissed Dalila's cheek. His lips lingered, and he whispered something into her ear.

Dalila placed her hands on his chest.

A slow song began, and Carter danced Dalila away from them.

"I hate that she's with Carter," Sudi said to Meri. "I tried to warn her."

Carter attended Lincoln High and was one of Sudi's best friends, in spite of his reputation as a heartbreaker.

"I know," Meri agreed, as a jealous ache filled her chest. "But it's not fair. Dalila has lived a sheltered life, and yet she's so natural with the guys."

"Maybe if you believed you were being reared to marry a king, a guy like Carter wouldn't be a challenge to you, either," Sudi offered and squeezed Meri. "Besides, all your fidgeting and giggles are adorable."

"I doubt that," Meri answered, trying to squelch her envy before it turned into bitterness.

"Let's go find the buffet," Sudi said. "Chocolate will make you feel better."

Meri started after her, but Michelle blocked their way. She had added lash extensions, and her skin had the glow of self-tanner.

"Meri, I'm so glad you brought friends," Michelle said, even though her heavily lashed eyes expressed anger. "Hi, Sudi," she added in a petulant tone as Scott pushed into their circle.

"Scott." Michelle posed seductively.

"Hi, Michelle," he said, and then, ignoring her, he turned to Sudi. "Do you want to dance? The singers aren't the best, but—"

"I wanted Sudi to sing," Michelle broke in. She pursed her lips in a babyish pout. "It's my party, and everyone has to perform."

"Sorry," Scott said, throwing Michelle a broad smile. "Sudi's taken."

Michelle watched Sudi and Scott until they disappeared behind other dancers. Then she wheeled around and scowled at Meri.

"Look at what you've done. Sudi's going to steal him from both of us. She's such a—" Michelle interrupted herself with a loud huff and ran her fingers over the hem of her ruffled pink mini. "I'd tell you what she is, but I don't use that kind of word, because it's too déclassé."

"She's really popular and well liked," Meri offered. "Is that what you were going to say? That she's such a great person?"

Michelle looked at Meri with the purest expression of hate. "Next time, don't bring any tagalongs unless you get my approval first." She stomped off.

But something other than Michelle was bothering Meri. She squeezed into the crowd, unmindful of the feet stepping on her toes, and continued shoving through the throng of dancers until she could see Scott and Sudi again.

When she had talked to Scott about Sudi at

school, he had said that she brought him bad luck. But at the moment, he was holding her and looking into her eyes as if he were about to kiss her. That worried Meri, and she wondered what had changed his mind. She hoped it was how gorgeous Sudi looked that night and not the demon growing stronger inside him.

An odd tingling on the back of Meri's neck made her turn around.

A man Meri recognized as the club owner stood at the edge of the dance floor, staring angrily at her. His head was shaved, and his scalp reflected the dim light. He wore a tailored suit and a black sweater. A large gold ankh hung from his neck, a talisman that kept him alive. Meri had seen him perform arcane rites while dressed in leopard skins, his eyes lined in kohl; she had also watched him die, when Sudi tore the ankh from its chain. He was the high priest of the cult. They had encountered him when they had rescued Scott.

Dancers bumped in front of Meri, crowding between her and the club owner.

When finally she made her way to the other side of the couples, the man was gone. Now she wondered how many of the kids at Michelle's party had joined the cult. And if they had, she hoped they weren't dedicated to bringing chaos into the world.

Unexpectedly, someone grabbed her arms. She flinched and turned around, expecting to see the club owner. Instead, Jeff smiled down at her. He was a junior at Lincoln High, and a friend of Sudi's. She had introduced him to Meri at Michelle's last party.

"You look pretty." He slid his hands around her waist. "I was hoping you'd be here tonight so we could dance."

But the way he caressed her made her think he wanted to do more than dance. She tried to ease away and keep space between their bodies, but he pressed closer, his jeans rough against her thighs.

She pushed against his chest.

In response he smirked. His fingers slipped under her tunic, and he ran his palms over her bare skin.

She stiffened.

"Why are you so nervous?" he asked, grinning at her jumpiness. "I thought you liked me."

"As a friend." Meri tried to slip away from him.

He leaned down and nuzzled her neck.

"Jeff!" someone shouted.

Suddenly, Sudi was there, forcing herself between them, her hips slinking against Jeff, making him drop his hold on Meri.

"You promised you'd dance with me," Sudi said with a flirty smile and purposefully stretched her arms, letting her lacy top and camisole rise in a tease that gave Jeff a peek at her flat stomach and hip bones.

Scott stood nearby, watching Sudi. He placed a comforting arm around Meri and spoke into her ear. "Sudi said we had to rescue you," he said. "Was she right?"

"Yes." Meri let out a long sigh. From the corner of her eye, she caught a blur of pink. Michelle was marching toward Scott.

Sudi grabbed Michelle's arm before she could latch on to Scott. "Michelle's been dying to hook up with you," she said to Jeff. Spinning around, she playfully shoved Michelle into Jeff's arms.

Michelle glared at Sudi, then smiled up at Jeff

and fanned her face with her hands. "It's too hot. I think I need to get a drink." She disappeared again.

Sudi pulled Meri over to the far wall. "Don't let a guy stampede you into doing more than you're ready to do," Sudi scolded. "You'll be sorry if you do."

"How did you know I was uncomfortable?" Meri asked.

"I know who your crush is. Even though Jeff thinks he's it, I know he's not," Sudi answered.

"You know?" Meri asked.

"Like Dalila and I haven't figured out that you're totally crushing on Abdel," Sudi said. "We were just waiting for you to say something."

"Why didn't you tell me I was being so obvious?" Meri ran her fingers through her hair. Then another thought came to her, and she felt ashamed and foolish. "Abdel must think I'm a total loser. I'll never be able to face him again."

"Yes, you will, and you'll get your kiss, too," Sudi answered confidently. "Come on, dance with us."

Sudi and Scott tried to pull Meri on to the

dance floor, but she eased back against the wall. She stared at the floor and started to zone with all the other rejects lined up beside her. If Abdel did know, then why hadn't he said something to her?

The music stopped abruptly, and she glanced up.

Michelle walked across the stage and tapped the mike. Feedback screeched across the room, and everyone covered their ears.

"Meri Stark has wanted to sing since she got here, but she's just too shy to take the stage on her own," Michelle yelled.

Meri's eyes widened. She gazed at Michelle, unable to believe what she was doing.

Everyone standing near Meri turned and looked at her, with huge, silly smiles.

"Let's give it up for Meri," Michelle squealed and began clapping.

Kids whistled and hooted. Hands were everywhere, pushing, pulling, prodding her toward the stage.

"Let's see you handle this," Michelle said as she handed Meri the mike.

"Michelle, you're going to feel worse if you make me sing," Meri warned. "You don't want to do this."

"Please," Michelle answered. "Why would *I* feel bad if *you* make a fool of yourself? Pick out your song."

Meri scrolled through the list, then punched in the numbers for a ballad she had sung back in California. She'd never told anyone that she'd been in a girl band. They'd even recorded a demo, *Bust My Heart*, which had been a hit on the local radio stations until her mother's campaign advisers had decided that it wasn't decent for the daughter of a presidential hopeful to sing about lust.

The music started. Pounding drums shook the walls, marking out the beat. Meri could feel the tension rising in the audience.

Michelle stood next to Brian. The two of them snickered and made faces.

Sudi held up her hands to show Meri her crossed fingers.

Meri closed her eyes and belted out the first note. The purity of the tone rose in the room. She finished singing the first few lines and looked at the crowd. Kids started dancing. Others edged closer to the stage and gazed up at her.

Slowly, she scanned the crowd. She loved to perform.

Then she saw Abdel and her heart took on a quicker rhythm.

He stood alone in the middle of the dancers, watching her. He wore a crazy porkpie hat that was different from his usual conservative style, and a slouchy gray coat that made her want to laugh. She wondered if he had dressed that way for her.

For the first time since she'd met him, his expression was unguarded, and she recognized the longing in his gaze; she had seen it on other faces when she performed.

Maybe he did like her.

She sang in a soft, low voice, crooning about love, and imagined his arms around her.

Gradually, she became aware that others were looking in the direction of her gaze. She had been so infatuated with Abdel that she had forgotten her audience. She pulled her mind back to her performance, but in her nervousness, she forgot the lyrics. That had never happened before. She stammered and foolishly tried to fill in with *la-la-la*s.

Brian laughed, and Michelle grinned triumphantly.

Meri hummed, distraught, and felt the heat of a blush rising to her cheeks. She looked down at the prompter, but she couldn't find her place, and when she thought she had, she sang the wrong words.

She set the mike in its stand and ran off the stage.

Kids clapped, stamped their feet, and yelled out their praise, some calling for her to come back and sing more. But she felt woozy from nerves and leaned against the wall, afraid that if she didn't hold on to something, she'd lose her balance and fall.

Dalila and Sudi joined her

"Why did you run off the stage?" Sudi asked. "You have an incredible voice."

"Everyone loved your singing," Dalila agreed, hugging her. "You should go back and sing another song."

Meri shook her head. "I think I'd better go home."

"Abdel came here for a reason," Sudi said, seeming to read her mind.

"Yeah," Meri said. "He came here to check out The Jackal." She pressed her fingers over her eyes. "I can't believe I made such a fool of myself in front of everyone."

"He came here to see you," Dalila reassured her. "Ask him to dance. He's probably as shy as you are."

"Maybe you'll get your first kiss," Sudi teased and nudged Meri playfully.

"I'll show you my secret for regaining composure." Dalila took Meri's hand and forced the fingers into a fist. "Now, tap on your breastbone, smile, and think of someone you love."

"You're not serious," Meri said.

"I warned you that you'd laugh at me if I shared one of my secrets with you," Dalila said. "It's called the thymus thump, and it's been proven to revitalize your energy. Say 'ha-ha-ha' with each tap."

Meri shrugged, then stroked her breastbone with quick, light blows, feeling foolish as she recited the "ha-ha-ha." But she did feel better.

"It works," she said, startled.

"Now, go," Sudi said, pushing her onto the jammed dance floor.

Kids smiled at Meri and complimented her singing as she squeezed between them.

Then she saw Abdel, and her heart dropped.

He was dancing with Michelle.

CHAPTER 8

Michelle caught Meri's gaze and smiled wickedly as she worked her fingers over Abdel's shoulders. Then she raised one eyebrow and mouthed the word *mine*.

After that, she pulled his head down toward hers and closed her eyes, parting her lips in anticipation.

Meri wasn't going to watch Michelle steal the kiss that should have been her own. She elbowed past the dancers, frantic to leave, and rushed outside before anyone could see her tears.

She charged down the sidewalk, expecting the pop of a paparazzi flash to blind her.

When nothing happened, she kicked off her sandals and ran wildly, her feet slapping against the cold concrete. She let her tears come.

A car engine started.

She glanced over her shoulder. She couldn't bear to have photographers stalking her. She darted across the street and hid in an alley, behind some empty mango and pear crates.

An SUV rolled past her. Thimble sat in the driver's seat, one hand on the steering wheel, the other holding his camera, ready to shoot.

When the car turned at the corner, she started jogging again, ignoring the stares of people watching her through restaurant windows.

She had gone only a few blocks when lightning streaked across the sky. Moments later, a thunderclap shattered the night. The boom reverberated down the street, setting off car alarms.

Clouds formed, billowing and growing with

uncanny speed, and soon the rain came, splashing into puddles left over from the last storm.

As she neared her house, the night took on a sinister feel. She quickened her pace, wanting nothing more than to be home, cuddled in bed with a glass of milk and a handful of cookies, reading and—

Something moved in the deeper shadows near the house just ahead.

Fear swept through her.

Instinct told her to run, but when she looked again, she saw nothing in the gloomy night that should have made her feel so afraid.

Wind whipped through the trees, lashing branches back and forth, and making gray shadows swirl.

Maybe a photographer was stealthily following her, hoping to get a picture of her running in the rain, barefoot, wet, and shivering in her skimpy California clothes.

But fear also made her senses sharper; if someone were stalking her, surely she'd have been able to hear him prowling through the wet shrubs and grass. She paused and tilted her head, concentrating, but the rain hid any noise someone trailing her might have made.

Even so, her feeling of danger did not go away.

Cautiously, she stepped backward. Her ability to change into a cat had also given her the feline instincts to sense a predator.

Something brushed against her leg. She cried out and turned, ready to fight.

Three cats wagged their tails, their fur drenched and clinging to their thin, trembling bodies.

She fell to her knees, and by an odd telepathy, sensed their rising terror.

"What is it?" she asked, knowing they couldn't understand her question.

And then, with a shock that made adrenaline race through her blood, she knew that an ancient evil had been slinking after her and hiding in the shadows near the houses.

The cats had seen the twisting snake and had come to warn her.

"Apep?" she whispered. No sooner had the name come into her mind than the cats scurried away, bellies low to the ground in fear.

At the same moment the stormy night filled with the scent of cucumbers and mold.

Meri stood and stepped between two cars parked near the curb. Runoff waters rushed over her feet. She willed her body to change, but not all the way. Whiskers prickled through her cheeks. Then, in a burst, her feline vision came.

The demon Apep swept toward her, leaving a trail of greenish foam in his wake. The snake had become larger; he was the size of an anaconda that could easily wrap around her chest and squeeze until she couldn't draw a breath.

The serpent opened his mouth, fangs exposed, tongue flickering, and shrieked as lightning seared across the night.

Apep flailed his tail, coiling eagerly toward her at a speed that seemed impossible.

She froze, trying to decide what to do. She couldn't outrun the creature as she was, but if she changed into a cat, she could climb a tree and flee across the rooftops.

Still watching Apep, she backed into the street and began reciting the incantation to change. She stepped onto the next curb.

Apep followed her. The sound of his scales scraping over the pavement became louder than the pounding rain, the rhythm quicker.

Meri concentrated and intoned the spell again. She moved on to her neighbor's lawn, near a tree. Her clothing disappeared, and she stood naked in the rain before black fur covered her.

The muscles in her back quivered; she began to shrink. When she was able to open her cat eyes, Apep was only two feet away, his fetid breath steaming around her.

The snake struck.

She jumped to one side and hissed.

The serpent's fangs caught in the wet ground. It furiously thrashed about, trying to break free from the mud.

Meri scrambled up the tree and crouched. She scanned the lawn below. Leaves and branches waved in front of her, making it impossible to see clearly. Still, she should have seen some trace of the snake. Where had he gone?

The tree swayed, and at first she thought the wind had made the movement. Then she looked down. The reptile had curled himself around the trunk and was spiraling toward her, his lurid green eyes hungry and focused on her.

Her heart pounded fiercely. She leapt to the roof of the nearby house, but rain had made the pitched slope slick and she slid backward, catching herself in the rain gutter.

Wind lashed around her. She struggled to keep her balance.

A flash of lightning startled her.

She lost her grip and fell, twisting and turning, to land on her paws. She hit the soggy ground, then shot off and raced down the street as Apep uncurled himself from the tree.

Thunder rumbled around her, making her ears ache. She sped to her front porch and desperately tried to change back into a girl. She sensed that Apep wouldn't be able to follow her inside.

She concentrated. Her bones ached, and her tendons quivered, but she remained a cat.

The sickening smell of Apep filled the air. The hair on her back rose in little spikes.

She turned and faced the demon. As she tried to decide whether to fight or try to outrun it again, someone picked her up.

She hissed and clawed, thrashing about, struggling to break free.

Whoever held her petted her, trying to calm her. She could feel the transformation starting, becoming stronger than her ability to hold it back. She couldn't let the person holding her witness her change.

She twisted violently as her bones began to stretch. Her fur dissolved, and slick, wet skin grew around her hands and arms. She had transformed.

The night spun dizzily around her.

The person holding her caught her before she fell.

Unexpectedly, Apep bellowed and turned away, but the hands holding Meri didn't let go.

Anyone but a cult member would have fainted or screamed when she changed. Apep hadn't been trying to capture her after all. The ancient demon had been chasing her toward the cult member waiting for her at home.

Defeated, Meri turned to face her captor.

The cloudburst ended, and the night filled with the sound of gushing water. Rooftops and trees shed the downpour, filling drainpipes and gutters. The lush fragrance of wet earth and grass scented the air but Meri still tasted fear.

"At least let me see your face," she grumbled and kicked. Her bare foot brushed over a pant leg and hit the porch step, jamming her toes. Pain shot up her leg.

"Soul of Egypt," a voice soothed. "Why are you still fighting me?" The hands released her.

Meri looked up and gasped. Abdel stared down at her. She had been rescued, not captured.

"You saved me," she said. Tension drained from her arms and legs, leaving her light-headed and weak. "How did you make Apep leave?"

"The demon's not yet strong enough to fight us both," he replied, "but soon he will be."

"Us?" Meri gazed up at him. "You did it. I couldn't—"

Abdel placed the tips of his fingers on her lips to quiet her. "You didn't need me," he explained. "You would have won this encounter."

"I doubt it," Meri said and started to shiver.

Abdel placed his hands on her shoulders. With a start she realized he was touching bare skin. Terror had consumed her, and she hadn't noticed that her lacy tunic and bra hadn't made the transition with her. She quickly crossed her arms over her chest.

She felt hot tears of embarrassment sting her eyes.

Abdel took off his coat and slipped it over her shoulders.

"I can't believe you saw me," she said, shaking her head.

"You're beautiful," he whispered and tentatively placed his hands around her face. "Why did you leave the party?"

She stared into his eyes. How could she tell him that she had been jealous of Michelle?

"I wish you had stayed," he whispered. "I wanted to dance with you."

Her mouth opened, but her brain couldn't find the words to speak.

"I think I know why you left," he said.

"You do?" she asked.

"You saw me with Michelle," he answered.

Meri felt her heart drop.

"Michelle kissed me, but I didn't kiss her," he said. "I pulled away from her, but then you were gone. She was trying to make you jealous."

"If you knew that, then why did you dance with her?" Meri asked.

Abdel hesitated. "I saw you with some-one," he confessed. "Michelle said his name was Jeff and that you liked him."

"I don't," Meri protested. "Michelle just wants to make my life miserable."

Abdel leaned down, his lips close to hers. Her heart raced with excitement.

She held her face up to his, anticipating his touch.

But then he hesitated, inches from her mouth.

Her mind whirled. Did he expect her to give him permission? She didn't know. All her friends had kissed guys, some had done more, but Meri had never asked for the details. Now she wished she had.

"It's okay," she whispered in a jagged voice, feeling suddenly too dizzy to stand.

He pulled back. "What is okay?"

"Kiss me before I faint," she said. Her heart lurched and skipped a beat.

He smiled. Then he closed his eyes and pressed his lips to hers.

She sighed, and her eyes widened. She wanted to remember everything about this kiss; the gentle ache of longing for him, the loving caress of his fingers on her temples and cheeks.

The kiss was over before she wanted it to be.

He pulled back and opened his eyes. A smile broke out across his face.

"You're supposed to close your eyes," he said, playfully shaking her shoulders.

"Of course, I know to close my eyes," she answered.

"Then why didn't you?" he asked.

She couldn't tell him that she had wanted to savor her first kiss.

"You've never kissed a guy before," he said softly. "I forgot that."

Her mind reeled. "Did Sudi tell you?"

"Of course not," he said. "Why would I talk to her about us?"

"Us?" she asked; and just as happiness started to buzz through her, another thought intruded. "Was the kiss that bad?" she asked. Then without pausing, she answered her own question. "That's how you knew it was my first time," she exclaimed. "Because the kiss was so terrible."

She pulled away from Abdel and rubbed her temples. She wished now that she had practiced kissing on the back of her hand or with pillows, as her friends had.

"Don't be upset," Abdel said. He tried to place his arms around her.

Meri jerked away from him, then fumbled in her skirt pocket, pulled out her key, pushed around Abdel, and unlocked the front door.

"What's wrong?" he asked.

She kept her head down, too embarrassed to look at him, and darted into the house.

"Good night." She slammed the door.

Abdel knocked. "Meri, at least talk to me. I didn't mean to upset you. I thought you wanted to kiss me."

"I do. I did," she said to the dark living room.

A miserable heaviness settled inside her. She leaned against the door and wiped her tears. She had wanted her first real kiss to be hearts-and-roses beautiful, a moment to remember for the rest of her life.

"Meri," Abdel called to her through the door.

"Go away," she said. She couldn't face him. She headed for the kitchen and opened the cupboard, pulled out a candy bar, tore off the wrapper, and took a big bite. Chocolate melted over her tongue.

She leaned against the counter and started to take off Abdel's jacket. Something rustled in the right pocket. She felt inside of it and pulled out an envelope. Her name was written across the front.

He hadn't actually given it to her, so maybe she should just leave it. She hesitated, then opened it anyway.

Divine one,

    Isis has sent her burning love fires to me, and all I think about is you. Even with potions and spells I am unable to stop this love that consumes me. What will happen if I make a fatal error because my mind is clouded with love? Worse, I fear that you do not share my feelings, because you act so strangely when I am near. You turn your face away as if you can't bear the sight of me. I have decided to return to Egypt. A new mentor will be sent.

                Fondly,
                Abdel

"No," Meri screamed, surprised at the depth of her emotions.

She ran through the house, opened the front door, and sprinted down the front walk, splashing through the puddles.

At the corner, she stopped and looked both ways.

When she didn't see Abdel, she yelled into the night, "I love you!"

Her words echoed around her, and she knew he was gone.

On Monday morning, Meri threaded her way among the guys clustered in small groups in front of the academy. She sipped her caffe latte, wishing she had added sugar to the bitter brew, and thought about Abdel. He hadn't responded to her e-mails or her text messages. Twice she had gone over to his house, but no one had answered the door.

A low snickering made her pause. She looked at the group of guys standing in front of her. Why were they all staring at her with such dreamy smiles?

"Hi, Meri," Cecil said, and nervously patted his black hair as if he were trying to impress her.

A chorus of hellos followed from the guys standing with him.

"Good morning," Meri answered, unsure why they were watching her.

They turned and stared at her as she headed up the front steps.

Michelle stood near the door, a stack of newspapers flung over her arm. She handed a copy of the *National Enquirer* to each student who entered the school. Gray newsprint covered her fingers; the tips of her French-manicured nails were tinged with black.

"Hi, Meri," she said with too much glee in her voice. She had rimmed her lids with silver, and her sapphire eyes looked brighter.

"What's up?" Meri asked. "It's spooky the way everyone looks so happy."

"You're front-page news," Michelle said with a wicked grin and handed Meri a paper.

The cup slipped from Meri's hand. Hot coffee splattered Michelle's legs and soaked into Meri's socks and shoes, but Meri didn't notice the burn.

"Ouch!" Michelle jumped back and hit the door with a loud bang. "You did that on purpose!"

Meri didn't answer. She stared down at the paper. Someone had followed her and taken her picture as she had transformed. In the first photo, she was walking in the rain, her wet clothes clinging to her body. In the second, she stood under the tree, completely nude as the change started. A flash of lightning had apparently blurred the third shot and, thankfully, it was impossible to make out her whiskers, tail, and shrinking size.

"What's up?" Scott asked, tugging the paper from Meri. His spicy cologne filled the brisk morning air.

"Dang." He glanced at Meri's boxy school jacket. "You should definitely wear tighter clothes."

"She probably posed for the picture," Michelle said. "Can you imagine anyone doing that?"

Scott chuckled. "Michelle, you're not going to win with this one," he said. "Meri looks drop-dead gorgeous."

"She's naked!" Michelle countered.

"Ye-e-e-a-a-ah," Scott said, stretching the word

out in a slow, easy way as he gazed down at the picture again.

"I hate you, Meri!" Michelle stormed inside, but not before Meri grabbed the remaining newspapers from her.

Meri bundled them up and hurried down the steps, ignoring the comments from the guys. When she was far enough away from school, she pitched the papers in a trash bin, keeping two copies. Then she ran out into the street and hailed a cab, already texting a message to Sudi.

Three hours later, Sudi, Dalila, and Meri sat in Meri's bedroom puzzling over the photographs in the *Enquirer*. Sudi had ditched her afternoon classes, and Dalila had had to climb out her bedroom window in order to avoid the bodyguard that her uncle had hired to protect her from the cult.

Dalila kicked off her jeweled thong sandals and leaned against the pillows on Meri's bed, engrossed in looking at the photos.

"A photographer must have followed you when you left The Jackal," Sudi said, gazing down at the paper that she and Meri shared. She looked up again and studied Meri. "No wonder the guys were gawking at you. I mean, you always look so tomboy, and you're really incredible. You should borrow some of my clothes and flaunt yourself a little more. My green—"

"Let's get back to the problem." Meri nervously brushed her fingers through her hair.

"Wow," Sudi said again.

Meri felt a blush rising.

"Your concentration would have been on Apep," Dalila said, "so it's possible you didn't see a photographer."

"I was looking at Apep," Meri added, "so whoever took my picture would have seen the snake, too, and should have been too terrified to take my picture."

"Unless one of the freelance photographers who chases after you has joined the cult," Sudi said. "Maybe the cameraman was hoping to get a more gruesome photo. You know, 'Giant D.C. Snake Eats Girl.'"

Meri shuddered. "I don't like that idea at all."

Dalila crinkled her copy of the paper, then spread it on top of the one that Meri and Sudi had been studying. "I think we have a bigger problem."

She pointed to another article on page three. "Tourists are disappearing near the FDR Memorial," Dalila said. "The memorial is next to the Tidal Basin, and bodies of water have always been entrances to the Netherworld."

"Do you think that's the way Apep is going back and forth to his lair?" Meri asked.

"I'm certain it is," she answered. "We need to find Abdel."

"That could be a problem," Meri said and fell back onto her bed. "I have something to confess."

By the time Meri had finished telling them everything that had happened between her and Abdel, she and her friends had eaten three bags of microwave popcorn and had gone downstairs to the kitchen to start on the chocolate-chip cookies that Georgie had baked before going home.

"We don't have time to wait for a new mentor to find us," Dalila said, frowning.

"You're right," Sudi agreed. "I think we should destroy Apep before he kills more tourists."

"Abdel said not to do anything until he found a protective spell," Meri countered.

"He deserted us," Dalila said with a flash of anger.

"It's my fault," Meri said guiltily.

"He's the mentor," Dalila corrected. "He should know better than to leave us, especially now."

"I agree." Sudi dipped her cookie in a glass of milk. "So how are we going to stop Apep?"

"According to legend, Apep must be dismembered until each bone in his body is separated from the rest," Dalila explained.

"Gross." Sudi set her cookie on a napkin. "That's disgusting. I can't do that. I can't even kill garden snails for my mother. I don't have the stomach to—" She didn't finish her sentence and grimaced.

"Can't we just look in the Book of Thoth?" Meri asked, feeling ill just from imagining getting close enough to Apep to cut through his scales. "Abdel was going to find a spell. So maybe we can."

"Besides, how can we slaughter something as big as an anaconda?" Sudi asked. "We'll have a thousand witnesses and probably become the lead story on the local news."

"We'll do it on Halloween night," Dalila said

calmly. "Then, if anyone sees what we're doing, they'll think it's only holiday shenanigans."

"I've never heard of anyone cutting up a snake on Halloween," Sudi answered.

"It's not exactly a holiday tradition," Meri agreed unhappily.

"The only problem is that we'll need to find sacred knives," Dalila said. She looked at the ceiling as if she were mentally going through museum displays. "Have you seen any in the Smithsonian?"

"You don't expect us to steal something from the Smithsonian, do you?" Meri asked.

"We're supposed to stand against evil," Dalila replied.

"I know we're supposed to do whatever it takes," Sudi said, "but we'll get caught. There's no way."

"All right," Dalila said reluctantly, "I'll look through my uncle's catalog of artifacts. Maybe he has something that he's studying now. Hopefully, he has borrowed a few knives from a museum that we can use."

"I've got to go home," Sudi said as she started for the front door. "Mom's planned a family night."

She shook her head. "Abdel chose the wrong person when he picked me over my sisters. They love this kind of weird stuff."

"He didn't do the choosing," Dalila said, correcting her. "Fate did, when the birthmark was given to you."

Sudi sighed. "Just my luck." She turned at the door and looked back at Meri. "I'm scared."

"Me, too," Meri replied.

Dalila didn't say anything. Tears rimmed her eyes.

Meri hugged them each good-bye.

After Sudi and Dalila left, Meri went back to the kitchen to rinse out their milk glasses. *Washingtonian* magazine lay open on the counter.

Fear raced up her spine. The magazine hadn't been there before. She would have noticed it. She walked over to it and stared down at a full-page advertisement for the Anubis Spa, announcing the opening of a special exhibit of ancient Egyptian relics that included ritual knives.

$\mathcal{S}$

$\mathbf{M}$eri stood on the street corner, all attitude and tough demeanor, even though her heart was racing. She stared up at the Anubis Building, then lifted the huge sunglasses she had just bought from a vendor and scanned the block behind her to make sure no photographers had spotted her in spite of her disguise.

She had slicked back her hair and redefined her eyebrows—not that anyone was going to see her eyes—but the arch jutting over her brow did not look like her. Neither did the tailored pantsuit that Roxanne had picked out for her. She fiddled with the collar to make sure her pink T-shirt wasn't showing, and waited.

After a car passed, she crossed the street and prayed that no one saw the outline of the Bermuda shorts she wore under her slacks. She carried a computer case in which she had packed a cotton hat, flip-flops, a moist cloth, and her papyrus from the Book of Thoth. She hoped that anyone who saw her would think she was a college intern who worked in the congressional offices.

Black glass covered the building facade and reflected the line of orange school buses parked at the curb. The front door opened, and children burst outside, running past Meri and shouting to each other about mummies and cat coffins.

Meri hadn't told Dalila or Sudi about her plan. She sensed that the advertisement so boldly left on her kitchen counter had been more trick than invitation. She was probably heading into a trap. Still, she had to take the risk. They needed the knives to stop Apep.

She stepped into the lobby, clutching the strap of the computer case so no one would see her hands trembling, and walked with purposeful steps through the flow of children still exiting the building.

Moments later, she entered the exhibit hall. The lights were dim, other than those focused on the artifacts in the display cases. She started forward and nearly bumped into a man before she realized he was the spa owner.

Adrenaline shot through her, and her mouth went dry with fear.

She strode past him, her back twitching, and pretended to examine the canopic jars.

The sound of rhythmic clapping startled her. Rattles and drums joined the noise.

She stepped between two large sarcophagi as a parade of eager children marched past her. Some shook sistrums, and others beat on drums. Those who didn't have instruments clapped and jumped. Their teacher beamed, enjoying their excitement.

Two security guards followed the group into the room. The larger one, with sunburned cheeks, checked his watch.

Meri turned her face away and pretended to read a plaque describing a blue glass headrest.

When the guards passed, she hurried down a hallway to the next exhibit room. She had gone only a few steps when she heard someone behind her. She turned abruptly.

Her sudden movement startled two young boys who had been creeping up behind her, probably bored with the artifacts and playing at being spies. They laughed and ran back to the first room.

Meri walked past more display cases, her urgency building. She sensed she was running out of time, and still she had not found the knives.

Then a distant voice spoke. ". . . The ancient Egyptians valued tranquility and order. . . ."

A guide was bringing another group of children through.

Meri needed to steal the knives and leave before the tour caught up to her. She quickened her pace.

In the next row, knives with slashing blades and lotus-flower handles sat in a display, along with jewel-encrusted daggers made from gold, bronze, and lapis lazuli.

She bent closer, studying the hieroglyphs engraved in the metal, until her breath fogged the glass. Then she saw what she wanted. A knife with a long, scalloped blade and an alabaster handle carved in the form of the fierce war goddess Sekhmet. Her name meant "the powerful one," and her fury was so devastating that other gods had had to intervene to save humankind from her destruction.

Meri looked around the room. She didn't see anyone, not even a security guard. That struck her as odd, but she couldn't think about it at the moment.

She shut the doors, closing the only entrance into the room other than an emergency exit, and quickly slipped a dead bolt into place.

She raced back to the display, unzipped the computer case, and pulled out the papyrus. Her heart pounded as she stared down at the spell she intended to use.

Both Dalila and Abdel had cautioned her about calling forth the goddess Sekhmet. Invoking her name could unleash terrifying power.

Meri closed her eyes and lifted her arms.

"Now I speak the terrible name Sekhmet," she

whispered, "and call forth her power. Open the seal, that I might have the knives to protect the world from the fiend Apep."

Then she read from the scroll. *"Behen a Sebau, se hetem na Apep,"* she intoned. "May I crush the evil one, may I destroy Apep."

Hot desert winds blew into the room, flapping her suit jacket as the scorching gust whirled around her.

The lioness-headed goddess appeared in a storm of sand, and with uncanny grace she walked over to the knife display and opened it.

The goddess vanished, and someone began screaming.

Meri whipped around.

The two boys who had followed her before stared at her, their faces covered with sand, screeching.

"No one is going to hurt you," Meri said, trying to reassure them. "Please be quiet."

When she lifted the knives from the display, an alarm went off. She clenched her jaw, bracing herself against the ear-piercing sound, and dropped the knives into her computer case. Shouting came from the hallway. The locked door shook as people on the other side banged against it, trying to break into the room. The boys ran to the door, sobbing and crying for help.

Meri set the papyrus on top of the knives, closed the case, and hurried across the room. She slammed through the emergency exit and rushed into a narrow passageway between the buildings. The stench of garbage was overwhelming.

She threw off her sunglasses, stepped out of her heels, and tore off her suit as sirens became louder than the alarms. With trembling fingers, she snapped her computer case open, grabbed the cotton sun hat and set it on her head, then yanked out the canvas tote and jammed the knives and papyrus inside it. Quickly she set her flip-flops on the ground, stepped into them, and grabbed the cloth. She left the computer case and ran toward the street, scrubbing off her fake eyebrows. Barely able to breathe, she turned the corner.

The alarms stopped, but her ears continued ringing.

At last she eased into the crowd that had gathered in front of the Anubis Building. She now wore the loose pink T and Bermuda shorts that she had worn under the suit and looked like any high school girl who had come to the District on her senior trip to the capital.

Something trickled across her palm. She looked down and saw her blood spattered on the sidewalk. She had cut her finger on one of the blades. Feeling dizzy, she wrapped the cut in the tail of her T-shirt. She needed to sit down before she fainted.

Her knees trembled, but she remained standing and mentally went back over what she had done. She had never had her fingerprints taken, so the impressions she had left behind could never lead the detectives to her. She had removed the labels from the pantsuit, so the clothing left in the alley wouldn't provide a clue. The computer case had been purchased at a garage sale in California: another dead end.

But the theft had been too easy, and that nagged at her. The priceless artifacts had been left unguarded, and that led her to only one conclusion. The cult wanted her to have the knives.

The rain had stopped, and the thunderous gray clouds had drifted away, leaving the night air moist and smelling of wet leaves. Halloween revelers paraded up and down Embassy Row, carrying trick-or-treat bags and eating candy.

Meri, Dalila, and Sudi walked away from the Australian embassy, clutching candy, and joined the throng, mostly college students, in costumes.

"Did you see the way that woman stared at

your whiskers?" Sudi said and brushed her hand over the cat ears poking through Meri's hair.

A pleasant feeling rushed through Meri, and a low rumble rose in her throat. She pushed Sudi's hand away.

"Be careful," Meri warned. "You almost made me purr."

"You need to purr," Sudi countered. "You're too nervous."

"Aren't you?" Meri asked. "I'm so jittery I could puke."

Instead of trying to hide the whiskers, tail, or feline ears that appeared when she was nervous, Meri had decided at the last moment to pull on a black leotard and dress as a cat. She wore a black velvet sash that held the Sekhmet knife close to her waist.

"But you stole the knives," Dalila said. "That's braver than I could ever be."

The wind caught Dalila's blue-silk veils and lifted them into the air, exposing the jewel-encrusted knife handle that lay flat against her smooth skin. The blade was tucked into the sequined band of her low-slung belly dancer's skirt.

"Great costume," said a guy dressed as a pirate.

In response, Dalila struck her finger cymbals. The brass plates pinged as she twirled with elegant grace. The skirt and veils swirled around her.

"I can't believe you did that," Sudi teased. "I'm the party girl."

"At least Dalila and I wore costumes," Meri scolded playfully. "I thought the plan was to look like trick-or-treaters in case someone caught us."

"I'm a tango dancer," Sudi said. With a sharp turn of her head, she embraced an invisible partner and took slow, slinking steps down the sidewalk, threading her way among kids dressed as witches, ghosts, and cheerleaders.

At the corner, Sudi did a quick foot flick through the slit in her skirt, revealing the ancient Egyptian knife, hooked into a lacy red garter that she wore above her knee.

Meri and Dalila laughed and ran up to her.

"Shouldn't we go to the Tidal Basin?" Dalila asked, gathering her veils tightly around her.

"I guess," Meri answered reluctantly.

Sudi grabbed their arms. "We have to stop at the Peruvian embassy first," Sudi said. "It's just across the street, and last year they gave out these incredible chocolate bars called Sublimes. We're not leaving until we each get one."

But as she started to step off the curb, a rusted old Cadillac rumbled down Massachusetts Avenue.

"That's Brian's car," Sudi whispered.

"So?" Meri asked.

"Why does he always show up wherever I am?" Sudi asked, looking after the car. Black smoke curled from the tailpipe.

"Maybe because you go to the same school and hang out with the same friends," Meri offered.

"No, it's not just coincidence," Sudi whispered with a haunted look. "It's something more."

"Why are you still afraid of Brian?" Dalila asked.

"I'm not," Sudi snapped. She scowled and started walking back the way they had come, her heels tapping out a fast, angry pace.

Meri and Dalila silently followed her down Sixteenth Street. No one spoke until they reached Lafayette Park and stood in front of the White House.

Then the strange mood Brian had cast over Sudi lifted, and her lively energy returned.

"When you're living there, Meri, we'll hang out, and watch all the cute Secret Service guys." Sudi hung her arm over Meri's shoulder. "My parents think your mom will win."

"She has to get the nomination first," Meri countered.

"Invite us for tea," Dalila added. "Can you imagine how elegant everything will be?" She clasped Meri's hand. "State dinners! You'll be entertaining kings."

Meri nodded but then she glanced up at the roof and saw the silhouette of a man. Since President Clinton had been in office, sharpshooters had kept watch from the White House roof. Meri's mother had already received death threats. Meri wondered what it would be like if she actually won the office.

Twenty minutes later, the girls stood on the western edge of the Tidal Basin, near the Franklin Delano Roosevelt Memorial. Moonlight reflected across the waters, and the rising tide made waves wash against the concrete and stone bank with a gentle whisper.

"Only a few visitors are walking around the

memorial," Sudi said. "I think most of the tourists are celebrating Halloween."

Meri glanced behind the gnarled trunks of the old cherry trees. Just one tour bus waited in the parking lot that was normally full.

"How do we even know Apep is here?" Meri asked.

"Since your last encounter with him, I've been keeping track of the storms," Dalila replied. "The thunder and rain this afternoon brought him into our world. He hasn't left yet."

"Do you think he's waiting for us?" Meri asked.

Sudi pointed into the dark behind the park bench. The wire-mesh fence had been twisted and bent until it was flattened against the ground. On the other side of the trees, the wooden slats of the second fence lay broken and scattered about the parking lot.

"Apep couldn't have done that," Meri argued, trying to ignore the ominous feeling building inside her. "A car must have plowed through the fences and plunged into the water."

"Then why aren't the trees crushed, too?"

Dalila asked. She set her finger cymbals down and unwound her veils, then tied them around a low-hanging branch. The wind whipped the silky scarves high into the air.

Dalila pulled out her knife, her eyes serious. She kissed the blade and whispered an incantation. She didn't look afraid.

"We should probably split up," Sudi said, slipping the knife from her garter. She held it as if she knew how to use the weapon.

"Shout if you find Apep," Sudi joked, with an unfamiliar catch in her voice.

"I'll scream, more likely," Meri said glumly as she headed south, walking away from her friends to the far end of the memorial.

A thin mist settled over the ground, leaving tiny droplets on the grass. The dew reflected the moon's glow and shimmered with eerie beauty. Meri studied the dark shadows around the back of the memorial and wished she had brought a flashlight.

A dry rustle came from behind the furrowed trunk of a weather-beaten tree.

Anxious, Meri crept toward the sound, her

heartbeat pounding in her ears. She clutched the knife handle in her clammy palm, tightening her grip, and stared down, searching for the snake.

Cautiously, she peered behind the trunk and then let out a long sigh.

A discarded lunch bag flapped back and forth, crackling as the brown paper brushed against dead leaves.

Meri breathed deeply and pressed her hand over her jittery stomach.

The slap-slap rhythm of a jogger made her wary; a lone man was running down the walkway, his cap pulled low over his forehead.

Meri slid behind a tree and waited for the runner to pass. She didn't want someone who might recognize her to see her skulking around the cherry trees, clutching a sharp-bladed, lethal knife.

Abruptly, the pounding footsteps stopped. She wondered why the runner had paused.

Minutes passed. Finally, Meri looked out. She didn't see anyone on the walk or resting in the grass. Maybe the runner had moved on.

Curious, she stepped forward. She had gone only a short distance when she saw a gray lump, no bigger than a squirrel, on the sidewalk. As she neared it, she realized it was a tennis shoe. She picked it up. The lining was still warm, the sole covered with a strange stickiness. She dropped the shoe. It bounced once and fell into the pool.

A soft scraping sound filled the night. The noise increased, then fell back, only to start again.

Maybe the runner had fallen and was dragging himself over dead grass and leaves, trying to find help. But even as her mind tried to override her fear and find a logical explanation for the sound, her body reacted in a visceral way. A spasm shot up her back, and adrenaline raced through her.

As she started to turn, a shadow passed over her.

At first, she thought a cloud had raced across the sky, blocking the moonlight, but then the brisk autumn air became filled with a musty scent, after which came the rancid odor of decaying cucumbers.

Meri readied herself to attack, then spun around. She looked up, inhaling sharply, and froze.

Apep had tripled in size since the last time

Meri had seen him. The giant snake reared, extending himself until his head towered above Meri.

She stepped backward, stumbling over her own feet. Her cat ears, tail, and whiskers abandoned her, leaving her to deal with her terror as a regular girl, without any comfort from her feline powers.

The serpent's head angled over her; his mouth poised above her, fangs exposed, ready to strike.

A scream gurgled in her throat, then died.

The knife slipped from her sweating palm and landed in the grass with a soft plop. She fell to her knees, frantically brushing her hands across the ground, searching for the blade.

Before she could retrieve the knife, Apep struck.

She rolled, dodging the sudden thrust of the head, then stood, waiting; when Apep drew back to strike again, she ran forward and ducked under his body.

Her hands squished against his scaly underbelly. The snake came down hard on top of her. She screamed in pain and twisted free, turning over and over until she had gotten away from the beast.

"Dalila! Sudi!" she shouted, but the words came out as no more than a puff of air. Her friends would never be able to hear her calls for help.

The foamy muck that Apep left in his trail covered her hands. Bile rose to the back of her throat. She swiped her fingers back and forth in the dew-wet grass, trying to get rid of the gluey slime.

Apep roared. The deep, prolonged cry thundered through the night.

Meri stood, trying to make her mind work and find a plan. She edged back, mentally scolding herself for not having the courage to face Apep. She had wanted to be fierce, like the goddess Sekhmet, rather than sniveling and afraid. Fate had chosen her to be a Descendant. She was supposed to be brave, but instead she was sick with terror.

Apep slunk closer, winding toward her, his piercing eyes trying to entrance her.

She took a clumsy step back, and her foot caught on a root. Her ankle turned. She lost her balance and fell down. Her head snapped back and hit the tree trunk. Pain shot up her spine. The soreness settled in her neck with a dull throb.

Apep hissed and slithered closer. The forked

tongue flicked in and out, darting up and down, tasting the air, a tracking device for locating prey. When it swiped over her face, she cried out. The tongue felt damp and left a sharp tingling on her skin.

The snake's mouth widened as his flexible lower jaw scooped up her feet. His fetid breath choked her, and the stench clung to her skin. She stared into the gaping mouth, down into the horrible darkness, and saw the jogger's cap.

A low and terrible moan escaped her lungs, her last desperate cry, as she watched the flicking tongue and imagined her death: swallowed, then suffocated as the reptile's digestive acids worked on her flesh.

CHAPTER 13

Slowly, Meri became aware of footsteps ham-
mering the ground. Voices called her name. Sudi
and Dalila grabbed her shoulders and, yelling
savagely, yanked her from Apep's mouth. Their
fingers dug into her shoulder and arm as they
tugged harder. Her leotard ripped, and the sleeve
unraveled as her back scraped over the rough tree
bark. Pain raced through her, and cuts stung her
back.

At last Sudi and Dalila pulled her to the other side of the tree.

Meri gratefully breathed the untainted air. "Thanks," she whispered in between coughs.

Enraged, Apep rose up. His jaws snapped violently around the tree. The trunk cracked and splintered. A branch fell. Twigs and leaves scratched Meri's face.

Dalila shoved the foliage away and fell down on her knees beside Meri. "You need to get up," she coaxed. "Apep will be coming after us."

Sudi let out a low whistle and handed Meri the knife with the Sekhmet handle. "You dropped this," she said, staring at the reptile. "No wonder. I thought you said Apep was the size of an anaconda."

"He grew," Meri said, choking back sobs.

The snake released the broken tree and bellowed, then slid toward them in smooth, wavelike motions, his scales glossy and white in the milky moonlight.

"He is huge," Sudi breathed.

"How did you know I was in trouble?" Meri asked as she got to her feet, weak and trembling.

"Your screams were a clue," Sudi answered. "We'd better get this done before the police get here."

"A queen must not show fear. . . ." Dalila muttered, trying to give herself courage. "She must always instill confidence and hope in her people." Then she turned to Meri and Sudi, a strange, blank look on her face. "We'll survive this," she said, but there was a question in her voice.

Meri looked down at her knife. The blade caught the moonlight and flashed with a supernaturally bright glow. "Even though Apep is evil, I hate doing this."

"There has to be another way," Sudi said.

"This is what is expected from us." Dalila stood taller and gripped the handle of her knife.

Meri took a deep breath and ran. An avalanche of fear sent adrenaline buzzing through her. Her feet hammered the ground, and she yelled as she attacked the snake. She dodged his thrashing head and continued running until she stood over his midsection. She plunged her knife into his glistening scales. As the blade cut through the reptile's body, the slick sound made her cringe.

Apep bellowed and thrust his tail, coiling it around Meri. She brought the blade down again, slicing through flesh.

The snake squeezed tighter, wrapping more coils around Meri. The pressure on her lungs made it impossible to breathe. Darkness pressed into her vision, and she became vaguely aware that Sudi and Dalila stood beside her, striking the reptile with heavy blows.

The tail went slack, and the beast squealed.

Meri took deep breaths and brought her knife down again. This time something warm splattered her face. She turned her mind from what she was doing and thought of Sekhmet. The goddess had been sent by the god Re to avenge evil for him. At his bidding, she had killed men and women until the slaughter became sweet to her heart and she waded about in their blood. For that reason and others, the goddess of destruction and war was a terrible force to summon.

Meri did so again.

"Behen a Sebau, se hetem na Apep," Meri intoned. "May I crush the evil one; may I destroy Apep."

The wind came as a soft murmur at first, the

hot air withering grass as it rushed across the Mall. The scorching gusts screeched around them and a pale image of the lioness-headed goddess appeared in the shadows, wavering over the slaughter and protecting the Descendants.

$\mathbf{M}$eri sat on the walk, her feet dangling over the edge into the Tidal Basin. The tide was at its highest, the water lapping around her ankles. She leaned forward and washed her hands in the cold, soothing liquid. Wisps of blood looped and curled into the moonlit water before dissolving.

"No more," Meri whispered. Her arm throbbed, and a stiff, painful feeling in her neck and back made it hard for her to bend low enough to clean her face. "I can't do more."

"It's over," Sudi said, dunking her bare feet into the water to wash the dirt and muck from her legs.

They had dropped the ritual knives next to the dead snake and left the carnage for others to find. Already, Meri could hear cries of alarm in the distance.

"Someone must have discovered Apep," Dalila said. Her hair was matted, her clothes stuck to her body, but in the moonlight, Meri wasn't sure if it was blood that covered her or the sticky film from the demon's underbelly.

"I think we should leave," Dalila said, standing.

"All right," Meri said, but she didn't get up.

Dalila made a sound: a mutter of disgust. She sighed and covered her eyes. "What did we do?"

"I'll tell you what we did." Sudi jumped up, dripping water on Meri's head. "We killed a monster, and now we can party."

"Party?" Meri turned to look at Sudi.

"Maybe being the protectors of the world won't be so bad after all," Sudi said, trying to sound happy.

Meri pulled herself up and limped over to her friend. "Are you all right?"

"Of course I am," Sudi snapped.

A hellish scream made them turn, and then a gun fired.

"Why would they need a gun?" Meri asked. "Apep is dead, a thousand pieces—"

"There!" Sudi shouted.

Meri followed her gaze.

Apep moved toward the water's edge, restored and larger than before, his scales smooth and gleaming. He slithered over a park bench and then the chain-link fence. The metal supports creaked and groaned under the reptile's weight as the bars bent. The snake dragged the wire mesh over the walkway, with a terrible screech of metal.

He splashed into the pool, and in the same moment, lightning streaked across the night. Thunder crackled and smashed, the low rumble shaking the ground. Rounded masses of clouds swept in from the east and began building, piling one on top of the other until they hid the moon.

"It's just as I feared," Dalila said at last. "When

destroyed, many Egyptian gods and demons simply regenerated. Apep is stronger now."

"The cult leaders let me steal the knives," Meri added. "They were taunting us. They knew we couldn't destroy Apep."

"They haven't won," Sudi said, gripping Meri's hand. "There has to be another way. We just need to find it."

"But how many people will Apep destroy before then?" Dalila asked softly.

Lightning shot jaggedly across the sky, and the rain fell in large drops as thunder rocked the night again.

Meri, Dalila, and Sudi started walking in the rain, ignoring the groups of people who had gathered.

The voices faded behind them, and then there was only the sound of rain.

When they reached the area where the tourist buses parked, they saw a huge, rusted Cadillac. Brian got out and grinned, resting his arms on the roof. Rain pelted his face.

"Do you need a ride home?" he asked with a chuckle in his voice.

"Brian," Sudi said, "have you been following me?"

"Why would I be following you?" he smirked and looked at Meri. "I liked that picture of you in the newspaper."

Meri rolled her eyes.

"That's unbelievable Halloween makeup," he said, no longer gazing into her eyes. "Where did you get it?"

"CVS," Meri lied, glancing down at her tattered leotard.

"Let's get a cab," Meri said to Dalila and Sudi.

"Like this?" Sudi asked. "No one will give us a ride."

Dalila looked back at Brian. "How did he know where to find us?"

"Come on!" Brian yelled, his voice rising with impatience. "I'm getting wet."

"Maybe he's joined the cult and he's watching us for them," Sudi said in a harsh, low voice. "I don't know. What else could it be?"

"Let's play along with him," Dalila said. "He's here for a reason. Let's find out what it is." She walked over to the Cadillac with a saucy stride.

"Do you think he just wants to get back with you?" Meri whispered to Sudi.

"Not likely," Sudi replied as she followed Dalila.

"We'll get your car dirty." Dalila tossed Brian a flirty smile as she waited for him to open the passenger-side door for her.

"I can clean the car," he said, staring at her bare belly.

Dalila slid inside, letting her skirt ride up and expose her perfect legs. She glanced at Brian, watching him watch her, and didn't shy away from his gaze. Instead, she stretched and posed seductively.

"Where did she learn that stuff?" Sudi said in a low voice to Meri. "I wish I'd been homeschooled by her teachers."

"She's amazing, isn't she?" Meri agreed. "And she knows just what she's doing. I bet she'll get Brian to tell us what he knows and he won't even know he's blabbing."

Meri crawled into the back as Brian pushed in behind the steering wheel.

The car rolled away. Windshield wipers made

a slick sound across the windows, and then Brian turned on the stereo. A rhythmic, pounding vibrated through Meri. She could feel Brian watching her through the rearview mirror, and when she glanced up, he was staring at her. His gaze returned to the road, and they drove to her house without talking.

"Sudi, are you going to be okay?" Meri asked as she got out of the car.

"I'm safe." Sudi nodded. "Dalila's with me."

Then Sudi leaned forward and spoke to Brian, "Go to my house next."

The car sped away, red taillights reflecting off the rain-slick street, and turned at the corner.

Meri splashed through the puddles and hurried to the back of the house. She unlocked the door, entered, and punched in the security code, then stood for a moment in the warm air, letting the heat embrace her before she undressed.

She curled her wet leotard into a ball and dumped it in the trash, then stepped naked into the kitchen just as the electricity went out. She grabbed the box of emergency candles and headed upstairs, grateful that no one was home.

Georgie had cleaned the bathroom earlier, and the scent of Clorox took Meri's mind off the odor clinging to her. She lit a dozen candles, setting the bases in the wet wax she had dripped onto the rim of the sink, and then she took a shower by gleaming candlelight. She sat in the tub and let the spray wash over her head. She didn't want to comb out her hair and find a piece of snake flesh clinging to a strand.

By the time she was finished and stood dripping on the rug, the thunder had quieted and a plan was running through her mind. She stepped into her bedroom and glanced at the flashing display on her clock. The electricity had returned, but she wasn't sure of the time. Still, she felt certain she could walk to Abdel's house and return before her mother got home.

She reasoned that Abdel would not have taken the Book of Thoth with him. It would have served no purpose; the next mentor would only have to bring the scrolls back.

Before she had even thought her idea through, she was pulling on her sweats. She grabbed a book of matches and her house key, punched a code into the alarm panel, and headed out the door.

She jogged down the sidewalk, her tennis shoes smacking against the wet pavement.

The sky was clear again, the moonlight bright, but the strange stillness in the air promised another storm.

As she neared Abdel's house she slowed her pace and looked around. Eerie Halloween music played in an apartment building on the next block, and jack-o'-lanterns set out earlier still had candles flickering inside them in spite of the storm. But she didn't see anyone.

Still her nerves thrummed as she jumped up on Abdel's front porch. She reached across the railing to see if she could force open the window, but when she pressed her fingers against the glass, she caught something in the corner of her eye. She turned, surprised.

The front door was open.

She pushed against the wood, letting the door swing wide. It bumped against the wall.

Caution told her not to call out. She slipped inside and closed the door, then waited. When she didn't hear anyone inside the house, she crossed to the stairs and started up the steps, her breathing shallow and loud.

As she reached the third-floor landing, she paused again. A gentle movement of air brought the faint scent of smoke. Had someone just extinguished the wicks in the oil-burning lamps?

A clammy cold filled the hallway, but other than that and the smoke, she didn't hear or feel anything strange. She entered the room, struck a match, and lit the wick floating in the first bowl of oil. The fire flared, leaving a thin black mark on the wall.

Meri blew out the match and then turned, not prepared for what she saw.

Papyri from the Book of Thoth had been unrolled and stretched across the floor, as if someone had been in a panic to find a spell. Had Abdel done this before he left? He had been searching for an incantation to protect the Descendants from Apep, but Meri couldn't imagine that he would ever have treated the ancient writings so irreverently.

Another thought occurred to her: the cult leaders also wanted the papyri. Maybe she had interrupted someone who was trying to steal the sacred writings.

She didn't think her sudden appearance could have panicked a cult leader. But she didn't understand why a thief would unwind the scrolls and leave them in such a chaotic jumble when he could have just taken them.

A shadow moved. Meri became aware that someone was standing behind her.

Adrenaline shot through Meri, preparing her exhausted body to fight. She turned around and grabbed her neck. "Ouch!" she yelled, rubbing the tender muscles.

Tiny red eyes gazed back at her from the dark corner. Then chirping filled the room, and a bird with an elegant, S-shaped neck waddled toward her, its blunt claws clattering on the hardwood floor. A long, daggerlike beak opened, and a loud trill came out. Meri covered her ears.

"Sudi?" Meri asked.

The flapping wings turned into graceful arms, and the bird grew taller. Sudi appeared. She wore clean jeans and a boy tank. Her wet hair was pulled back in braids. She hugged Meri, and the musky fragrance of her shampoo filled the air.

Meri's tension eased, and she let out a huge sigh.

A tweet escaped Sudi's mouth. She coughed and tried again. "You scared us to death," she said, brushing fine, fluffy feathers from her arms.

"Where's Dalila?" Meri asked. She looked at the shadows hovering near the back wall.

A cobra slid forward, twisting and curling until it stood on the tip of its tail; then, still whirling, its body thickened, and Dalila appeared, spinning out of control.

Sudi and Meri grabbed her and stopped her from hitting her forehead against the bookshelves.

Dalila pressed her hands on either side of her head. "I'm so dizzy," she said. "I think I'm going to be sick." She wore Sudi's clothes: a denim miniskirt with a pink baby-doll top and flip-flops.

"At least you didn't become that devourer monster with the big butt when you transformed," Sudi said. She turned her attention back to Meri. "We asked Brian to leave us both at my house," Sudi explained. "My parents and sisters are still at a Halloween party, and Dalila couldn't let her uncle see—"

"—What a mess I'd become," Dalila said. "Besides, I didn't want to be alone in the car with Brian. His behavior is unacceptable."

Meri raised an eyebrow and glanced sideways at Sudi. "Translation?"

"He rubbed Dalila's knee," Sudi said.

"And my thigh," Dalila said, her eyes huge. "I thought he was Carter's friend."

Sudi wrapped her arm around Dalila's shoulders. "The thought of getting caught making a move on you made it even more fun for Brian."

"He can't be trusted." Dalila shook her head and shuddered. "I never want to be alone with him, ever."

"I know that feeling," Sudi answered, and pulled a tube of gloss from her pocket. She opened it and spread tangerine color over her lips, then puckered and passed the gloss to Meri.

"Does he know anything about the cult?" Meri asked.

"We're still not sure," Sudi said. When Meri didn't apply the gloss, Sudi took the tube and put it on her lips for her. "But after we showered, we decided to come back here. We figured Abdel would have left the scrolls and—"

"—We wanted to find a spell to stop Apep from coming into our world." Dalila held her lips out for Sudi to shine. "There has to be an incantation—something. After all, the ancient Egyptians wrote the *Book of Overthrowing Apep*. It gives spells and instructions for stopping the monster; so why can't we find anything to help us?"

"That's why I came here," Meri said, but secretly she felt hurt that they hadn't called her. She looked at the scrolls spread across the floor. She couldn't believe that Sudi and Dalila had done that to the sacred text.

Dalila began rolling up a papyrus. "We thought we could find the answer," she said with a look of remorse, "but that's not an excuse to treat the Book of Thoth this way. I don't know what made me act so disrespectfully."

"Maybe trying to stop a giant snake that can swallow you whole requires extreme behavior," Sudi said. "We did the right thing."

Meri placed a comforting hand on Dalila's arm. "It's okay," she whispered.

But Dalila appeared truly ashamed. "I'm so sorry. I hope I didn't hurt anything. The hieroglyphs are so fragile." Her eyes were glassy with tears.

"It was mostly me, anyway," Sudi said, stepping forward to take the blame.

All three began to pick up the papyri and roll them. Meri dropped hers in a leather case and set it inside a trunk.

"So what did Brian tell you?" Meri asked.

"Just like always, he talked about how cool he is," Sudi answered, and then she sighed heavily. "If he did join the cult, and now I'm not sure that he has, I can't imagine the leaders entrusting him with any secrets anyway."

"He's exceptionally foolish," Dalila added, and then she collapsed on a stool. "What if we can't find the spell? What happens if we don't stop Apep?"

"Our next mentor will know what to do," Meri said, with a confidence she didn't feel.

A sound from downstairs made them stop.

The front door shut with a definite *clack*.

"Could the wind have done that?" Sudi asked.

"I closed the door," Meri whispered. "Someone just came inside." Her heart hammered. She hoped it was Abdel.

But then she heard the footsteps. A shuffling step was followed by a loud tap. After that came the shuffling noise again, of someone dragging a hard-soled shoe across the floor. Then another knock hit the floorboards, and immediately the shuffle sounded again. It didn't sound like Abdel's easy stride.

Meri looked at Sudi and Dalila.

"Do you think that's our new mentor?" Sudi asked.

Whoever it was started up the stairs, pounding heavily on each step. The old wood creaked under the visitor's weight.

"If that's our mentor, then the person is an old geezer," Meri said, trying to figure out the odd mix of sounds. "And whoever it is must weigh at least a thousand pounds."

"How are we going to get all of this cleaned up?" Dalila whispered frantically, panic in her face. Her fingers worked another papyrus, rolling it. "We can't let our new mentor see what we've done."

Sudi grabbed her hand. "We don't have time to pick everything up," she said.

"Then what are we going to do?" Dalila asked with a wild look in her eyes. "Should we transform?"

"I don't know about you two," Meri whispered, "but I'm definitely too tired. I'd get stuck in some in-between phase."

"We can't let our mentor find us," Dalila said. "How are we going to explain this?"

"We're not going to," Sudi said. "We'll hide, and after our mentor gets settled in for the night, we'll sneak out."

"Where are we going to hide?" Meri asked, looking at the stacked trunks and bookcases pressed against the walls.

"Here." Dalila slid beneath the table.

Sudi joined her. Then Meri squeezed between them.

The person had crossed the second-floor landing and was starting up the third flight of stairs. The harsh scraping sound made Meri cringe.

"We forgot to put out the light." Dalila gripped Meri's arm. "Our mentor will wonder why the oil lamp is burning."

"How are we ever going to kill a monster snake when we can't even handle something like this?" Meri muttered under her breath.

She scrambled across the floor to the shelf that held the oil lamp, then stood, licked her fingers, pinched the wick and put out the flame. The smell of smoke floated into the air.

As she started back to the table, a flashlight shone on Meri's face.

CHAPTER 16

Stanley Keene stood in the doorway, holding the flashlight in one hand and leaning heavily on Meri's wand with his other. His breathing made a harsh, annoying sound.

"Light the lamp again, Meri," he said, apparently not surprised to find her in Abdel's house. "Please, light them all."

Meri struck a match.

Stanley hobbled into the room, using the

wand as a cane. He stopped and gazed down at the scrolls still lying on the floor.

"Fascinating how these little drawings can be used to indicate sounds as well as the objects they depict." He tapped the tip of her wand on a hieroglyph that looked like an owl staring sideways at the reader. "That tiny creature represents an *m* sound."

"You know how to read Egyptian hieroglyphs?" Meri asked, lighting another wick and wondering why Stanley was there.

"Now," he whispered. "If only I'd known then."

She struck another match and watched him wander around the room, looking at the scrolls.

At last he found a papyrus, which had been tied with a string. A lump of mud covered the knot and was stamped with a seal. He picked it up and carried it back to the table. Then with a slow, strenuous effort, he sat on a stool.

He glanced down at Dalila and Sudi, still hiding under the table, and regarded them contemptuously.

"Cowering beneath the table," he said and

frowned. "How do you expect to save the world?"

Sudi crawled out from under the table, and Dalila eased out after her.

His focus swung back to Meri, who was lighting the last line of lamps. Flames darted and curled, casting an orange glow about the room.

"Your wand doesn't work," Stanley complained. With a surge of wild anger, he beat the snake head against the floor. "It's supposed to ward off evil, and it didn't."

"I never said it would," Meri answered, bewildered, and stepped back to the table. She stood over him. "You *stole* the wand from me."

"Yes, my little cat," he said, calm again. His swollen fingers gathered her wet hair, then squeezed the ends and let go. Heat radiated from him, and she wondered if he had a fever.

"You knew the cat following you was me?" Meri asked.

"Of course," he answered. "I'm the one who sold the photos of you changing into a cat to the *National Enquirer*." He smiled in a way that made Meri wince. "One of my better assignments," he said.

"Why weren't you afraid of Apep?" Meri asked, trying to turn the conversation away from what he must have seen that night when she transformed.

"You could say I have special protection," he answered mysteriously.

"But why were you following me?" Meri asked.

"It's not just you." Stanley glanced around the table. "I've been watching the three of you since the day you were summoned, and now I've come to help you, before you destroy the world with your bumbling."

"You're our new mentor?" Sudi asked.

"We have so many questions," Dalila added eagerly.

"I said I've come to help you, not guide you," Stanley answered in a maliciously superior tone. "I pity anyone who is saddled with teaching the three of you the old ways," he sniffed.

"Then how will you help us?" Dalila said, adopting a tone and posture that made him blink.

"I know how to stop Apep," he said.

Meri sat down on the stool beside him. Dalila and Sudi drew closer.

"How do you know about Apep?" Sudi questioned.

"How do I know?" he whispered. For a moment, Meri thought he was going to cry. He sighed instead and rubbed his eyes.

"It started as an assignment," he said at last. "I had to cover the opening of the Anubis Spa. A fluff piece, I thought, but then I discovered, too late, that the cult leaders are a group of determined women and men who have used ancient rites in order to gain terrifying power."

"What do you mean, 'too late'?" Dalila asked, and rubbed his hand to comfort him.

"Because I didn't believe what I saw," he replied. "Who would believe that the ancient conflict between good and evil continues today? I doubted my own eyes. Is everyone so blind? And then, when I did believe, the cult had already cast its curses upon me."

He looked at Meri and sighed. "The three of you are nothing compared to the powers they have, and yet the Hour priests have called on you to do the impossible. What kind of misguided faith must they have?"

"We'll learn what we need to know," Dalila said firmly.

"Perhaps," he answered. "I'll pray it's so."

"Tell us about Apep," Sudi interrupted. "You said you know how to stop Apep."

"The cult summoned Apep to destroy the three of you," he said.

"We know," Meri answered.

"The demon was small at first," Stanley continued, "and sent to kill you with its venom while you slept, but your cat Miwsher stopped it."

"Miwsher fought Apep," Meri said, remembering the storm, and how she had awakened to find a stray animal in her room.

"A lot of bad things happened that night," Stanley said, with unfathomable misery in his voice. "Apep has his own will, and the cult has lost control over the demon. Now only Seth can stop Apep. The three of you must summon the ancient god of chaos and storm."

"The cult worships Seth," Dalila put in, "so why don't they call him?"

Stanley frowned. "I'm surprised you don't know such a simple thing," he said. "Long ago, the goddess Isis cast a spell that still imprisons Seth in the chaos at the edge of creation. The god can't enter this world in physical form unless he is summoned by the divine pharaohs. You three are the only ones who can release him from that spell and call him into our world."

Meri looked at Dalila and Sudi, wondering if Stanley were telling them the truth.

"We'll never do that." Dalila folded her arms over her chest.

"To save the world from Apep," Stanley said, "you must."

"How do we know you're telling us the truth?" Sudi asked.

"We won't do it," Meri said firmly.

"If that is your decision," Stanley said, "then you alone will pay the consequences, and I've done my job."

He placed the scroll under his arm, shifted his weight, and, using the table edge as a brace, stood.

He started for the door, shuffling his feet, and tapped the wand on the floor.

Meri joined him at the top of the stairwell.

"Why did you visit my mother?" she asked. "You were with her the morning after the storm, and I heard you mention the Cult of Anubis when you got into the car with her."

"I thought your mother could help me," he said, starting down the steps. "Especially after I discovered the way she stole you out of Egypt."

Meri bristled at his choice of words. "She adopted me," she said, following him down the stairs.

"Hmph," he snorted, taking another step. "'Kidnapped' is a better word."

"What do you mean?" Meri asked.

Dalila and Sudi hurried down the steps so they could listen.

"I was the late-night visitor you were asking about that day after the storm," he explained as he started across the second-floor landing.

"You were the one who knocked on the door?" Meri asked. "Then that means you stayed until morning talking to my mother."

Stanley grinned. "When I mentioned the Cult of Anubis to her, she opened the door to make sure no one was outside listening."

"Why would my mother be so cautious if she truly believes the cult is no more than a silly fad?" Meri asked as they walked down the last flight of stairs.

"Precisely," he answered, stopping to catch his breath before he spoke again. "Why did she become so nervous? I assumed she knew something that could help me."

Sudi and Dalila joined Meri and put comforting arms around her.

"Did she?" Meri asked at last.

Stanley started to answer, then stopped and wheezed. He labored to pull in air. His cheeks turned from red to an odd purplish color.

"Maybe you should sit down on the steps," Dalila suggested. "You don't look very well."

He shook his head sharply and quickened his pace. "I've said too much," he whispered. "That's all."

By the time he reached the front door, he had a strange desperation in his eyes.

"Help me," he whispered as he fell on the stairs with a loud thump. He clutched the wand and papyrus tight against his chest.

Meri placed her hand on his forehead. The skin felt cold and wet.

He pushed her hand away.

"I think you're having a heart attack," Meri said.

"Don't you know anything?" he asked. "Can't you see what is happening to me? You're supposed to use the magic of the gods to protect the world, and yet you don't know?"

Sudi flipped open her cell phone. "I'll call an ambulance."

"Doctors can't help me." Stanley grabbed the phone from her and snapped it closed. "Since the beginning of time, the divine pharaoh has been charged with keeping the cosmic order and stopping the forces of chaos that threaten the world. As royal Descendants, you're failing."

Suddenly, Meri felt the presence of another force building around them, something cold and ancient and evil.

Stanley looked up, and his jagged breathing gave way to silence. His eyes widened as his arms and legs stretched and a guttural sound came from his throat.

Meri screamed and shielded her eyes.

When she looked again, Stanley had dissolved into a cloud of specks that fell like a powdering of dust on the floor.

Meri jumped back and batted the particles away from her, trying not to inhale them. She opened the door, stepped out onto the porch, and took a deep breath.

"Yuck," Sudi squealed and ducked, rushing toward the door. She joined Meri outside.

Dalila groped through the dust until she was outside, too; then she leaned over the porch railing, coughing and crying.

"How could he just disappear?" Meri asked, trying to blot out the image of Stanley vanishing.

"Even though we possess our own identity," Dalila explained, "the gods can still use us to deliver messages. I think Seth was trying to use Stanley, but when Stanley fought to tell us what we needed to know, Seth called him back."

"What did we need to know?" Meri asked. "That we're failing?"

"No," Dalila said. "Stanley managed to tell us that Isis had cast a spell imprisoning Seth. I doubt that Seth wanted Stanley to give us that information. And I think Stanley was trying to tell us more in spite of what was happening to him."

When the particles had settled over the floor and stairs, Meri stepped back inside, grit crackling under her feet, and picked up the scroll and the wand.

"I can't believe it," Sudi said. "Just like that, Stanley's gone."

Dalila bent down and touched the grains. "I think this was more a show, to frighten us and convince us of Seth's power. Stanley was probably transported to another location."

"I hope so," Meri said as she stepped outside again and rejoined Sudi and Dalila on the porch. "I hate to think that I was just walking over what's left of Stanley."

Sudi pointed to the seal on the papyrus. The hieroglyph for Seth, an erect tail and a pair of angular, raised ears, was imprinted on it. "Open it, and see what Stanley was trying to steal."

Meri broke the seal, untied the string, and unrolled the scroll. The papyrus felt heavier and the fibers rough, different from the ones she'd touched before. She winced, wondering if the magic within was more powerful because the spells were used to battle the lord of chaos.

"*Sexem a xesef a madret a,*" Dalila intoned, reading the first spell aloud. Then she translated: "I gain power over and repulse the evil which is against me."

"It looks like all the spells are ways to free oneself from Seth's control," Sudi said.

"Poor Stanley," Meri whispered. "He was probably stealing this so he could get out from under Seth's control."

"Maybe Seth is the only answer," Dalila said. "Wall paintings in tombs show him on the prow of the sun god's barge, fighting Apep."

"Seth stands for evil and destruction," Sudi reminded her. "He's too dangerous to call forth."

"We'll find the same incantation that Isis used to imprison Seth," Dalila said confidently. "Then, after Seth has destroyed Apep, we'll send him back to the chaos at the edge of the universe."

"Are you sure?" Meri asked. "If Seth was

controlling Stanley, then how can we trust anything that Stanley told us?"

"You're holding a scroll that proves that Seth can be overpowered," Sudi said.

"I know," Meri said, hating the way her fingers quivered.

"Tomorrow night," Dalila said firmly. "We'll meet at the Tidal Basin and summon the god."

"And if we do bring him here, will he really obey us and destroy Apep?" Meri asked.

"He's destroyed Apep before," Dalila answered.

"But so have we," Meri said, feeling doubtful. "It feels so risky. We could end up with both Apep and Seth loose in our world."

"The Book of Thoth gives us the power to command the ancient gods," Dalila argued.

"It hasn't helped us with Apep," Meri countered.

"That's the reason we need to summon Seth," Sudi added.

"All right," Meri said at last. "Tomorrow night." But she didn't feel convinced.

After a moment, Meri went back upstairs and

extinguished the lamps. Then, downhearted, she started home, carrying her wand, and the papyrus that Stanley had tried to steal. She wished she had the answers.

M̶eri stepped into the front room. Her mother was sitting in the rocking chair near the fireplace. She didn't look like a future president of the United States, wrapped in her purple afghan. She looked vulnerable and small, and in the firelight Meri saw a mix of fear and sadness on her face.

Meri dropped the papyrus in the umbrella stand and set her wand against the wall; then she walked across the room.

Her mother turned.

"Have you been crying?" Meri asked as she stepped toward the hearth and kissed her mother's cheek.

"No, of course not," her mother said and sniffled. "Have you ever seen me cry?"

Meri shook her head. But then her mother's eyes brimmed with tears.

"What's happened?" Meri asked.

A jangling sound made Meri look down. A pile of red, green, and blue beads was cupped in her mother's hands. The semiprecious stones glinted in the firelight.

"I need to tell you the truth before it becomes headline news," her mother said. "Sit down."

Meri pulled a chair up next to her mother. She sat beside her and watched the fire. The embers pulsed within the pile of ash.

"I want to be president," her mother began softly. "You know that better than anyone, but it's another kind of power that has always interested me."

"What other?" Meri asked.

"The power of spells and incantations," her mother answered. "Does magic really exist?"

Meri held her breath, then blurted, "Why are you asking me?"

Her mother turned and took Meri's hand. "Because ten years ago, when I saw you on the streets in Cairo, I stepped into another realm, or at least I think I did. I'm certain not everything that happened that day was my imagination."

"I remember the afternoon," Meri whispered. She had been holding Miwsher and meandering through the crowds outside the Cairo museum. Tourists had given her money in exchange for having their picture taken with her.

"You need to know everything that happened," her mother went on, "so you'll understand why I did what I did. When I walked past you—maybe it was the glint of sun—I don't know, but I saw your birthmark, like a brilliant white light, beaming from you. I know I couldn't really have seen it, because your hair was thick and long, like it is now."

"You never told me this before," Meri countered. "You always said you saw my little face and fell in love with me."

Her mother looked away from her and stared

into the fire. The shadows on her face stuttered in the firelight and made her look old.

"You have an odd birthmark on your scalp," her mother said quietly. "It's the sacred eye of Horus. Do you know what that is?"

Meri nodded.

"If I hadn't seen the birthmark," her mother confessed, "I probably would have walked past you."

Meri looked down and blinked to keep the tears from her eyes.

"I'm sorry," her mother said. "I was with a delegation, and we didn't have time for such—"

She stopped, but Meri knew she had almost said, "nonsense."

"That day I crossed a threshold into a world of magic," her mother said, and gazed back into the fire. "As strange as it sounds, I sensed that evil forces were trying to kill both you and Miwsher. Maybe too much sun was giving me heatstroke. I don't know, but I decided to adopt you. And it was more than a decision. I felt as if my entire life had pushed me to that moment. I told the Egyptian officials who were with me that if you were an orphan, then I wanted to adopt you and take you home with me."

Her mother paused and wrapped the afghan more tightly around her shoulders and across her chest, even though the room was overheated.

"The translator asked you about your family," her mother stopped and laughed, not aloud, but to herself, in a sad tone that sent a shiver through Meri. "You told her that Miwsher was your mother."

Meri gasped. "Why haven't you told me this before?"

Her mother ignored her question and continued, "The officials loved your story and called you a child of royal blood. Then one of the government men told me the story about the cat goddess Bastet mothering the pharaohs. They thought you were delightful."

Meri had vague memories of her life in Cairo—the kindness of the neighborhood women, their warmth and love—but she had no memory of a home, a mother, or of Miwsher being more than her pet.

"It was a while before you spoke English, and even after you did, you insisted that Miwsher was your mother, that your cat turned into a woman."

"I don't remember saying that," Meri said, feeling her chest tighten. "I would remember something so strange."

"Sometimes at night, even now," her mother went on. "I hear prowling around the house—sounds only a human can make by opening the refrigerator or the sliding glass door, and when I investigate, I always find Miwsher alone."

As if the cat understood, she stretched and meowed, then sat and blinked at them.

"Yes," her mother said to Miwsher. "I find you staring up at me with that smug little feline smile that probably exists only in my imagination, but still, late at night, I've wondered if you really do transform into the goddess Bastet."

Then her mother laughed again, and her laughter sounded strange. "Can you imagine if the opposition party could hear me say that?" She shifted the beads to one hand, and a strand fell across her lap. That was the first Meri had noticed that the beads were strung together.

Her mother leaned closer. "I forged documents

and brought you both home with me," she whispered. "I broke the law."

Meri took in a deep breath. Her mother's reputation was impeccable. The opposition party was always trying to create a scandal or find something in her past, but without success. What would happen if they discovered her secret?

"By the time the plane landed in California, the magic was gone, and I couldn't believe what I had done," her mother went on, "but I adored you. I had never been as happy as I was when you were in my arms."

Her mother began rocking. The curved slats of the rocker creaked noisily.

"I don't believe it was a coincidence that brought us together that day," her mother said, staring up at the ceiling. "I think the universe was weaving our lives together, purposefully, and with a plan."

Meri felt a sudden urge to tell her mother the truth, but she held back. Her heartbeat quickened, and she waited to hear what else her mother had to say.

"Over the years, one lie built on another," her

mother said. "I was always amazed that no one found out, and then, somehow, Stanley Keene did."

"Did he tell you how?" Meri asked.

"No," she said. "He threatened to print the story unless I joined the Cult of Anubis. Why would he want me to do such a silly thing?"

The wood crackled, and flames shot up the chimney.

"Did you join the cult?" Meri asked, aware that her voice was trembling. She changed her position so her mother couldn't see the shaking in her knees, and wondered if Seth had been controlling Stanley even then. Or maybe Stanley had been hoping that if her mother saw the truth she'd use her position in the government to stop the cult.

"Of course not," her mother answered. "I think Stanley was having mental problems. His family has reported him missing. He hasn't been home since that night. And whoever heard of black-mailing someone into joining a spa? Ridiculous."

"I'm glad you didn't," Meri said in a weak voice.

"I won't be blackmailed, and I told him so," her mother said. "I don't care what it costs me, even if I lose my seat in the Senate. I only wanted you to hear the truth before the rest of the world knows."

Meri knew Stanley wasn't going to run the story, because he didn't exist anymore. Or, if he did, Seth had taken him someplace far away. At the same time she sensed that her mother wasn't telling her everything. After all, Stanley had spent half the night with her. They must have discussed something more.

Her mother leaned over and poured the beads into Meri's hands. "This is the necklace you were wearing the day I found you," she said.

Meri examined the large amulet attached to the strings of beads. "I don't remember it."

Her mother stood and dropped the afghan on the rocker.

"Why are you giving it to me now?" Meri asked.

"Because I sensed that you needed it now," her mother answered mysteriously.

"What did Stanley tell you that you're not saying?" Meri asked.

"I belong to the intelligence committee," her mother said. "I know that some things must be left unsaid, because to speak them could create more problems than already exist."

"You have to tell me," Meri pleaded, following her mother across the living room. "Mom, I have to know what Stanley told you."

"Why?" her mother looked back at her. "Should I believe the things he said?"

"You gave me the necklace," Meri replied, "so you must believe."

They stared at each other for a long moment.

"I love you, Meri," her mother said. "If something happened to you, what I would have left in my life wouldn't be enough."

"Mom, you're scaring me," Meri said, but her mother was already heading up the stairs. "Do you know who I am?"

"Yes," her mother answered. "You're my beautiful daughter."

CHAPTER 18

Night pressed against the windows, and the changing pictures on the six TV screens reflected off the glass, flashing and jumping as one story changed to the next. The sound was off.

Meri sat in her mother's chair, alone in the room, the necklace spread out on the table in front of her. She studied the hieroglyphs etched in the amulet. Her fingers began to tremble as she traced over the symbols.

"*Heka,*" she whispered, reading out loud. "Divine magic."

"*Sia.*" She read the second word aloud and translated it as well. "Divine knowledge."

And then she uttered the last word, "*Hu;* divine utterance."

She didn't understand why the words filled her with such hopelessness. Maybe it was because she didn't have the answers but knew she should. She turned the amulet over, hoping to find a clue on the back.

The words *medou netjer* were written there. The hieroglyphs meant "the words of the gods." But that didn't help her, either. She wondered what her mother knew, if anything, and why she hadn't told Meri more.

Carefully, she placed the necklace around her neck. A clasp was missing, or one of the lengths was broken, because she couldn't figure out how to wear it. She took it off again and wrapped the strands of beads around her arm, then placed the amulet in her palm and returned her gaze to the television sets.

The topic on channel seven changed to the weather.

Meri grabbed the remote and turned up the volume.

A commentator's voice filled the room.

She wished the noise would wake her mother. She didn't want to be alone, but her mother had a full schedule tomorrow, ending with a fund-raiser at the Willard Hotel, and she needed her sleep.

Meri sighed, disheartened, and stared at the TV.

Geologists, meteorologists, and volcanologists had come to D.C. to study the freak storms. Scientists agreed that the current temperature, moisture, wind velocity, and barometric pressure could not produce cumulus clouds, but as of yet, no one had a theory to explain what had.

The next segment showed silver weather balloons being released and floating into the clear turquoise sky near the Washington Monument.

Meri muted the sound from that program and turned up the volume on a second.

A reporter's voice boomed, "Tomorrow, geologists will send a probe under the earth's crust to see if magma is building and releasing gases that are affecting the local climate."

Meri pushed a red button and turned off that television.

Most stations were interviewing people who had gathered in front of the White House with signs. A family stood behind a handmade poster that proclaimed the end of the world. Other groups carried banners that blamed global warming for the freak storms. A few men and women held placards that said aliens from outer space were changing the atmosphere.

Meri was about to turn off all the sets, when the words *breaking news* flashed across the bottom of the last TV screen.

In the picture, a reporter stood in front of the Tidal Basin.

Meri turned up the volume and watched.

The reporter stepped next to the broken fence, then leaned over and ran her fingers through the slime that covered the walkway. She crinkled her nose, seeming to smell something disgusting. "Is this a Halloween hoax, or is there a monster loose in the District?" she asked, staring solemnly into the camera. "Tourists reported seeing a snake that was as long as a city bus."

Then the camera panned, and, under the harsh lights held by the TV crew, the reporter followed the trail of dead grass and mucous that led to the broken chain-link fence. She held a handkerchief over her nose and joined a group of tourists who didn't look very happy to be standing next to a splintered tree. Their eyes kept shifting in a watchful way, appearing terrified that the creature might return.

The reporter took the white piece of cloth away from her mouth and spoke to a lady whose sagging belly was covered with a long green T-shirt.

"Tell us what you saw," the reporter said.

"It looked like a giant slug," the woman answered, waving her hands, "and I think it bit that tree into pieces."

No sooner had she spoken than a man pushed in front of her.

"I sure hope the government hasn't been doing some weird biological research," he shouted, "because I saw something that doesn't belong in the natural world!"

Meri turned off the last set and sat in the dark, wishing she heard the soft steps of her mother coming into the room to comfort her. But the house remained silent. Slowly, she stood up and walked outside. She sat on the edge of the rock garden and looked up at the starry night. Staring into that vast dome of space, she felt as if she knew the secret of all secrets: the divine did exist. The universe wasn't an accident, and knowing that, the immensity of what she had to do overwhelmed her. What would happen if they couldn't stop Apep?

Abdel had said that Descendants who failed were sent to live in the chaos at the edge of creation. But, her fear wasn't for her own fate; she was afraid of what she and her friends were going to unleash on the world. They needed a solution, and she didn't think Seth was the right one.

"You've put too much on me," she whispered to the night sky and wiped at her tears. A breeze curled around her, bringing dampness from the Potomac River. Glistening drops of moisture settled on the lawn.

If Meri and her friends did summon Seth tomorrow night, she feared that they wouldn't be able to control the ancient god. What if releasing him from the old spell and allowing him to come back were the spark that started the end of the world?

"Help me," she prayed. Closing her eyes, she confessed, "I'm afraid."

A hand touched her shoulder.

She cried out and turned.

Miwsher sat on the stone ledge behind her, looking very much like an ordinary cat. Had Meri only imagined the touch, or had Miwsher tried to comfort her? She picked her cat up, petted the soft fur, and cradled Miwsher against her.

Miwsher nestled against Meri's neck and purred loudly, trying to console her.

The birds began to twitter before the sky had even turned gray with morning light. And by the time the rising sun had tinted the tree branches pink, the smells of bacon and coffee were coming from the house. Meri had spent the night outside, trying to come up with a plan. She had none. That meant in twelve hours she and her two friends were going to summon an arcane god, the lord of chaos and storm, who had tried once before to destroy creation.

"Good morning," Meri said as she stepped inside the kitchen.

Georgie gave a startled jump and dropped her spatula. She bent to pick it up, then looked at Meri and stopped.

"Were you locked outside all night?" she asked, as she hurried around the kitchen island. "You look ill." She placed her warm hands on Meri's face and gasped. "You're as cold as death."

"I'm not going to school today," Meri replied and pulled away. "I need to sleep."

Georgie followed her into the living room. "Do you want me to bring you some breakfast?"

Meri shook her head and picked up the wand from the place near the door where she had left it the night before. "I think I might have a touch of flu," she lied as she took the papyrus from the umbrella stand. "I'm going to spend the day in bed so I won't miss the fund-raiser tonight."

"That's a good idea," Georgie said, but anxiety laced the old woman's voice, as if she sensed that something unthinkable had happened to Meri. She leaned against the newel post. "You'll call me if you need anything?"

"I'll call you." Meri continued up the stairs. She felt too tired to shower or even take off her sweats.

In her bedroom, she unwound the necklace from her arm. The beads clattered into a pile as she set them next to the papyrus on the nightstand. She prayed for guidance and hoped a plan would come to her in her dreams. Then she crawled into bed and snuggled under the covers, wanting nothing more than to have sleep take her.

She had just fallen asleep—or thought she had—when a familiar voice awakened her. "Your mom said you needed help getting ready for the fund-raiser."

Roxanne leaned over Meri, her flowery perfume filling Meri's lungs.

"I guess I can see why," Roxanne went on. "Did you sleep all day? What are we going to do about those swollen eyes? Everyone is going to think you've been crying."

"I can dress myself," Meri said, trying to tug the covers back over her head.

"Then why aren't you dressed?" Roxanne asked. "It's almost time to leave."

Meri sat up with a jolt, and they bumped heads.

"Ouch!" Roxanne jumped back and pressed her hand against her forehead.

"What time is it?" Meri asked, looking at the dark sky outside her window. She imagined Sudi and Dalila waiting for her at the Tidal Basin.

"It's almost seven," Roxanne said. "But I'll have you ready in time. Don't worry."

"Were there any storms today?" Meri asked as she threw back her covers and sprang out of bed.

"If we'd had one, it would have awakened you," Roxanne said. "That thunder is the worst I've ever heard."

Meri reached for her phone to see if she had any messages.

Roxanne grabbed it first and held it against her chest. "You have to get ready," she said. Then she set the phone down and handed Meri some lacy black underwear, still wrapped loosely in pink tissue. "Go shower," she ordered, "and put these on."

Meri locked herself in the bathroom and turned on the water. She stripped and grabbed a bottle of honeysuckle-scented soap, then doused it over her belly and scrubbed. She washed her hair, and then turned off the shower. After drying off, she put on the silk panties and the push-up bra and walked back into her room with the towel wrapped around her. She was still dripping wet.

Roxanne took the tail of the towel and patted at the soap bubbles sliding down Meri's arms. "I know I said to hurry, but we have enough time for you to dry off. I'll get you there on time. I promise."

Roxanne stepped back and proudly held up two slinky black dresses, different from the boxy clothes she had purchased that were hanging in the closet.

"When I saw your picture in that scandal rag—"

"Has everyone seen it?" Meri asked, feeling a blush rise.

"You have a gorgeous body, and obviously I misjudged your style," Roxanne said, taking a dress off its hanger. "All those clothes in your closet are for a whimpering, fearful, young girl. I'm taking them back and giving you a sassy style that fits more with who you are." She handed the dress to Meri.

Meri held it up and stared at the plunging neckline.

"What were you doing, anyway?" Roxanne asked. "The photo looks like you were jogging naked in the rain,"

"No," Meri answered emphatically. "I wasn't. Is that what everyone thinks?"

"Who cares what they think? It must have felt incredible. If I ever get gutsy enough I might try it myself." Roxanne tossed a flimsy jogging suit on the bed. "And just in case the press asks about your midnight run in the rain, your mom wants you to tell them that this is what you were wearing,"

Meri wondered why her mother hadn't mentioned the photos in the *National Enquirer* to her, the night before.

"Just say you didn't realize it was so see-through when it got wet." Roxanne smirked. "I love your style, and it's time you showed the world your true self."

"Okay," Meri said, wanting to hurry so

she could meet her friends. Suddenly, she saw something dark wiggling across the carpet.

A cobra lifted its head. The skin of its neck spread into a hood.

Meri let out a startled cry.

"What?" Roxanne asked, turning around.

Meri stopped her. "I'm just so excited about the dress," she lied.

"I thought you'd love it," Roxanne said. "It's going to make your waist look even smaller. You might as well flaunt what you've got. Everyone's seen what you have anyway, so it's not like you're showing off."

"Right," Meri said. She waited until the snake slid into her bathroom. Then she let the towel fall to the floor, and she slipped the dress over her head. She stared at her reflection, awestruck. The bodice revealed more than her bathing suit.

"Has my mother seen this dress?" she asked.

"You look lovely," Roxanne cooed. "Why wouldn't she approve?"

"I need an Alka-Seltzer." Meri dodged back into the bathroom, slammed the door, and leaned against it.

Dalila stood in the corner, transformed. Her brown eyes widened, and she shot a surprised look at Meri.

"You look stunning in that dress," she said. "Is your mom going to let you wear it?"

"I guess." Meri opened the medicine cabinet. She pulled out the box of Alka-Seltzer and a glass.

"Sudi and I were so worried," Dalila said in a rushed voice. She stopped Meri before she put the box away. "The transformation makes me sick," she explained. "My stomach is still spinning."

Dalila grabbed an extra glass and dropped two tablets into it. "Where have you been?" she asked as she turned off the faucet. "We needed to talk to you. You didn't answer your phone, and you weren't at school."

"I was sleeping," Meri said.

Roxanne knocked on the door. "We really need to get started on your makeup," she said. "Are you okay?"

"I'm fine," Meri replied, and then she whispered to Dalila, "How did you get in?"

"I slithered in," Dalila said with a smile. "No

{ 465 }

one expects to see a snake climbing up the stairs."

"What did you need to tell me?" Meri asked, not sure she wanted to hear the answer. She sipped the drink, the fizzy bubbles tickling her lips.

"People with cameras are camped out at the Tidal Basin near the broken railing," Dalila said and chugged her drink. She placed her fingers over her mouth to cover a burp. "They're all waiting for Apep. They think D.C. has its own Loch Ness Monster, and a radio station has even started a contest to name it."

Roxanne pounded on the door again. "Meri, are you sure you're all right? I can hear you talking to yourself."

"I'm practicing a speech," Meri lied, saying the first thing that came into her mind. "It's a surprise for my mother. I want to tell everyone at the fundraiser how much she means to me."

A long, heartfelt *aaahhhh* came from the other side of the door.

Meri shook her head. "I can't believe I said that," she whispered, and then she asked Dalila, "So what are we going to do?"

"We'll still meet at the Tidal Basin, but on the other side, near the Jefferson Memorial," Dalila said. "Be there by ten."

"I'll be there," Meri answered, feeling her chest tighten, because that also meant she was going to have to walk out of the fund-raiser in the middle of her mother's speech.

"Summoning Seth is the right thing to do," Dalila said, sensing Meri's hesitation. "The newspaper said nine more tourists disappeared."

"I know we're doing what's right," Meri agreed, even though intuitively she didn't feel that they were. "Do you have the incantations?"

"I found the papyrus," Dalila answered. "The spell for summoning Seth is really long. It will take at least twenty minutes to recite." She frowned. "I hope no curious bystanders get in the way."

Meri shrugged. "We'll do our best."

"I'll see you later," Dalila whispered. Then she began reciting the spell, to transform herself.

A magic glow spun around her, lighting the room. A flurry of sparks shot into the air, and Dalila began to shrink.

Someone tapped on the door.

"Just a sec, Roxanne, please," Meri said. "I'll be out in a moment."

The door opened, and Meri's mother peeked inside.

Meri sprang forward, trying to bar her mother from coming in.

"Mom, I can explain," Meri said, even though she couldn't think of a lie to account for the reason that Dalila was twirling in the middle of the bathroom.

Her mother switched on the light. "Roxanne told me."

"She did?" Meri blinked in the harsh glare. When she looked back, Dalila was gone. A black snake wiggled across the tiles and hid behind the clothes hamper.

"I didn't know the fund-raiser was upsetting you so much," her mother said. "And you shouldn't feel nervous."

"Nervous doesn't even begin to describe what I'm feeling," Meri answered.

"You look beautiful," her mother said. "Everyone will be staring at you."

"Yeah," Meri agreed, but she had a feeling

they'd all be looking at her neckline. "I'm all right, Mom, really. Just a little queasy. If I don't feel better I might have to leave the dinner early."

"Not before you give your speech," her mother said with a broad smile.

"My speech?"

"Roxanne told me," her mother went on. "She said it was a secret, but she knows how I hate surprises. Don't worry. This one I love. I'm so touched."

"I can't believe she told you," Meri said, feeling her heart flutter. "I can't give the speech now. It won't be a surprise."

"Of course you can." Her mother stepped toward the doorway. "I wouldn't miss what you have to say for the world."

Meri groaned. How was she going to have time to write a speech?

"What's wrong?" her mother asked.

Meri placed her hands over her stomach. "Just the flu, I think," she said and promised herself that after this night, if she survived, she wasn't going to tell another lie.

"You'll get used to the nerves," her mother

said. "Be down at the car in twenty minutes."

"My hair's still wet," Meri said. "Maybe I should just stay home and wait until next time."

Her mother laughed. "Wet hair is not a challenge to Roxanne." She left the bathroom.

"Great," Meri said glumly and watched Dalila, as a cobra, slink through the doorway.

Meri stepped back into her bedroom as Roxanne came into the room, holding a pair of spiky sling-back shoes. She almost stepped on Dalila, not noticing the creature squirming near her ankle.

Ten minutes later, Meri stared at her reflection in the mirror. Her hair was pulled back in a knot at the nape of her neck, and her chandelier earrings tickled her bare shoulders.

"The person in the mirror doesn't even look like me." Meri wished Abdel could see her smoky eyes and glossy cheeks. She looked like a true Sister of Isis, a goddess and queen of Egypt. Maybe Abdel would have loved her enough to stay if he had seen her this way.

"That's you, sweetie." Roxanne stepped toward the door. "I'll give you a moment to go over your speech. I can touch up your makeup in the car." She paused in the hallway. "I almost forgot. Good news. Your mom said we can hire a makeup artist next time."

"Goody," Meri said, trying to fake enthusiasm. She doubted there'd be a next time.

As soon as the door closed, Meri went to her nightstand, grabbed the papyrus, and examined it again. Abdel had told her that the ancient Egyptians had used marsh reeds to make the strong, thin paper. They had split the stalks, then laid them across one another and pounded them into thin sheets. But this papyrus felt thicker and heavier than the others had. She studied the edge, then slipped her fingernail in between the fibers and ran it down the length of the scroll. Carefully, she pulled the two sheets apart.

Beneath the first papyrus was another.

Her heart raced as she began reading. Stanley hadn't been trying to find a way to release himself from Seth's command. He had been trying to steal the magic that Meri stared at now, so that the girls would have had no option but to summon Seth.

According to the ancient writing, Apep had

escaped Duat once before, but that time, Isis had stopped him without any help from Seth. She had traveled down to the Netherworld and found Apep while the creature was still in his lair. Then she had spoken the demon's secret names and ordered the serpent to remain in the land of the dead and not bother the living.

"Meri," Roxanne called from downstairs.

"Coming," Meri yelled back. She rolled up the scroll, grabbed her purse, and stuffed the papyrus inside, but as she started to leave her room, Miwsher meowed, and the sound made Meri stop. The feline cry came out very clear; enfolded in the yowl, her cat had said, *wait*.

Meri turned slowly, expecting to see a woman standing behind her.

Instead, Miwsher jumped on top of the nightstand and batted at the necklace until it fell on the floor.

"I'll take it with me," Meri said, rushing back to grab the beads. She opened her purse and slipped the necklace inside. "But I don't know what good it will do me. Can't you tell me what I'm supposed to do?"

Miwsher stared up at her, and a purr rumbled in her throat.

"All right, then, keep your secrets," Meri said and tenderly touched the tip of Miwsher's nose.

As she hurried from the room, she was already forming a plan.

Meri tensed as the sedan pulled up in front of the Willard Hotel. News reporters and photographers crowded the stairs and carpet under the awning. A valet opened the car door, and when Meri stepped out, the photographers jostled one another to get closer.

Meri felt hesitant and shy, suddenly self-conscious about her neckline.

A noisy burst of flashes blinded her. People

shouted at her, each question overlapping the last.

She stood disoriented, wondering how she was going to climb the steps in her spiky heels with the explosion of afterimages clouding her vision.

A gentle hand clasped her elbow.

"Step and step again," her mother said jovially, guiding her up the stairs. Then they were inside.

"You're magnificent," her mother spoke in a soft, tender voice. "You can handle anything."

"I wish," Meri answered, feeling restless about what she had to do in less than an hour.

Mrs. Autry, one of her mother's aides, greeted them. She was dressed in a black pantsuit and held a clipboard filled with ruffled pages.

"We've had a lot of cancellations," Mrs. Autry said as she led them down the spiraling staircase to the ballroom.

Two men quietly joined their entourage. Meri assumed they were Secret Service agents or privately hired bodyguards.

"With all the media coverage on the weather and that Halloween snake," Meri's mother said, "I'm grateful that anyone showed up."

Nerves twittered in Meri's stomach. She wished she could tell her mother about Apep. Maybe the military could get rid of the beast.

Just before the doorway, her mother paused. She took a deep breath and straightened her back, then walked into the ballroom with long, elegant, presidential strides.

People at the banquet tables stood and applauded.

Meri peeked into the room. The gathering didn't look small to her. The crowd greeting her mother would distract her for another ten minutes. That gave Meri the opportunity to sneak out through the rear entrance, on F Street. She doubted any photographers would be waiting there.

As she started up the stairs, she heard someone crying in the women's restroom. Meri couldn't ignore anyone who sounded that miserable. She crossed the short hallway and tapped on the door, then pushed inside.

A girl wearing a shimmering white dress stood in front of the mirror, her hands covering her face. The long blond extensions looked like Michelle's, and so did the three-inch high heels.

"Michelle? Are you all right?" Meri asked.

"That's a stupid question!" Michelle wailed. "Why would I be crying if I were okay?"

She turned around, and Meri gasped.

Bright orange blotches covered Michelle's face. Rust-colored slashes ran across her forehead, and now reddish-yellow spots on her chin were starting to swell.

"I wanted Daddy to be so proud of me," she said, turning back to the mirror. She swept more powder over her face with a fluffy brush. "I just used a little self-tanning lotion to enhance my color so I'd glow tonight."

"Maybe you mixed products that shouldn't be used together," Meri offered.

"I'm always careful," Michelle answered and sniffled. "After all, it's my face. How did this happen?" She groaned and didn't wait for an answer. "Daddy will be so angry. He said this dinner was going to be crowded with people who matter, and he wanted me to look spectacular."

"Why would your dad care how you look at a reception for my mom?" Meri asked.

"Don't you know?" Michelle spun around and

stared at Meri. "Your mom hired my dad to be the fund-raiser for her campaign."

Energy drained from Meri, leaving an unpleasant emptiness in her chest. Even if she survived this night, which she doubted she would, her life was going to be filled with still more of Michelle's taunts and snide remarks.

"Don't look so unhappy," Michelle said, appearing glad the news upset Meri.

"I think that's great," Meri said, with fake enthusiasm. She wasn't supposed to use magic for her own advantage, but if she did something nice for Michelle, maybe Michelle would be grateful and stop harassing her.

"You probably just need to use a little soap on your face," Meri said, determined to give magic a try.

"Since when do you know about glamour?" Michelle asked unpleasantly.

Meri ignored the taunt and grabbed a paper towel. She added a little soap and turned Michelle away from the mirror.

"Close your eyes," Meri ordered.

Michelle did.

Beautiful Isis, queen of magic, hear my words, Meri said to herself as she wiped the towel across Michelle's forehead and down her cheeks. *I entreat you, goddess of love and healing, let the blemishes leave this one here and end her weeping.*

Michelle's skin glistened and changed back to her normal color and glow.

"The soap worked like magic," Meri said and turned Michelle back around to face her reflection.

"Wow!" Michelle whispered. She started to say thank you but stopped and looked at Meri as if she were seeing her for the first time that night. A scowl replaced her smile. "That dress is too risqué for you, don't you think?"

Meri glanced down, self-conscious again.

"The décolletage." Michelle shook her head pensively. "You helped me, now I'll help you," she said, tossing her makeup bag into her purse. "Maybe one of the waitresses has a sweater you can borrow."

"Does it look that bad?" Meri asked.

"Trust me." Michelle raised an eyebrow. "You need to cover up."

Meri touched her chest. Maybe she had

exposed too much. "I was leaving anyway," she said, turning to go.

"You can't leave." Michelle clutched Meri's wrist. "What will people say if you do?"

"But I don't feel well," Meri lied and tried to pull away.

Michelle caught her hand and led her back to the ballroom as Scott came down the stairs. He brushed his curly hair back and stared at Meri with a naughty tease in his eyes that surprised her. When he kissed her cheek, his lips lingered before he pulled back.

"You look amazing." He glanced at her chest, then hurriedly looked back at her face. "I don't know what you've done, but you should keep doing it."

His fingers slipped down her arm, and she wondered if he was flirting with her.

"She didn't have anything to do with her look," Michelle said with a pout. "It was her stylist."

"You know about Roxanne?" Meri asked, surprised.

"Daddy told me," Michelle answered as she added more gloss to her lips.

Meri wondered if Michelle's father was going to tell Michelle everything he found out about Meri's private life. She sighed. She didn't need to worry about the future until she knew for sure if she would have one.

As Michelle and Scott headed in to the ball-room, Meri turned to dash up the stairs, and bumped into Mrs. Autry.

"The senator has been looking for you," Mrs. Autry scolded. "Where did you go?" She didn't wait for an answer but marched Meri back inside the ballroom to the table near the front where Michelle and Scott were already seated. The room was filled with the luxurious smells of expensive perfumes and the lush fragrance of warming rolls.

Meri took her place, wondering how she was going to excuse herself and leave. Her stomach felt jittery, and she sensed she was already late.

She took deep breaths to calm herself, then pulled the necklace from her purse and studied the amulet. The bright light glinted off the gold and illuminated an indentation that she hadn't seen before. She pressed it, and the amulet opened.

Inside, engraved on the flat surface, was a curling snake. The goddess Isis in her avian form stood over it.

A waiter used tongs to set a piece of bread on a plate in front of Meri. She hadn't eaten since the night before. She grabbed a knife, buttered the bread, and took a huge bite, loving the rich butter melting over her tongue. As she chewed, she translated the hieroglyphs to herself: *the goddess Isis, beloved of the great living sun disc, did imprison Apep, using these secret names of the demon.*

"I can't believe you don't know the difference between a fish knife and a butter knife," Michelle said, holding up the proper utensil and buttering a morsel of bread.

Meri glanced up, then returned her attention to the list. Each name had been carefully defaced so that the writing of the names would not give Apep power. But the markings still left the names legible. Meri felt suddenly optimistic; possessing Apep's secret names would give her the power to command the demon and make him stay in his lair.

"I don't want your mother to lose the election because you have bad table manners," Michelle went on. "And why do you have those dirty beads on the table?"

"Because I'm going to save the world," Meri answered and glanced around. Maybe she could just stand up and walk out. Everyone would think she was only going to the restroom until time passed and she didn't come back.

Michelle sniffed. "You could at least use your napkin."

"I'm tired of being nice, Michelle, and I don't have anything left to lose," Meri warned and closed the amulet.

"What is that supposed to mean?" Michelle asked.

Meri dropped the necklace back into her purse. "I have more important things on my mind tonight and—"

"Like what?" Michelle asked snidely. "How to get another nude photo of yourself printed in the paper so you can show off your body?"

Scott reached over and rubbed Meri's shoulder. "Ignore her," he said.

Meri pushed back her chair and started to walk away. Suddenly her mother's voice boomed

over the microphone. "My daughter had been practicing a speech for tonight, and I can't wait to hear
it. Meri, would you like to give it now?"

Meri dropped her purse back on the table and
held her hands to her cheeks, trying to push back
the cat whiskers that were already prickling under
her skin. What was she was going to say?

But as she started toward the podium, thunder
shook the room. The dull, heavy sound rumbled
beneath Meri's feet.

Lights flickered, and voices rose in fear and
wonder.

Meri paused. Either Dalila and Sudi were
summoning Seth, or Apep was coming back into
this world. Whatever it was, Meri needed to be
with her friends.

An elderly man with a curved spine raised his
hand and stood. His poise and authority took the
attention away from Meri.

"Senator Stark," he said, in a loud clear voice,
"everyone is saying that the military has a new war
technology that allows them to control the weather.
Are these freak storms the result?"

"I can guarantee you that this weather is not

something the Pentagon has created," her mother answered with confidence.

"But if the information is classified," the man said, "you wouldn't be able to tell us if these storms were machine-made."

"I assure you," her mother replied.

As the diners began talking about the weather, Meri hurried back to the table, grabbed her purse and started to leave.

"I can't believe you're sneaking out when your mother asked you to speak," Michelle said loudly. "My father is right. Your mother needs a daughter like me if she expects to win this campaign."

"Michelle, get off it," Scott said. "That's not true. Everyone loves Meri."

"I don't," Michelle replied.

Meri spun around. Abdel had told her that she could never use the magic in the Book of Thoth for her own advantage. She took a deep breath and spoke an incantation anyway, knowing that for the second time that night she was violating a cosmic law.

"In the name of Isis, queen of magic, I return all the evil wishes and unkind thoughts you have sent me," Meri said under her breath. Then she turned her invocation to Isis and murmured. "Goddess of many names, I entreat you. May the thoughts that Michelle sends to me find a magical path back to her."

Meri hadn't even finished her whispered spell when a waiter holding five plates of salad lost his balance. Leafy greens slid over Michelle as the plates clattered to the floor.

"You did that," Michelle screamed, picking endive off her nose. "I don't know how, but—"

"I didn't do it," Meri said. "That's what you wished for me. So be careful what you think."

Michelle picked up her glass and tossed the water at Meri, but the water magically curled back and splashed over Michelle's face. She screamed.

The ballroom became silent. Everyone turned and looked at Michelle.

She pointed at Meri and shouted, "She did this to me, because she's so jealous!"

Meri left the room and didn't look back.

Meri ran to the back entrance of the Willard Hotel and, ignoring the surprised looks on the security guards' faces, kicked off her shoes, swung her purse over her shoulder, and bolted outside. The night pulsed around her with a strange quiver, and she wondered if the sensation came from something other than her fear. She sprinted down the sidewalk, then cut across Fifteenth Street and headed toward the Mall.

The pungent odor of grilling onions filled her lungs as she raced past tourists who were waiting to buy hot dogs from a street vendor. They stood in her way, gawking and pointing up. At first, she assumed the president's helicopters were passing overhead, but when she didn't hear the familiar thump of the rotary blades, she glanced up, and her heart skipped a beat.

Black mist bled into the night sky, seeming to come from an opening beyond the stars. A vein curled over the moon, and the vapor continued toward earth. Instinctively Meri knew it was the primal darkness seeping from chaos, carrying Seth to Dalila and Sudi.

Time was against her. She only had minutes to find Dalila and Sudi and stop them before they finished the spell. Adrenaline surged inside her. She intensified her pace and ran wildly, her purse bumping against her back.

Her thighs burned as she pumped harder. The fire in her muscles spread to her lungs. She raced up the hill past the Washington Monument, then down again to the water. Her breath came in jagged bursts. All at once she caught a glimpse of her friends through the trees.

Dalila and Sudi stood on the bank of the Tidal Basin, dangerously close to the edge, staring down at a papyrus. An eerie, convulsing shadow encircled them, but no tree, post or building accounted for the dark patch of shade hovering over them.

"Dalila! Sudi!" Meri yelled as she followed the path through the twisted trunks of the cherry trees. Branches slapped against her face.

They didn't stop or look up, but continued to intone a spell, seemingly lost in a trance. They didn't even respond when she was close enough for them to hear her rasping breaths.

The shadow thickened and closed around them, in a tight sphere, seeming to sense Meri's approach.

Meri shot her hand through the dark circle and was surprised when the shadow bit back. Her skin scraped over something that felt like the pointed scales of a horny toad lizard. She pinched an edge of the papyrus and ripped it away.

Dalila gasped and staggered back, stumbling out of the shadow.

Sudi blinked, then squinched her eyes and

shook her head. She looked around, disoriented, and waved her hands, struggling to fan the darkness away.

The shadow squirmed and writhed, trying to shroud Sudi and Dalila again. Meri lunged forward and swept her hands through the black cloud. It wiggled up into the air, then caught a gust of wind and whipped away.

"What was that?" Sudi asked, looking stunned.

"I don't know," Meri answered. "It was surrounding you."

Dalila shuddered and brushed her hands over her forehead. "The spell that summons Seth has power of its own," she said. "It dominated my will and forced me to continue chanting the invocation even after I wanted to stop."

"That happened to me, too," Sudi said, her eyes widening. "But I didn't want to stop, because something deep inside me wanted to please the lord of chaos."

"I don't think it was the spell," Meri said and pointed up to the sky. "I think Seth had control over you from the moment you spoke the first word."

Near the moon, the black vapor was recoiling,

the thin tentacles turning in and slipping away from the world, back beyond the stars. The natural rhythms of the night took over, and a gentle autumn breeze replaced the abnormal quivering of the atmosphere.

"We never would have been able to command Seth," Sudi said.

"What did we almost do?" Dalila asked. "If we'd been successful in summoning him . . ." She stopped. Whatever she had envisioned was too horrible to say. Then she leaned against Meri. "I'm glad you came late and were able to stop us."

Meri started to roll up the papyrus, but Dalila plucked it from her hands and threw it into the water. The ancient writing dissolved, and the papyrus floated away, no more than a piece of trash.

"I can't believe you did that," Sudi said.

"It was the best thing to do," Dalila said confidently.

"So, what now?" Sudi asked.

"I want to show you the papyrus that was hidden under the one that Stanley tried to steal," Meri said, opening her purse.

She handed the scroll to Sudi and Dalila. They unrolled it and began reading.

"It gives us another way to stop Apep," Sudi said. "But where are we going to find his secret names?"

"I have them," Meri said. "At least, I think I do." She took the beads from her purse, opened the amulet, and showed them the list.

"A *menat* necklace," Dalila said. "Where did you get it?"

"My mother said I was wearing it when she found me," Meri explained. "But a clasp must be missing, because I can't figure out how to wear it."

"I'll show you." Dalila took the necklace and placed the shorter strands of beads across Meri's chest. Then she lifted the longer chain, with the amulet, over Meri's head and let it fall down her back. "The amulet hangs down your back as a counterbalance to the beads in front and gives you divine protection."

Meri could feel the talisman dangling behind her.

"Then, when you need its power," Dalila went on, "you reach back, grab the amulet, and pull it forward, surprising your enemy." Dalila threaded the amulet through the space between Meri's body and her arm, finally placing it in her palm. "The pharaohs used the *menat* as a counterbalance to the huge gold collars they wore. I wonder who gave this one to you," Dalila said. "It looks as if it was blessed by the goddess Bastet."

Meri thought of her cat, but, instead of saying anything, she shrugged.

Sudi handed the papyrus back.

"To work the spell, we have to find Apep while he's still in his lair," Sudi said. "How are we going to do that? The last time we went into the Netherworld, a pissed-off god flung us there."

Meri stepped to the water's edge and looked down. "We're going to swim."

"No way," Sudi said. Her expression grew solemn. "We'll drown before we find Apep's underwater tunnel."

"I'm certain the entire Tidal Basin is the entrance Apep uses to come into our world," Meri answered. "We can dive down anywhere, and we'll eventually break through to the other side and enter Duat."

"The Netherworld is reversed," Dalila added, seeming to agree. "Legend says that the damned walk upside down. If this is the entrance, then the bottom of the Tidal Basin will be the surface of a lake in their world."

Sudi didn't look convinced.

"When the cult cast a spell and called Apep here," Meri went on, "I doubt that they created a single tunnel for him to use, because after he adjusts to our world he'll be able to come here exactly as he exists in the Netherworld. You remember how immense he was the first time we saw him?"

Sudi was quiet for a long while. "It's risky," she said. "What if you're wrong, and we swim down and find only mud? Will we have enough air to swim back?"

"We can't summon Seth," Meri countered. "What else can we try?"

Sudi looked away. "I hate this," she said in a small voice.

"I know," Meri answered.

Lightning flared across the sky, its reflection flashing and flittering over the tide pool. The wind picked up, and the water churned. Whitecaps lashed back and forth.

"Apep's starting to come into our world," Dalila said. "We need to stop him before he leaves his lair."

"Let's go," Sudi said, not sounding happy about what they were about to do. She took off her boots, then peeled down her jeans and stepped out of them.

Meri stripped off her dress and started to jump in, holding the papyrus tight against her chest.

Dalila stopped her. "You can't take the scroll," Dalila warned. "It won't survive the water. You just saw what happened to the other one."

Meri bit her lip. "I didn't memorize the spells."

Dalila and Sudi snatched the papyrus from her, unrolled it, and began studying the hieroglyphs.

"I'll take the first incantation," Sudi said. "Dalila, you memorize the second."

"I've got the last one." Meri started repeating the words in her mind.

"We can read the names from the amulet together," Sudi added.

Meri tried to focus on her incantation, but Sudi was reading hers aloud, and Dalila's teeth were chattering so noisily she couldn't concentrate. She should have thought of this before.

Cumulus clouds continued building into towering heads. Lightning stroked the earth, and the water throbbed and pulsed, reflecting the strobing light. Thunder ricocheted across the night, and raindrops spattered the papyrus.

"We have to go." Dalila took off her jacket and let it fall on the sidewalk.

Reluctantly, Meri rolled up the papyrus and put it back inside her purse. She worried that she hadn't memorized all the words she needed.

Sudi splashed into the water. Meri started after her, but Dalila still held back.

"What's wrong?" Meri asked.

"I never learned how to swim," Dalila said.

"We'll jump in together." Meri held out her hand. "Don't be afraid. I'm a strong swimmer, and I can take you with me."

"I know you'll protect me," Dalila said bravely, but her eyes showed fear. She took off her long skirt and stepped over to the edge.

Meri clutched Dalila's wrist. Dalila screamed as they plunged into the Tidal Basin. Icy waters slapped against them, and Dalila started to panic.

"Grab on to my shoulders," Meri said.

Dalila shivered violently. Her fingers trembled as she held on to Meri.

Meri curled and dove, swimming steeply downward.

Sudi swam beside them, her cheeks round, full of air. Then darkness engulfed them, and they swam blind, continuing down.

Meri pushed her arms forward, then stroked back. Her ears began to ache from the pressure, and her chest became strained. If they didn't break through the water on the other side soon, then she had brought her friends to their deaths. They were too far below to return without another breath.

Light filtered through the murky water, and bits of debris floated past Meri. She knew at once that the surface was near. Strength swelled inside her. She stretched her arms in front of her, swept her hands back, and burst upward into the air. She gasped and drew a huge breath, then quickly looked around, searching for danger.

When she saw none, she concentrated on filling her starved lungs.

Dalila popped up beside her. Greenish-black scum covered her face. She held on to Meri's shoulder as brackish water spewed from her mouth; she gagged and spit, then dunked her head, getting rid of the slime.

"We made it," Sudi said breathlessly, as she dog-paddled toward them. "But I don't think that's a reason to celebrate." She turned over and did a backstroke toward shore, each breath followed by a short, broken cough.

Meri swam after her, pulling Dalila with her.

Bones bobbed in the water, knocking against something that looked like chum. Meri wouldn't allow her mind to consider what else drifted past her.

They sat on the muddy bank and stared out at the cavern. The lake was black and dull, and didn't reflect the flames that burned up the sides of the cave walls. Foul-smelling smoke rose from the fires, twisting into the dense haze that wreathed the long, pointed stalactites.

"It looks so different from what I remember before," Sudi said miserably.

"When we went into Duat the last time, we passed through the gates," Dalila explained. "The sun barge and the blessed dead, as well as the damned, go that way. But this time we used an entrance that leads only to Apep's lair."

"My emotions are all wrong," Meri broke in, wondering why such profound unhappiness had come over her. "I should be afraid, but instead I feel homesick, like I've been abandoned."

"Something's missing," Sudi agreed and tapped her chest. "I feel lost."

"The condemned are denied the revivifying light of the sun god," Dalila explained. "God pervades the world above, and we don't notice the divine presence, because it's always around us. Here we feel the complete absence of God."

"It's horrible," Meri whispered, fearing that if they stayed too long they'd lose all hope and never be able to return home.

"Let's get this over with," Sudi said, standing. "I hate it here."

Meri stood up and started walking away from the water. Soft, sticky mud sucked at her feet and oozed between her toes. Sudi and Dalila slogged along beside her.

An eerie humming filled the air—a dirge of

human cries from far away that blended into one constant sound. The wails grew louder until the keening became unbearable.

"Where are all those voices coming from?" Sudi asked.

"The condemned," Dalila answered. "In the ancient texts it says that the songs of the condemned rise in the morning and in the night, in a never-ending plea to the sun god for mercy."

They stepped through a craggy opening in the rocks and stared out at a wasteland of stagnant pools and filth, crowded with hundreds of bone-thin people.

The cries turned into shrieks as the condemned became aware that Sudi, Dalila, and Meri stood among them. Skull-like heads turned, and hollow eyes watched them.

"Jeez," Sudi whispered. "I don't think I have the strength to walk past them."

"It's the only way to find Apep," Meri answered with grim determination, stepping over a cadaverous man who tried to clutch her ankle.

Fires spit through the soggy soil, exploding around them.

A wail of immeasurable pain made Meri cover her ears.

A man dragged himself through the flames toward her. His skin blistered and split, peeling back like blackened petals. But Meri couldn't feel any heat radiating from the blaze.

"Help me," the man gasped, as he lifted his bony hand. His charred fingernails clawed at the air, trying to grab Meri.

She started to help him, but Dalila yanked her back.

"Don't touch him," Dalila warned.

The man screamed his outrage.

"But he's stuck in the fire," Meri answered.

"You mustn't pity the condemned," Dalila countered. "They did something atrocious once and knowingly excluded themselves from eternity."

But Meri's sympathy didn't go away. "He's suffering; they all are."

"They want you to feel sorry for them so you'll help them escape," Dalila said. "Even now they don't repent."

"They seem remorseful," Meri said.

"They're trying to convince you that they are,

so they can manipulate you," Dalila answered sternly. "Don't let them touch you. They'll steal your body and use it to return to our world, and your soul will be left here for Apep."

"Then stay close to me," Meri said, shaking violently. She locked arms with Dalila and Sudi. They stepped forward, trying to ignore the pleading looks and skeletal hands grasping for them.

They had gone only a short distance when the moans became chaotic, the voices wild with fear. The condemned squirmed and writhed over each other, trying to get away.

"What happened?" Meri asked. As she spoke, a strange and frightening tension wrapped around her.

"Apep is near," Dalila warned.

From the distance came the sound of something swishing over the mud.

Adrenaline shot through Meri; a cold sweat prickled her skin. Her breath came in rapid draws as her muscles tightened.

Apep appeared from behind a stony hill and sloshed toward them, through filth and decay, his massive girth wiggling and looping, circling over and around itself.

"Start the spell," Dalila ordered.

Sudi stepped forward. Her arms and legs were trembling, but her voice was strong. She raised her hands and shouted, "Fiend of darkness, demon of the west, we have the power of the goddess Isis and her magic. We are her sisters, the Descendants, and we come to speak your secret names, that you must obey us."

Even though Sudi was the one invoking the spell, Meri could feel the energy from the words.

Apep drew back and glared at them, trying to entrance them with his gaze. When they didn't look into his eyes, he opened his mouth, exposing his fangs, and bellowed. His roar shook the cavern walls. Fire spilled from the rocky perches and rained over the girls.

Undaunted, Dalila stepped beside Sudi, raised her arms and yelled, "Our magic comes from the great Isis, she of many names, who gave us the Book of Thoth. We command you to remain in Duat and not venture up into the world of light."

The words materialized, shimmering and re-forming into a lance that shot through the air and encircled Apep with white energy. The giant snake recoiled, then thrashed and rolled, splattering mud, trying to get rid of the spell that was melting into his scales.

Sacred magic quivered through Meri as she opened the amulet. She held it up so that all three girls could read the hieroglyphs inside.

"We call out these secret names," Meri said, "so that the serpent, who feeds on the dead, must obey us."

Then together, Dalila, Meri, and Sudi read: "Shat ebut. He te tebe te she. Art ebu haya."

"We demand that you remain forever bound to the underworld," Meri shouted, finishing the incantation.

Apep stopped. He cocked his head to one side, his tongue flickering, seeming to anticipate more.

"Something feels really wrong," Sudi whispered, taking a step backward and pulling Meri and Dalila with her.

"I sense it, too," Meri said as they continued backing up. "What did we forget to do?"

"I'm sure we said the right incantation," Dalila added. "I'm positive we did."

Apep inched forward, testing them. His tongue shot out and wagged, inches from Meri's face.

"Do you think the incantation worked?" Meri asked.

"I don't think we should worry about that now," Dalila said, "because if the incantation did work, then the entrance to Apep's lair is starting to close, and we need to hurry."

"Let's go," Sudi said. "I definitely don't want to get stuck here." She turned to leave and nudged Meri. "Come on."

Dalila took the lead, sloshing through the mud, but when Meri started to follow, a soft, swooshing sound made her glance back. She didn't like what she saw.

She whirled around, and her feet sank into the silt. "Why is Apep following us?"

Sudi and Dalila joined her, each clutching one of her arms.

"We didn't tell him that he had to stay in one place," Dalila offered, and as she spoke Apep threw his body forward, squirming toward them.

"What do we do now?" Meri asked.

"Run!" Sudi yelled.

Meri tugged her feet out of the mud and tromped forward. "I think I forgot to add one little part when we cast the spell," she called out.

"What?" Dalila shouted, running clumsily. Grime splashed over her legs.

"I forgot to command Apep to allow us to leave the Netherworld without harm," Meri answered as she darted around a fire.

"It's not like we had time to memorize the spell," Sudi complained. She leapt over a woman sitting in her path. "We probably all messed up the words."

"It doesn't matter," Dalila answered, panting and gasping for air. "We'll outrun Apep. He'll never catch us."

Meri ran with her head down, her arms pumping at her sides. She felt grateful that her friends didn't blame her, but she also knew that she was the one who had forgotten to say the words that would have ensured their safety.

"Be careful!" Dalila shouted.

Meri looked up.

The condemned had crawled from their

hiding places and were crowding the path back to the lake. They squeezed against one another, weeping and howling, their hands reaching for Sudi, Meri, and Dalila.

"They want to use us to return to the world above," Dalila warned.

Meri hurdled over an outstretched hand. When she landed, she skidded in the mud and almost fell. Sudi caught her, and with a burst of energy, half dragged, half carried Meri forward.

Apep whipped over the thin bodies of the condemned, relentless in his chase.

The girls held hands and raced away.

By the time they reached the water's edge, Meri could feel Apep behind her, his fetid breath surrounding her.

"We can't fight him in the water," Dalila said. "He's too strong there."

"He'd swallow us whole," Sudi agreed. "Let's cast the spell again."

But already bubbles and waves agitated the surface of the lake. Something turbulent was rocking the depths below.

"There isn't time." Meri shoved Sudi into the

water. Before Dalila could turn, Meri pushed her hard, and she tumbled in with a huge splash after Sudi.

Sudi grabbed Dalila, and they stared up at Meri, surprised.

"I'm the one who forgot the words," Meri explained. "Leave while you still can."

"We're not going to go back without you." Sudi treaded water, holding Dalila.

"You have to," Meri said, hopelessly. "Don't let my death be for nothing."

Reluctantly, Meri turned and faced Apep.

The monster coiled around her, ravenous, eager for her soul. His breath, a bitter, venomous cloud, misted over her. She breathed in, and her lungs froze. Why had she believed she could possibly command the ancient gods and fight demons? Abdel was wrong. She was nothing: a nameless orphan from the streets of Cairo.

Through her stupor, Meri became aware of a sharp twinge in her temple. Her birthmark throbbed, awakening her, forcing her to rise and stand. The soul of ancient Egypt pulsed within her—the power of the ages. Her chest heaved. She wiggled the numbness from her fingers, then reached behind her back and grabbed the amulet. As she brought the charm forward, her pain gave way to courage.

With her remaining strength, she jabbed the talisman into Apep's side.

The monster shrieked, releasing her from his deadly coils.

"I am a Descendant, a Sister of Isis," Meri said, her lips still sluggish, the words jumbled and slurred. "I command that you allow us to leave the Netherworld."

She pulled back her amulet and opened it, then recited Apep's secret names: *"Shat ebut. He te tebe te she. Art ebu haya."*

Apep recoiled. His tongue twitched irritably.

Meri stepped away, her feet numb, her thoughts groggy. This time, the demon had to let her leave. But when she reached the embankment, Apep's head shot around, and the tip of one fang stabbed her shoulder. Poison stung her and streamed under her skin, down into muscle and bone.

She cried out and fell to her knees, bending over in anguish.

Apep drew back, screeching his victory, his giant tail switching jubilantly as he curled over and around his massive body, sweeping away from her.

Meri groaned. She had failed again. She had

forgotten to add "without harm" to her command, and that mistake had left her without magical protection.

She dragged herself to the edge of the bank and rolled off, splashing into the water near Dalila and Sudi. The cold hit her chest and stole what little breath she still had.

"We'll help you," Sudi said, and tried to take her hand.

But Meri shook her head. "I'm all right," Meri lied. "You take Dalila back. I can make it on my own."

She filled her lungs and dove below the surface. She'd only slow her friends down, and she wanted them to survive, even if she couldn't. She extended her arms, ignoring the pain, and swam into the black depths.

Sand and pebbles roiled around her as the entrance to Apep's lair closed. Currents lashed back and forth, tumbling her about, and then the waters calmed. The barrier between the two worlds was again solid and secure.

Meri rose to the surface and floated on her back to the edge of the Tidal Basin, breathing in the aroma of an autumn night. The skies were clearing, the moon shining through the thinning clouds.

Sudi and Dalila pulled her from the water and helped her lie down on the walkway.

"You don't look very good," Sudi said. "I'm going to find help." She started to stand, but Meri grabbed her wrist.

"No one will know how to treat Apep's venom," Meri whispered. "Stay with me. I don't want to—"

Dalila pressed her fingers over Meri's lips before Meri could say, "die alone."

"Don't say it," Dalila pleaded, and began mumbling prayers.

Sudi wept quietly, her warm tears falling onto Meri's face.

Meri grasped her amulet as blackness clouded around her. She held the talisman against her motionless chest.

"Medou netjer," she whispered to herself. She had spoken the words of the gods to save the world, and now she needed their divine help. She wanted to live.

"*Heka. Sia. Hu.*" She repeated the words inscribed on the amulet, calling forth the benevolence of the universe to let her stay.

The night became windless, the world still, and Meri started to rise out of her body.

A woman walked through the silence toward her and held up her hand.

"It is I, the great Isis, speaker of spells, divine protector of the Descendants," the woman said. "I come to you as mistress of charms and enchantments, to remove the serpent's venom."

She touched Meri's shoulder, placing her hand over the snakebite. "I have made the poison fall out on to the ground. You shall live, and the poison shall die."

Meri fell back into her body and sucked in air. She let it out with a jagged cough. Her lungs began working. Air wheezed in and out. A fire burned inside her, but she welcomed the pain; she knew it was life, coming back to her.

She blinked and the night became filled with noise again: the rumble of traffic and planes, and the excited voices of photographers camped on the other side of the Tidal Basin.

Dalila screamed with joy. "You're back!" she yelled. "I prayed we wouldn't lose you."

Sudi grabbed Meri and planted big kisses all over her face.

"Quit with the mushy stuff. You're suffocating me."

"How did you return to us?" Dalila asked as she helped Meri stand up.

"Isis was here," Meri said, feeling dizzy. She craned her neck to get a look at her shoulder. "She healed me."

"You have a mark," Sudi said, "but the wound is gone. It doesn't look like a snakebite, it—"

"Cool tattoo," someone behind them said.

All three girls froze.

Meri became suddenly aware that she was standing outside in wet, clinging underwear.

"Brian?" Sudi shouted.

Meri picked up her dress and yanked it over her head.

"Brian, why are you here?" Sudi demanded as she struggled into her jeans. A blank look crossed Brian's face. He shrugged. Then he glanced at the photographers across the lake. They had gathered their equipment and were racing down the walkway toward Meri, Sudi, and Dalila.

"I came here to save your butts," Brian said gruffly. "Just get in the car."

He turned and started walking back to the giant Cadillac that was parked illegally on the grass, belching smoke.

"How did he drive his car into the park without getting caught?" Sudi asked as she picked up her boots. "I can't even toss a banana peel without having a dozen cops telling me to pick it up."

"Right now, I don't even care," Meri said. She grabbed her purse and started after Brian. "I just want to get away from here."

"Brian, did you join the cult?" Sudi asked.

"Hell, no," he said as he squeezed in behind the steering wheel. "You know I hate that touchy-feely junk."

"I think there's something magical about Brian," Dalila said, zipping up her skirt.

"Brian?" Sudi and Meri exclaimed in unison.

"Isis is using him," Dalila explained. "I'm certain that she is. The same way Seth used Stanley.

The goddess has provided us with a chauffeur and a ride home."

"Isis might be the goddess of many names," Sudi said. "But she's definitely got bad taste in boyfriends."

They crawled into the back seat of the Cadillac, and before Meri had even closed the door, Brian sped away.

Sirens sounded in the distance, but Meri was more concerned about the photographers who stood in their path.

Brian jerked the steering wheel to the left, and the car jounced wildly. The back wheels spun chunks of mud and grass into the air, hitting the photographers who were chasing after them.

Meri sank low in her seat and tried to hide her face.

"I'm going to be in so much trouble!" Sudi squealed. She bowed her head. "I'll be grounded until I'm twenty-one."

"The hell you will," Brian shouted, speeding through a red light. "No one's going to catch us. I borrowed the license plates from a black sedan parked by the FBI building before I did this deal." He grinned, proud of his cunning.

Dalila smiled, enjoying the reckless ride. "Isis knew that Brian wouldn't falter. Of all the young men we know—"

"—He's the biggest fool," Sudi finished for her.

"The one with the criminal mind, you mean," Meri said, praying no one ever found out about this night.

"But he is doing exactly what is needed to protect our secret," Dalila countered, with a satisfied look.

The tires squealed as Brian drove the car around the corner, and again at the next intersection. Meri glanced out the back window. The street was empty.

Finally, Sudi leaned forward. "Brian, no one is chasing us. Can you just take us home?"

Meri turned back in time to catch Brian's reflection in the rearview mirror. He looked disappointed.

"Yeah, sure," he said. The car slowed.

"Drop me off in Georgetown," Meri said.

"Why are you going back to Abdel's house?" Sudi asked.

"I'm not ready to face my mom yet," Meri explained.

Moments later, Meri was at Abdel's front door. She stole inside and climbed the stairs to the second-floor bedroom. She sat on Abdel's bed, then snuggled down into his pillows and breathed in the scent of his cologne.

As she started to fall asleep, the front door opened downstairs. She sat up in alarm, her heart beating frantically. She had been foolish to think that Seth would allow her to survive. The lord of chaos would demand revenge, and he undoubtedly knew that she was alone in Abdel's house, unprotected and vulnerable. A chill raced through her as she wondered who the ancient god had sent to destroy her.

Meri crept across the carpet, her amulet clutched in her fist. She hid in the shadows at the top of the stairs and then slowly leaned over the banister, peering down into the room below. Abdel stood near the hearth, staring at the fire. Flames sputtered and sparked, and the faint smell of smoke filled the air.

"Abdel!" Meri cried as she ran down the steps.

He spun around, startled. "Meri, what are you doing here?"

She fell against him, loving the feel of his body. "I'm so glad you didn't leave after all." She hugged him harder. "I have so much to tell you."

"What happened?" he asked, still looking stunned. He touched the ends of her wet hair.

"You'll be so proud of what we've done," she said excitedly and began telling him everything, starting with the letter she had found in his jacket pocket.

When she had finished, he placed his hands on her shoulders and looked at her with something close to misery in his eyes. "The three of you promised me that you wouldn't act on your own," he reminded her. "What you did was dangerous."

"People were dying," she explained. "How could we wait?"

He shook his head. "Even the smallest ritual, when done without thought, can have unexpected consequences," he said. "Dalila and Sudi started to summon Seth, but then you stopped them before the spell was complete. The three of you failed to offer a counterspell to close the magic that Sudi and

Dalila opened. What will be the final outcome from that breach? You could have altered the very structure of the universe."

"We thought we were doing the right thing," Meri said, looking down.

"Meri, you were the reason I became an Hour priest," he confided.

"Me?" she asked. "How can that be?"

"You haven't lived those memories yet," he answered. "I never thought I would see you again, and now that I have . . ."

He didn't finish his sentence but instead kissed her with such tenderness and longing that she knew he thought this would be their last embrace. She closed her eyes and let her hands move up his sides. He gently pushed her back, before she was ready to end the kiss. She leaned forward for another.

"I can't let my feelings for you interfere with what I've been sent to do," he said. "I will fulfill my sacred vow to Isis."

"Isis doesn't care," Meri insisted. "She's the goddess of love, among other things. I know it's allowed."

"It's impossible," he answered.

"Nothing's impossible for me," she said adamantly. "I stopped the lord of chaos from coming into the world, and I battled the ancient demon Apep. I almost died tonight. I deserve more from you."

Then she realized what she had said, and she rushed outside, feeling foolish. Abdel came out onto his porch and joined her. His hands slipped around her waist, and he pulled her to him. He kissed her again.

That was what she loved about D.C.; the possibilities were endless. Magic happened here.

"Go home, Meri," Abdel whispered. He kissed her gently once more; then he went back inside.

She stepped into the shadows and changed herself into a cat, then stretched, enjoying the luxurious pulse of ancient Egypt that rushed through her. She didn't care what her mother, or Michelle, or Abdel thought. She had done the right thing, and had been true to her real self, a divine Descendant, an Egyptian goddess who had repelled the dark forces of chaos and saved the world. For a night.